Dear Readers,

Many years ago, when I was a kid, my father said to me, "Bill, it doesn't really matter what you do in life. What's important is to be the *best* William Johnstone you can be."

I've never forgotten those words. And now, many years and almost two hundred books later, I like to think that I am still trying to be the best William Johnstone I can be. Whether it's Ben Raines in the Ashes series, or Frank Morgan, the last gunfighter, or Smoke Jensen, our intrepid mountain man, or John Barrone and his hardworking crew keeping America safe from terrorist lowlifes in the Code Name series, I want to make each new book better than the last and deliver powerful storytelling.

Equally important, I try to create the kinds of believable characters that we can all identify with, real people who face tough challenges. When one of my creations blasts an enemy into the middle of next week, you can be damn sure he had a good reason.

As a storyteller, my job is to entertain you, my readers, and to make sure that you get plenty of enjoyment from my books for your hard-earned money. This is not a job I take lightly. And I greatly appreciate your feedback—you are my gold, and your opinions *do* count. So please keep the letters and e-mails coming.

Respectfully yours,

William W. Johnstone

WILLIAM W.
JOHNSTONE

DESTINY
OF
EAGLES

PINNACLE BOOKS
Kensington Publishing Corp.
http://www.kensingtonbooks.com

Prologue

New York, February 14, 1884

The house servant who opened the door recognized J.P. Murray, and stepped back quickly to allow him to come in from the snow.

"Hello, James. Is the Assemblyman in?" Murray asked, taking off his snow-flecked coat and handing it, and his hat, to the servant.

"Yes, sir, Mr. Murray. He is in the library."

"How is he?"

"He is brokenhearted, as I'm sure you can imagine," James said. "But you know Mr. Roosevelt, he keeps his suffering to himself."

"Do you think it would be all right if I went in?"

"Yes, sir, I'm sure Mr. Roosevelt will take comfort in your visit," James said.

Murray walked down the long hallway from the foyer, then into the library, where he saw Teddy Roosevelt standing at the window, looking out at the falling snow.

"Teddy?" he called from the door.

Roosevelt looked around upon hearing his name called. His eyes were red, the more so because they seemed enlarged behind the pince-nez glasses that he was wearing. His face, always round, seemed a bit more so now because there was a puffiness under his eyes.

"Hello, Joe," Roosevelt said. "It was good of you to come."

"I came as soon as I heard," Murray said. "God in heaven, man, your mother died this morning and your wife this afternoon? How can one man be asked to endure so much?"

"I just made an entry in my diary," Roosevelt said. He handed the diary to his friend.

There was a huge X at the top of the page. Beneath the X was a simple entry.

THE LIGHT HAS GONE OUT OF MY LIFE

"She died in my arms," Roosevelt said. "I . . . I take some comfort from the fact that her last awareness as she left this world was feeling my arms around her."

"And the baby?"

"The baby survived," Roosevelt said. "Bless her little heart, she knows nothing of the sorrow that happened in this house today. She's just a little girl, a fighter, I might add, taking her place in this new world of hers."

"I sent word of your bereavement to the Governor, and the Speaker," Murray said. "You being a member of the Assembly, I'm sure they will want to acknowledge it in some way."

"Thank you. And thank you for coming over, especially in the snow."

"I wasn't going to let a little snow stop me," Murray said.

"Ironic that it would be snowing today," Roosevelt said.

"Oh? How so?"

"Some of my fondest memories of Alice are with the

snow. We liked to walk in it, to catch the snowflakes on our tongue, to play in it like children. I just reread one of my earlier entries in my diary, made when I was still a student at Harvard. That's where I met her, you know."

"You met Alice at Harvard?"

"Well, not Harvard, of course. But in Boston. Read the entry for February third, 1880."

Murray thumbed through the pages and started to read.

"Read it aloud, if you don't mind," Roosevelt asked.

Murray cleared his throat, then began to read. "Snowing heavily, but I drove over in my sleigh to Chestnut Hill, the horse plunging to his belly in the great drifts, and the wind cutting my face like a knife. My sweet wife was just as lovable and pretty as ever; it seems hardly possible that I can kiss her and hold her in my arms; she is so pure and so innocent, and so very, very pretty. I have never done anything to deserve such good fortune."

Murray looked up again. "That is a very touching entry, Teddy."

"Do you believe in the survival of the soul, Joe?"

"Yes, of course I do. Don't you?"

"Yes, I do. I believe the soul is kept in God's memory. And that means that, after we die, we can revisit any part of our life that we wish, any time we wish. I have no doubt in my mind but that . . . right now . . . this very minute, my Alice and I are riding together in that sleigh, pressed against each other under the warm lap robes. For me, here, now, it is but a memory. But for Alice it is real, it is actually happening this very minute. And I am there with her, Joe. I am there with her."

"That's a nice thought," Murray said.

"But," Roosevelt said, holding up his finger, "here is the wonder of God's mystery. Even as Alice is reliving that moment with me, my dear mother may be holding me on her lap when I was her infant. I am in both places at the same time. And in both cases, it is really happening. It is like our life is a single stream, everything we have ever done we are still doing, and when you are in God's memory, you can dip into that stream at any place you wish."

"I'm sure you can take comfort from that," Murray said, clearly not comprehending everything Roosevelt was telling him.

"You will come to the funeral?" Roosevelt asked.

"Yes, of course I will."

"It will be a double funeral. Then, we shall christen the baby."

"Have you a name for the baby?"

"Yes. I am calling her Alice, after her mother."

"What are you going to do now, Teddy?"

"Now?" Roosevelt replied. He shook his head. "Funny you should word your question that way, for now is all I have. I cannot, for the life of me, project myself beyond this very moment in time. I don't know what the next year, month, day, or even minute will bring. For joy or for sorrow, my life has been lived out."

"No," Murray said, shaking his head. "Your life isn't lived out, Teddy. It's just beginning. I know it's hard for you to think such a thing now, especially after today. But I've known from the moment I met you that you were something special. You have a bright and brilliant future in politics, my friend. I think I can promise you a spot at the national Republican Convention in Chicago, this year."

"I will not support James Blaine," Roosevelt said.

"You could do worse than hitch your wagon to a rising star," Joe said.

"I consider the man corrupt, and I will not support him," Roosevelt said.

"Well, at this point it doesn't matter. All that matters is that you find some way to get on with your life. And let's face it, Teddy, your life has been Alice and politics. With Alice gone, you have only politics left."

"And my integrity," Roosevelt insisted.

"Yes, of course that."

Chapter 1

MacCallister

It had been three years since Falcon MacCallister stumbled across the settlers' wagon. The buzzards were still circling when the big man on a tall black horse came on the scene from the south.

One man lay on his blankets, his head back, his throat cut, a pool of coagulated blood around him. Owen Blanchard looked like he had gone down fighting; he had three bullet holes in his gut. There were three females, one adult and two girls, ages twelve and thirteen. The young ages not withstanding, all three had been raped before they were murdered.

Dismounting and brushing his long, wheat-colored hair back from his blue-steel eyes, he read the sign as clearly as if a newspaper reporter had witnessed the event and wrote the story. He found the family's name, Blanchard, in a trampled Bible, picked up a piece of a map, saw a few scraps of paper and a woman's locket. Immigrants from the East, the little family had started west to get a piece of the American dream.

What angered Falcon more than anything was the realization that this was not the work of Indians, defending their land. The Blanchards were killed by their own kind in some sort of savage blood lust.

Falcon buried what was left of them, then stood over the rough grave, bowed his head, and said a little prayer over them.

"Lord, in case you're paying any attention now to what you let happen here, these were the Blanchard family, from east of Neosho. I don't know anything to say about them, good or bad, except they didn't deserve this."

They didn't deserve it, his deep grief echoed, any more than his wife, Marie Gentle Breeze, deserved what happened to her back then. But then, things happen all the time that folks don't deserve.

In that moment, Falcon MacCallister felt an anger deeper than any he had known in a long time. "I couldn't do anything about you, Marie," he continued aloud, raising his eyes toward the sky, where his beloved wife now dwelt among the spirits. "Lord," he growled, "there's a limit to what any man can tolerate, and I believe I just found it. Help me if you want to, or not if you don't care, but I guess I have to go after those men. Somebody else tracked down those savages who should have been mine, but there's another score here to settle and there's nobody else here right now. Just me. Amen."

That had set Falcon on a personal quest for revenge, a quest that didn't end until a gut shot shattered his ribs and nearly killed him. But during his quest, he uncovered a land-fraud scheme that extended all the way back to Washington, D.C., at the highest echelons of government. Head of the scheme was Asa Parker, said by many to be the fastest and deadliest gunfighter in the West. It was Asa Parker's men . . . he called them his vigilantes . . . who were responsible for the massacre of the Blanchard family.

Falcon finally caught up with Parker in the little town

of Paradise, caught him in the middle of a stolen herd of horses.

For a big man, Asa Parker was quick. Elusive and cunning, he moved among the milling horses, and it was all Falcon could do to keep track of where he was.

But when the horses were bunched in the middle of town, then set off with some shots in the air, only dust remained to hide a man.

Holding Diablo on a tight lead, Falcon had backed off around the corner of the hotel. But when the thunder of the stampede had passed, he dropped the reins and stepped out into the street. There was no need to shout orders, and no one to shout them to. The Mason boys knew what to do, and they were doing it.

While Jude headed off to knock down the fences at the livery and corrals, Jubal prowled the edges of the town, looking for snipers. He had already found one, and the man lay sprawled under the rickety water tank. Now Jubal was hunting for more of them, keeping pace from building to building, setting fire to everything that would burn.

Fading babble, punctuated by shouts, dimmed as the various noncombatant residents of Paradise fled for their lives.

Falcon strode the firelit street, his hunter's eyes cutting this way and that. The street was a littered shadowy clearing where the dust still swirled on the breezes like mist on a pond. From knee-level down, it was hard to see anything.

Down the street Jubal yelled a warning and Falcon ducked, feeling a jab of lingering pain from his wound as his .44 came up. It bucked once, licking at the gloom

with a fiery tongue, and a man pitched headfirst from
the roof of the old trading post.

Falcon was past the big wagon when some impulse
made him turn and duck. A bullet sang past his ear.

There in the street, rising out of the settling dust, was
a man as big as Falcon himself . . . a man with a spit-
ting gun in his hand.

Falcon dodged, tumbled, and rolled, and the pain in
his middle was a living thing. But there was no giving
there, no feeling of things tearing loose. It was only
pain. Two more bullets kicked up dirt beside him as he
rolled again, coming up on his elbows to return fire.

The specter in the dust dodged wildly, and ran. In an
instant he was out of sight beyond the wagon.

Falcon came to his feet, advancing. A broken-down
trough hid the underside of the wagon, and he started
around it, then doubled back and went the other way.

Asa Parker was waiting for him, crouched in shadows
behind a tall wheel. He held a ready .45 and leaned out-
ward, ready to shoot the instant Falcon cleared the
water trough.

Falcon circled around the lashed-up tongue and
stepped past the iron tire of the off fore-wheel.

"Time's up," Parker," he said levelly.

If he expected Asa Parker to react suddenly, he was
disappointed. The big outlaw didn't even move for a moment. Then he raised himself slowly. His hands went up,
and his .45 dropped to the ground.

He turned slowly. "I guess you got me, MacCallister,"
he said. "I'll come along peaceably."

Falcon stared at the outlaw for a moment, then lowered his gun as though accepting his surrender.

Parker's eyes glittered in the gloom. Slowly, he lowered his hands and extended his right hand as though to

shake it. The flicker of motion at his sleeve was almost undetectable.

Falcon's .44 roared once, then again. Both shots took Asa Parker front and center, forming two dark little holes that could have hidden behind a playing card.

The outlaw stood for a second, weaving on braced feet, then fell facedown in the dust. In his outflung right hand was a nasty-looking little .41 derringer, exposed as his dead fingers uncurled from it.*

The Blanchard family was avenged, but even with Asa Parker and the outlaws who had worked with him rotting in their graves, Falcon still did not know peace. For three years after his run-in with Asa Parker, Falcon lay low while he nursed his wounds, both physical—he still had twinges of pain from the bullet Billy Challis had put in him—and emotional. Marie Gentle Breeze had been dead for several years now, but sometimes he could hear her laughter in the still wind that was her namesake. And at night, wrapped up in his bedroll out on the plains, he could feel her warm body next to his.

Falcon hung up his guns and lived a quiet life, fully intending to spend the rest of his days quietly enjoying the fortune in gold that his father had left him. The first thing he did was go to New York. His brother and sister, the twins Andrew and Rosanna MacCallister, were performing in a Broadway play. He could remember, before the war, how they would entertain, not just the family, but all the people of MacCallister Valley.

Everyone said they were good enough to be profes-

---

*Blood of Eagles

sionals, but no one really believed the twins would actually follow through with their ambition. After all, MacCallister Valley was a long way from New York.

But follow up they did, and Falcon went to New York to see them for the first time in many years.

Falcon MacCallister was not a man who was easily impressed, but it was hard not to be awed by New York. The streets were crowded with a steady-moving stream of conveyances of all kinds, from wagons to carriages to horse-drawn omnibuses. In addition, trains moved back and forth through the city, sometimes on elevated rails, sometimes on the ground.

"What do you think of our city, little brother?" Rosanna asked.

"I'll be honest with you," Falcon said. "I don't like it."

"You don't like it?" Andrew replied. "How can anyone not like New York? Why, this is the most exciting city in the whole world."

"MacCallister is too crowded for me," Falcon said. "And New York is much worse than MacCallister."

Rosanna and Andrew laughed.

"Andrew, were you and I ever such country bumpkins?" she asked.

"Surely not," Andrew said. He smiled at Falcon. "But country bumpkin or not, I can't tell you how happy we are to see you."

Again, Andrew and Rosanna embraced Falcon.

Falcon didn't say it out loud, but just as they wondered how he could be such a bumpkin, he wondered how they could be such dandies. If he hadn't known for a fact that they were his blood kin, no one would have been able to convince him of it.

* * *

He looked at the theater marquee.

THE POWER AND THE PRIDE

A Drama in Three Acts

Starring

ANDREW AND ROSANNA MacCALLISTER

In a rare

Joint Appearance

There was quite a line waiting for tickets. Andrew had told Falcon that he didn't have to stand in line, that he could just come right inside the doors, show his letter of introduction, and he would be taken right to his seat.

Following his brother's instructions, Falcon opened the door, but was approached by a stern-faced man in uniform.

"Get back in line, you!" he said.

"But I've got . . ." Falcon started to say, holding up his letter.

"I don't care what you have," the uniformed man said.

"You must return to the line."

Not wanting to cause any trouble, Falcon returned to the line, where he waited patiently.

A carriage stopped and three young women got out, then joined the line behind him. They were speaking excitedly about the play, and during the course of the conversation, he realized that they were college students.

When he reached the box office, he showed the letter to the ticket agent. The agent looked at it. Then his eyes grew wide and he looked up at Falcon.

"You are Mr. MacCallister?" he asked. "You are the brother of the MacCallisters?"

"Yes."

"My goodness, sir, there was no need for you to stand in line. The private box is yours, please, go in."

"Thank you," Falcon said. He'd started to turn away when he heard the ticket agent tell the three young women behind him that there no more seats available.

"Oh, but I must see it," one of the girls said. "I love Andrew and Rosanna MacCallister. Can't we be allowed to come in and stand in the back?"

"I'm sorry, that isn't possible."

Falcon stepped back to the ticket window. "Excuse me," he said. "Did you say I have a private box all to myself?"

"Yes."

"How many seats are in that box?"

"There are six, I believe, Mr. MacCallister."

"MacCallister?" one of the young women said with a gasp. "Is your name MacCallister?"

"Yes," Falcon said. "And if you are interested, I would like to invite you and your two friends to join me in the box."

"Oh! Oh, how wonderful of you to ask! Yes, of course we would love to join you. That is . . . if you are serious."

"I'm serious," Falcon said. "What man would not want three pretty girls to join him?"

"Thank you," the girl replied. "But biologically speaking, we aren't girls. We are of the age to be considered women."

Falcon chuckled. "Of course you are," he said.

"I am Anna Heckemeyer of Medora, Dakota Territory," the young woman said. "These are my two friends, Miss Gail Thorndyke of New York, and Miss Emma Lou Patterson of Richmond, Virginia."

Shortly after Falcon and his young guests reached the box, the gaslights in the theater were dimmed, the lights on the stage came up, and the curtain opened. Rosanna was standing at center stage, reading what appeared to be a letter. The audience applauded.

After a moment of silent reading, she thrust the letter down by her side with her left hand, while with her right, she pinched the bridge of her nose.

"Oh, what terrible news to bring me! I have word of the death of my betrothed. I feel as if my heart has been ripped from my body!"

The audience reacted with an audible "Ohhh."

Andrew came in, and again, the audience applauded. Andrew was in the costume of an army officer.

"Claire, my sister. I have come to you with terrible news! My friend, your beloved Filbert, was slain upon the field of battle."

Falcon watched the entire play, more engrossed by the reaction of his guests, and of the audience, than he was by the play itself. He was no drama critic, but it seemed to him like all the lines were delivered too loudly, and with something of a forced emotion. The last lines were the most overemoted of all.

"I shall find comfort in the knowledge that honor brings both the power . . ." Rosanna said.

"And the pride!" Andrew finished.

As they finished their lines, both faced the audience, and Rosanna curtsied as Andrew gave a sweeping bow. The curtain fell to a thunderous applause.

"Oh," Anna Heckemeyer said, clasping her hands over her heart. "Oh, that was the most wonderful thing

I ever saw." She turned to Falcon. "Thank you, sir, for you generous hospitality."

"You are welcome," Falcon replied.

Falcon enjoyed being able to share his box with the young women, and afterward he enjoyed introducing them to his famous brother and sister.

Both Andrew and Rosanna were used to the accolades of adoring fans, and they were warm and cordial to the three young women, entertaining them with humorous stories. Falcon, who was inexperienced with the fawning expressions of fans, sat quietly in the corner of the reception room until the theater managers told the girls they must leave.

"Wait just a few minutes until we are out of makeup and costume, Falcon," Andrew said to Falcon. "Then we will take you out to dine at Delmonico's. I assure you, there is nothing back home that can compare with this."

Delmonico's was a fine restaurant and Falcon ate well. But it didn't take long for him to realize that New York just didn't agree with him, and though Andrew and Rosanna begged him to stay longer, he left after another week, promising to return someday soon. Even as he was giving the promise, though, he doubted that he would ever keep it, and he knew that his brother and sister didn't expect him to keep it either.

Returning to Colorado, Falcon tried to settle down, but the restless discontent that had driven him for many years did not go away.

Then one day, out of the blue, Falcon got a letter from a man he hadn't seen or heard from in a long time.

Dear Falcon MacCallister,
   My name is Billy Puckett. I don't know if you remember me. Back in '52, I was attacked by some

Indians who didn't take too kindly to my trapping in their hunting ground. They killed my horse and left me with a couple of arrows sticking out of my gut. Your pa found me up in the mountains, more dead than alive. He brought me back down to MacCallister Valley, where your ma nursed me back to health.

You were the youngest of all the MacCallister children as I recall, probably no older than eleven or twelve at the time. Even then I knew that someday you would make a name for yourself.

I've heard a lot about your exploits over the years, such as how you tamed Asa Parker, Billy Challis, and that lot of outlaws. But the only thing I've been hearing recently is lot of rumors, some of which are just too wild to believe. Those rumors have caused me to start worrying some about you, though.

One reason I worry is because I am a sheriff now, and from time to time over the years I remember seeing dodgers come across my desk with your name on them. In every case the wanted posters were pulled back, but there is always the possibility that someone might not get the word. And when there is a reward of five thousand dollars, dead or alive, it wouldn't take much for someone to ambush you.

I know your pa used to get his mail at general delivery in MacCallister, so I am hoping that you do as well. If you are still alive, and if you do get this letter, I would like to invite you to come up to Belfield, Dakota Territory, for a visit. I'm going on to seventy years old now, and I think it's about time I got something off my chest.
Billy Puckett

Falcon decided to throw the letter away without even answering it, so he wadded it up and started to toss it into a wastebasket.

Then he hesitated, stared at the wadded paper for a moment, and finally smoothed it out to reread it.

He did remember Billy Puckett, remembered him as sort of a short, stocky man who laughed a lot. He remembered him as being a physically strong man too, though he didn't know if he really was that strong, or it just seemed so from the perspective of a twelve-year-old.

Falcon hoped that he had made a good life for himself, and he wondered if Puckett had ever heard about what happened to Falcon's father . . . how he had been murdered by an assailant who mistook Jamie MacCallister for his son Falcon.

What did he mean when he said he had something he needed to get off his chest? Whatever it was, was it something Falcon even wanted to know about?

Damn.

He needed to know now, just to satisfy his curiosity.

Falcon had become somewhat of a recluse over the last three years, protected by his small circle of friends from inquiring reporters who wanted to write his story for the big newspapers back East. It was only natural then that rumors would start. One story had it that he had been killed in Abiline, shot in the back as he played a hand of poker. Another insisted that he had been hanged out in Tucson. The wildest and most improbable rumor suggested that he'd joined the crew of a windjammer and was sailing the seven seas. Falcon got quite a laugh from that one.

One thing those rumors did do, though, was help him maintain his privacy over the last three years. And in order to preserve that privacy, he'd been about to discard this letter until he started having second thoughts about it. Finally, he decided that three years was long enough to wallow in self-pity. It was time to step back into the world, and how better to do so than to answer an invitation from an old friend?

Falcon went down to the telegraph office and sent a wire back to Belfield.

> *THANK YOU VERY MUCH FOR THE INVITA-*
> *TION STOP I ACCEPT STOP WILL ARRIVE BY*
> *TRAIN AS SOON AS ARRANGEMENTS CAN BE*
> *MADE STOP FALCON MAcCALLISTER*

Chicago, June 5, 1884

The Convention Hall in Chicago was crowded with people, filled with cigar, cigarette, and pipe smoke, and festooned with American flags and red, white, and blue bunting. In addition to the hall decorations, each delegation was identified by a placard that identified its particular state, while large posters, photographs, and banners were thrust up on poles over the various delegations. Most prominent were the names of those men who had put themselves forward as candidates for the nomination of their party for President of the United States.

RE-ELECT PRESIDENT CHESTER ARTHUR

JOHN A LOGAN, OF ILLINOIS,
A MAN WE CAN TRUST

JAMES G. BLAINE, THE ROCK OF MAINE

SENATOR JOHN EDMONDS, FOR
HONESTY IN GOVERNMENT

In addition to the primary delegates who were seated in chairs on the floor, alternate delegates crowded the balcony that encircled the auditorium.

A man wearing the hat of a Western Union messenger was walking the floor, calling aloud for "Mr. Powers, of the Third District of Michigan! Telegram for Mr. Powers, of the Third District of Michigan!"

Many others were roaming the floor too, most of them working the delegates for their particular candidates. Amos Crockett from Maine was one such delegate, campaigning for fellow Mainer James G. Blaine. He, and Joe Murray, who wasn't a delegate but was present at the convention, and also campaigning for Blaine, had called Roosevelt to one side. Roosevelt was a delegate from New York.

"Teddy, I'm going to ask you again to switch your support from Senator Edmonds to James G. Blaine," Murray said.

"I can't do that, Joe," Roosevelt said. "I believe Mr. Blaine to be a corrupt man."

"I'll have you know, sir, that Mr. Blaine is from Maine," Crockett said. "You call him corrupt?"

"I call him corrupt because he is corrupt," Roosevelt said. "Everyone knows how he manipulated those railroad stocks to enrich himself at the expense of the smaller stockholders. I know that, you know that"—he pointed to the crowded floor of the assembly hall behind them—"everyone on this floor knows that. And yet the sad truth is many, if not most, of the delegates to this convention will vote for him for reasons that have nothing to do with what is best for the country."

"You are stating opinion, Mr. Roosevelt. Not fact," Crockett said.

"I'm sorry," Roosevelt replied. "I'm supporting Senator John Edmonds."

"I am curious. Why Edmonds over President Arthur?" Crockett asked.

"President Arthur did a good thing when he did away with the spoils system by establishing a civil service, but that's as far as he went. There is more to be done, and John Edmonds is a reformer who will do it," Roosevelt said.

"John Edmonds is a radical who will lose the support of half the people in the nation who call themselves Republicans," Crockett said.

"Do you really think Blaine can win the election?" Roosevelt asked.

"He'll win the nomination tomorrow," Murray replied.

"I didn't ask that, Joe. I asked if you thought he would be elected President of the United States."

"Of course he will," Crockett replied.

"I'm asking you, Joe."

Murray got a pained expression on his face, then turned to Crockett. "Mr. Crockett, would you excuse us for a moment while I talk to my friend?"

"I hope you talk some sense into him," Crockett said. Then, as he left, he shouted out to those nearby, "Blaine, boys! Don't forget to vote for James G. Blaine!"

"Mr. President! Mr. President! Virginia requests the floor!" someone was shouting close to where Roosevelt and Murray were standing. Above the shout of the delegate from Virginia could be heard the almost incessant pounding of the gavel.

Three delegates walked by, laughing and talking loudly, obviously drunk.

"It pains me to think that the future of our nation might

be in the hands of people like that," Roosevelt said, nodding toward the inebriated delegates.

"You aren't going to switch your vote, are you?" Murray asked.

Roosevelt shook his head. "No."

"Then let me ask you this. If Blaine wins the nomination tomorrow, will you support him in the general election?"

"As God is my witness, the Democrat, Grover Cleveland, is a better man," Roosevelt said.

"Surely you won't bolt the party and vote for a Democrat?" Murray asked with some alarm.

"No, I won't do that," Roosevelt said. "I will support Blaine in the general election."

"Then I can tell Crockett and the others that you will support Blaine once he gets the nomination?"

"Yes."

"I hope that will be enough."

"Enough?"

"To save your political career," Murray said. "Teddy, you are a practical politician, for heaven's sake. Since you know Blaine is going to get the nomination, and since you have already said that you will support him in the general election, won't you please reconsider and switch your vote tomorrow?"

"No, I can't do that."

"You realize, don't you, that if you don't switch your vote tomorrow, you will have absolutely no place in Blaine's campaign this year?"

"I know," Roosevelt said. "But that doesn't matter. I have other plans."

"Other plans?"

"I'm going West."

"What do you mean, you are going West?"

"I'm going to the Badlands."

"You are going to bad lands? Why on earth would anyone go to land that is bad?"

Roosevelt chuckled. "The Badlands," he said. "Not land that is bad. I'm going to my ranch in the Dakota Territory."

"Wait a minute? That's . . . that's a long way from New York, isn't it?"

"Yes, a very long way."

"What are you going to do out there?"

"Why, I'm going to ranch, of course," Roosevelt replied.

Murray shook his head. "Teddy, don't do this. If you do, you are saying good-bye to all hopes of any future in politics."

Roosevelt sighed, then put his hand on his friend's shoulder.

"Can't you tell, Joe, that I am just paying lip service to these entire proceedings? Oh, I'm making my own little statement as to integrity by honoring the pledge that I made to Edmonds to stay with him until the last ballot. But I am here in shadow only. I can't really explain it. My heart and soul are still back in New York with the lingering ghosts of my wife and my mother."

"How will your going to the Badlands help that?" Murray asked.

"I hope to become so immersed in my new life out there that the memories of my dear Alice will stop being painful and become beautiful. And I believe that hard work and fresh air are just the ticket I need to accomplish that."

"You're serious about this, aren't you? You really are going West."

"Yes, I'm serious," Roosevelt said.

A loud cheer erupted on the floor as the Virginia delegation pledged all of its votes to James G. Blaine.

"All right," Murray said. "When are you going?"

"Right away. As soon as this convention is over."

Murray extended his hand. "I wish you the best of luck on your journey," he said. "And if you need anything, if there is anything I can do for you, write to me. In fact, write to me anyway, just so we can keep in touch."

"I will," Roosevelt promised as he shook Murray's hand warmly.

Chapter 2

Three men were mounted; a fourth was dismounted, holding the reins of his horse as he relieved himself against the piling of the trestle. It was dark, but the moon was full and bright, and the twin ribbons of iron gleamed softly as they stretched east and west along this part of the Dakota Territory.

"Damn, Thad, how long you plannin' on peein'?" Rufus Wade asked. "Seems to me like you been peein' now for the better part of half an hour."

Buddy Taylor and Curly Latham laughed.

"I ain't done no such a thing," Thad Howard answered. Finished, he buttoned his pants and remounted his horse.

"Hey, Rufus, you ever seen them hydraulic mining operations?" Buddy asked. "You know, the way they use steam power to build up the water pressure, then squirt these big pipes of water against the mountain?"

"Yeah, I've seen 'em," Rufus answered. "What about 'em?"

"You think we could get any money by rentin' ole Thad here out for such an operation?"

Rufus and Curly laughed.

"Well, boys, I'm glad my pecker's providin' you with all this entertainment," Thad said. "But damn if it don't make me worry a mite about what kind of fellas I've done hooked myself up with."

They heard something in the distance, a high, keening, lonesome sound.

"Is that the train?" Curly asked

They heard the sound again.

"Coyote," Rufus said.

They heard the sound again, and this time there was no mistaking it. It was a train whistle.

"No, by damn, that's the train," Curly said.

"Curly's right," Thad said. "We'd best get ready."

"Buddy, you got ever'thing you need?" Curly asked.

"I've got torpedoes on the track," Buddy said. "And I've got this here red lantern."

"How do you know that'll stop him?"

"I was a fireman for a while, remember? I give it up because the work was too damn hard. Believe me, this'll stop him. When the wheels hits them torpedoes and the engineer sees the red lantern, he'll figure the bridge across Heart River is out. Torpedoes and a red lantern will stop any engineer who doesn't want to run his train into the river."

They heard the whistle again, and this time, as they looked off in the distance, they could see the faint glow of the gas headlamp.

"I wonder how much money she's carryin'," Buddy said.

"My brothers said it would be carryin' a couple thousand dollars, or maybe more," Thad said. "They'll meet us in Sheffield."

"To get their cut," Rufus said. There was an edge of sullenness in his voice.

"You got a problem with that?" Thad asked.

"I ain't got no problem," Rufus said. "Only thing

is . . . we're takin' all the risk, and they're gettin' the same cut as we are."

"They're the ones that found out about the money shipment, and they're the ones who planned it," Thad said. "If you don't like the way it's set up, why, you can just ride off now."

"I ain't pullin' out now. I was just sayin', that's all," Rufus said.

"Don't say," Thad replied. "Just do your job."

The train whistled again and now, for the first time, they could also hear the puffing sound of escaping steam from the engine.

If anyone had been out on the plains alongside the track witnessing the passing of the Midnight Special, they would have been treated to a sight to stir the soul. Thousands of tiny, glowing, red sparks lifted from the stack and drifted up to join the stars. Smoke, blacker than the night, streamed back along the top of the train.

A great, gleaming gas lantern threw a beam ahead of the train, while a flickering orange glow bathed the interior of the engine cab.

Clyde Baker was the fireman, and having just thrown in several loads of coal, he closed the door to the firebox and sat down to catch some of the breeze generated by the forward progress of the train.

"What's the pressure like, Cephus?" he asked.

The engineer checked the gauge. "One hundred sixty PSI," he said. "You've got a good fire going, Clyde. We're running high, wide, and handsome." Cephus held a tin cup under the water keg and drew a cup of water, then handed it to his sweating and panting fireman. "Here, have a beer. You earned it," he said.

"Thanks," Clyde said, taking the proffered cup. He

drank the tepid water, then smiled. "Best beer I ever had," he teased.

Cephus pulled the cord to blow the whistle, playing with it to alter the pitch.

Clyde laughed. "Ain't nobody can make music with a whistle like you can."

"Yeah, well, I always did want to play me one of them calliopes," Cephus said.

"A what?"

"A calliope. It's a big thing, sort of like an organ, only it has steam whistles. They have 'em on riverboats sometimes."

"I'll be damned. I never heard of such a thing." Clyde smiled. "I expect it's somewhat louder than an organ."

Cephus laughed. "Well, I don't think you'd be wantin' to play one in a church," he said. To accent his point, he blew the whistle again, again coaxing two long, sweet, mellow tones from it.

Behind the engine and tender came the dark baggage car, then the express car. Behind the express car was a stock car wherein, in comfortable stalls, were six horses, belonging to passengers who had paid the extra fare to bring their mounts with them.

There were only two windows in the express car, but they were shining brightly because inside the moving post office, Fenton Bowles, the mail clerk, was busy sorting mail and putting it into the pouch for delivery at the next town. In a safe in the corner of the mail car, there was an oversized white bag. Bowles had signed for the white bag when he came aboard, so he knew that it contained exactly $1,817. That was a lot of money, almost two years of his salary, and he was responsible for it. Being responsible for so much money made him nervous, and he would be glad when they reached Belfield, so he could be rid of it.

There were four passenger cars behind the express car. Although this was a night train, there were no parlor cars on this run because, essentially, it was a local, stopping at just about every town along the route. Vance Dexter, the conductor, was in the last seat of the last car. There was light in this car, as there was in the other passenger cars, but it was soft and unobtrusive. The illumination came from low-burning kerosene lanterns that were mounted on gimbals on the walls of the car. Some of the passengers were awake and talking quietly among themselves, but most seemed to be trying to grab some sleep, though, as the seats did not recline as they did in some of the more plush parlor cars, sleep was rather difficult to come by.

Dexter took out his pocket watch and examined it in the light of the lantern that was just over his seat. It was just after midnight. They weren't due in Belfield for nearly two hours.

He felt himself growing drowsy, so to ward off falling asleep, he got up and took another walk through the entire length of the train.

When he reached the second car, he stopped and looked at the man halfway up on the left side. He was a big man, with hair the color of straw. His hat was pulled down over his eyes and his chest was forward on his chin. His arms were folded across his lap.

From time to time, Dexter had celebrities ride on his train, and this passenger fit that category. He wasn't sure that Falcon MacCallister would qualify as a celebrity in everyone's book, but as far as he was concerned, MacCallister was as famous as any passenger he had ever carried. He was said to be one of the most accomplished men with a six-gun to ever roam the West. Stories about him were told and retold until they reached legendary proportions and Falcon MacCallister seemed larger than life.

When Dexter learned that Falcon MacCallister was to be one of his passengers, he was actually quite surprised. He had heard so many stories about him that he wasn't sure he really existed, or if he existed, was still alive. Many of the later stories told of MaCcallister's death. One insisted that he had been surrounded by a gang of thirteen outlaws, but had killed twelve of them, succumbing only when the last bullet from his two guns had been fired. And even as the thirteenth outlaw shot him, MacCallister, according to the story, killed him by throwing his knife at him as he fell.

Dexter learned who his passenger was only because MacCallister paid extra to have his horse transported in the stock car ahead.

Although MacCallister had neither done nor said anything to suggest that he might be dangerous, Dexter was somewhat frightened of him. He was leery each time he walked by MacCallister's seat, and he paused now to study the noted gunman while he took a deep breath to steel his courage.

"Come on by me, conductor, I'm not going to bite," MacCallister said quietly. He neither lifted his head nor opened his eyes, and Dexter wondered how he knew he was there.

"Thanks, uh, I just didn't want to disturb you, is all."

Dexter passed him by, then walked all the way up to the front car. When he reached the front car, he stepped out onto the platform for a moment to let the fresh night air help revive him.

That was when he heard the torpedoes.

There were three warning torpedoes on the track, and they popped loudly as the engine ran over them.

"Cephus! Torpedoes!" Clyde shouted, but even as he did so, Cephus was already on the brake lever.

"I heard 'em!" he called back. "There's a red lantern wavin' ahead too!"

"Damn!" Clyde said. "The trestle must be out!"

"See if you can see anything!"

Clyde leaned out of the side of the cab and stared ahead, but though the headlamp threw its beam through the night, it showed only an unbroken line of track.

The wheels squealed as they skidded along the track, steel sliding on steel. Behind them, the Westinghouse Air Brakes had automatically set the brakes on all the cars, so the train was losing momentum rapidly.

"If I was you, I wouldn't be standin' in the middle of the tracks like that," Thad said.

"I want to be sure he sees me," Buddy replied.

"Well, hell, you know he did. He's slowin' down now, you can hear the wheels a-squealin'," Thad said. "Ever'body, get your masks on."

The four men had kerchiefs tied around their necks, and they lifted them now so that their noses and mouths were covered. Then they watched as the train, though slowing noticeably now, continued its forward momentum. Finally, it came to a complete stop about thirty feet down the track from where Buddy stood with his lantern.

"Okay, boys, that's it!" Thad said. "Buddy, you go up to talk to the engineer and keep him busy. Rufus, you and Curly come with me."

Buddy walked directly down the track toward the train, which now sat puffing rhythmically as the relief valve vented off the unused steam. Thad and the other two moved up the other side of the track, staying out of the light of the headlamp.

The engineer stepped out onto the platform at the rear of the engine cab.

"What is it?" he asked as Buddy came walking up alongside. "Is there a bridge out?"

Buddy raised his pistol and pointed it at the engineer.

"Nah, there ain't no bridge out. This here is a holdup," Buddy said. "You and the fireman step on down from that engine cab," he ordered.

"The hell we will!" Cephus stepped back into the cab and pushed the throttle forward. Even as he did so, Thad and Rufus were climbing up onto the engine from the other side of the track. Thad shot the engineer, hitting him in the back.

"Get this train stopped!" he yelled, turning the gun toward the fireman.

Clyde closed the throttle and applied the brakes. The train, which had started forward when Cephus opened the throttle, once more jerked to a stop.

"Let all the steam out," Thad said.

"I'm just the fireman," Clyde said. "That's not my job."

Thad fired at Clyde, and the bullet shredded an earlobe. With a cry of pain, Clyde slapped his hand to his ear.

"Now let all the steam out like I told you," he said. "Or I'll shoot your other ear, and I'll take it clean off."

Shaking in fear, Clyde pulled the relief-valve cord and steam began rushing from the valves. The steam pressure dropped to way below 100 PSI.

"Now, you sit there and be a good boy while we take care of our business."

"Can I see about the engineer?"

"Sure, look over him if you want. He's not going anywhere," Thad said. "And without the steam, neither is this train."

By now the conductor was out of the train, walking up alongside the track to see what was going on.

"What's going on here?" he called when he saw Buddy standing beside the engine. "What'd you stop us for? And why is the steam being vented?"

Buddy turned toward Dexter. It wasn't until then that Dexter noticed that he was wearing a kerchief over his nose and mouth and was holding a gun. He raised it, and pointed it toward Dexter.

"Wait," Dexter said in sudden fear. He threw his hands up and backed up a few steps. "Wait," he said. "Don't shoot me. Please don't shoot me."

Thad stepped to the side of the engine then and stood there, bracing himself with his right hand on the back of the engine cab and his left raised up to the cab roof.

"Well, now, Mr. Conductor, I'm just real glad you are here," Thad said. "Open the door to the express car."

"I can't do that," Dexter said.

"You want to die for someone else's money, mister?" Thad asked. He nodded at Buddy, who cocked his pistol.

"No, no, I mean I can't open it from out here. The mail clerk has to open it from inside."

Thad jumped down onto the ground. "Then tell him to do it," he said.

Nodding in assent, the conductor walked back to the express car, followed by both Thad and Buddy. He knocked on the door.

"Mr. Bowles, open the door, please."

"I can't do that, Mr. Dexter."

Dexter looked at Thad.

"Ask again, real nice-like," Thad said.

Again, Dexter knocked on the door. "Please, Mr. Bowles, open the door."

"I can't," Bowles said again.

"If you can't get him to open that door, I'm going to kill you and we'll dynamite the door."

"Bowles, for God's sake, man! Open the door or they will kill me!" Dexter pleaded, by now his voice a high-pitched squeal.

There was a moment of silence, then the sound of a lock being turned. The door slid open and Bowles stood in the doorway, a small man, balding and with small, wire-rim glasses.

"When I show up in Belfield without the money, you're going to be the one who takes the responsibility for it," he said. "They're not going to take that money out of my pay."

"Oh, for heaven's sake, Bowles, they aren't going to do that," Dexter said.

"Get up there and get the money, Buddy," Thad said. "Rufus, you and Curly go through the passenger cars to see what we can get there."

"All right," Rufus said. "Curly, you go back to the last car and start coming this way. I'll get on this car and start back toward you."

Nodding, Curly trotted alongside the track to the rear of the train.

Chapter 3

Falcon had been asleep when the train was stopped. Opening his eyes, he looked out the window expecting to see a depot, or at the least a water tower. Seeing neither, he got curious, so he walked up to the front vestibule, then leaned out just far enough to see what was going on. That was when he saw four armed and masked men standing alongside the conductor.

Drawing his pistol, Falcon stepped out of the car on the opposite side of the train from the four men, then ran up the right side of the train until he reached the engine. Looking up into the engine, he saw one man lying on the floor and the other squatting down beside him. From the coveralls they were wearing, he knew that one was the engineer and the other the fireman, but he didn't know who was who.

Falcon examined the inside of the cab as best he could from his vantage point, to make certain none of the train robbers were there. Deciding that it was empty except for the train crew, he climbed up and, suddenly, barged in.

"What the hell!" Clyde shouted in alarm.

Falcon put his finger across his lips.

"Who are you?" Clyde asked.

"Just a passenger," Falcon answered. He nodded toward the man on the floor. "How is your friend?"

"Dead," Clyde answered.

"How many of them are there, do you know?" he asked.

"Four, I think," Clyde answered.

"Do you know where they all are?"

"No," Clyde said. "I didn't see where any of them went."

Falcon leaned out from the engine cab to have a look. Just as he did so, one of the train robbers happened to look in his direction.

Thad saw Falcon look out from the engine cab, and reasoned correctly that he was someone from the train. Whoever he was, he had no business being there.

Thad fired at Falcon, and the bullet hit the steel frame of the engine cab, then careened and ricocheted around inside. It had the effect Thad wanted, for it caused Falcon to duck back inside. When he did, Thad ran away from the relative light alongside the track, and out into the shadows.

"Conductor, in here!" Falcon shouted.

The conductor hesitated. "MacCallister? Are you one of them?"

"Do you really think I'm one of them?" Falcon said. "Why would they shoot at me if I'm one of them?"

Seeing the logic of Falcon's question, the conductor hurried to the engine. The muzzle flash of another shot lit up the darkness as someone was shooting at the conductor. The bullet slammed into the side of the cab, raising sparks but doing no damage. Falcon fired back at the muzzle flash, providing cover for the conductor as he closed the distance between himself and Falcon.

Falcon reached down and grabbed him by the wrist, and half-assisted, half-lifted the conductor into the engine cab.

"Get this train going!" the conductor shouted to Clyde.

"I'll have to build the steam up again," the fireman protested.

"Don't tell me what you have to do. Just do it!" the conductor said.

"Yes, sir," Clyde answered, glad to acquiesce to someone who seemed confident enough to take control.

Leaning out the side of the engine cab, Falcon saw Buddy standing in the doorway of the express car, holding a white bag.

"Buddy, I've got your horse! Throw me the bag and let's get out of here!" a voice shouted from the darkness.

"Bring my horse here."

"And get him shot? Throw the bag!"

Buddy threw the bag and Falcon shot it, hitting it twice. The impact of the bullets stopped the bag in midflight, and it fell just at the outside edge of the ambient light.

Buddy shot at Falcon, and Falcon returned fire. Buddy went down.

Jumping down from the engine cab, Falcon started up the side of the tender. That was when someone from the first car leaned out and shot at him. The bullet cracked by his head; then his would-be assailant disappeared back inside.

Falcon walked out to recover the bag, keeping his senses alert to the fact that someone was out there in the darkness. That was when he heard the sound of galloping hooves.

Thinking his adversary had fled the scene, Falcon relaxed somewhat and started toward the bag. That was a mistake, because two more shots came from the darkness, both of them dangerously close.

"You ain't gettin' my money, mister," the voice called from the darkness.

"It's not your money," Falcon replied.

"Well, now, it looks like what we've got ourselves here is a Mexican standoff," Thad called from the darkness. "The money is just lyin' out there in the dark, and can't neither one of us get to it."

At that moment, Falcon heard a shot coming from inside one of the passenger cars. The shot was followed by a woman's scream.

Thad laughed, his laughter evil-sounding from the dark. "Sounds like my men are killin' your passengers," he said. "That means you got yourself a decision to make, Mr. Hero. You can stay out here and keep an eye on that money bag, or you can get back on the train and rescue the passengers."

From inside one of the passenger cars there was another shot, and another scream.

"So, which will it be? The money or the passengers?"

With a frustrated sigh, Falcon turned back toward the train. He slipped back on board as soon as he had a chance to do so. Laughter from outside told him that the train robber had retrieved the money bag.

In the first car, he saw that everyone was awake, and sitting in their seats, terrified by what was going on. But one man in the back was looking out the window as if totally uninterested in the drama playing out around him.

Falcon wondered how the man could be so unafraid, unless he was the cause of everyone else's fear. He stared at the man as he walked down the aisle.

Either because of Falcon's intense stare, or because he was just nervous, the man suddenly raised his pistol and fired at Falcon. Falcon saw the finger of fire leap from the barrel of the pistol, and felt, rather than heard, the crack of the bullet as it slammed by him.

A woman screamed as Falcon fired back, and he saw

a small, dark hole appear right between the man's eyes. The man fell back across the seat.

Falcon ran through the cars until he reached the last car. As he ran up the aisle, gun drawn, several people reacted in fear, but one of the passengers called out to him.

"He got off the train!"

Nodding his thanks, Falcon started toward the rear exit. Because the car was lit from inside, and it was dark outside, the windows acted as mirrors. That little fact saved Falcon's life, because glancing at the window nearest the exit, he saw a man aiming a gun at him. It was the same person who had just told him that the outlaw had left the train.

Hawk jerked to one side just as the man fired, and the bullet from the assailant's gun went through the very window in which Falcon had seen the reflection.

Falcon fired back, hitting the shooter in the throat and sending him crashing through the window by his seat, half in and half out.

Falcon stood there for a moment with smoke curling up from his gun, commingling with the smoke from the outlaw's gun. He walked over to check the man out, but saw that he was dead. He put his gun back in his holster, then looked up at the anxious passengers.

"It's all over, folks," he said.

"There may be others," someone said in alarm.

Falcon shook his head. "No. There were only four. One got away."

"What about the other three?"

"You won't have to worry about the other three," Falcon said.

After retrieving the money bag, Thad waited around for a while until he saw five bodies put into the baggage car. Three of the bodies were his men, Buddy Taylor, Curly Latham, and Rufus Wade. And, by the coveralls the man was wearing, he recognized the engineer's body. He had no idea who the fifth body was, but figured it was probably one of the passengers.

"Well, boys," he said with a silent salute. "Too bad you aren't going to be around to help me spend the money." He laughed, then leaned forward and patted the money bag, which now hung from the saddle pommel.

"Mr. MacCallister?" the conductor said, gently shaking Falcon awake.

Falcon opened his eyes and ran his hand across his face. "Yes?"

"We're coming into Belfield," the conductor said.

Falcon nodded, then looked through the window. It was light now, and he reached into his pocket and pulled out his watch. It was five after eight.

"I hated to wake you, you were sleeping so soundly, and Lord knows you earned it," the conductor said. "But you did say you wanted me to wake you at Belfield."

"Yes, thanks," Falcon said.

The train slowed with a series of jerking moves, rather than the smooth way it normally slowed. That was evidence of the fact that the man at the throttle was the fireman, and not the engineer.

Falcon thought of the man who was driving this train. While Falcon slept, Clyde had been forced into the position of being both fireman and engineer. It was a backbreaking task, and he'd kept it up all through the night. Falcon hoped the railroad would reward him in some way.

Reaching overhead, Falcon retrieved his saddlebags and rifle, the only luggage he had. He walked to the front of the car and stepped down onto the wooden platform. The depot was a small, red-painted building with a black-on-white sign that read BELFIELD.

Behind Falcon the train, temporarily at rest from its long run, wasn't quiet. Because Clyde kept the steam up, the valve continued to open and close in great, heaving sighs. Overheated wheel bearings and gearboxes popped and snapped as the tortured metal cooled. On the platform all around him, there was a discordant chorus of squeals, laughter, shouts, and animated conversation as people were getting on and off the train.

Dickenson was the only scheduled stop between where they were robbed and Belfield, but as no one on the train was ticketed for Dickenson, and the stationmaster didn't have a stop signal out, Clyde had barreled on through. As a result, no one in Belfield knew of the robbery until the train arrived. But within minutes after arriving in the station, the news spread quickly.

Falcon could measure the speed with which the news was traveling according to the change in conversation. He knew also that the arriving passengers were telling of his participation in the excitement, because soon he could feel many sets of eyes staring at him.

Looking up toward the baggage car, Falcon saw that five bodies were being taken down and laid out side by side on the wooden platform.

"Don't you dare!" Falcon heard Clyde shout, his words clearly audible even above the sound of popping metal and vented steam.

"What's that?" someone called back up to him.

"Don't you dare lay Cephus's body alongside those other sons of bitches!"

"That there is Micah Peters. He was a passenger; he don't belong with them outlaws either," someone said.

"All right, move Cephus and Mr. Peters away from the others," another said.

The curious began to gather around the bodies then, and while Falcon had no particular interest in them, he found himself there as well, because the bodies had been placed very close to the stock car and Falcon was waiting for his horse to be off-loaded.

"Hey, I know one of them boys," someone said. He pointed to one. "That one there is Rufus Wade. Me'n him cowboyed together last year. That is, till he got drunk and set fire to the bunkhouse. Mr. Eddington fired him for that."

The one identified as Rufus Wade was the one Falcon had shot through the throat. There was a hole in his throat, as well as cuts and gashes on his face, sustained when he crashed through the window. One of Rufus's eyes was open and one eye was shut. His lips were pursed and open, showing yellow, crooked teeth.

"He's young," the man who identified him said.

"He ain't young," another said.

"Yeah, he is too. He's only nineteen."

"He ain't young," the other insisted. "He's dead. You can't get no older than dead."

"Who are the other two?"

"I don't know. Onliest one I know is Rufus Wade."

"That is Buddy Taylor, and that's Curly Latham," a new voice said. The speaker was a short, stocky, gray-haired man wearing a badge.

Even after all these years, Falcon recognized him, and he walked over to the man whose life his mother and father had saved so long ago.

"You'd be Billy Puckett?" he asked.

"I am."

Falcon extended his hand. "As near as I can reckon,

it's been thirty-two years since I last saw you. But you haven't changed that much."

For a second Sheriff Billy Puckett looked confused. Then a wide grin spread across his face. "You're Falcon MacCallister," he said. He reached to shake Falcon's hand. "Welcome to Belfield."

"Thanks," Falcon said. "When did you take up sheriffing?"

"Comin' up on twenty years now," Puckett said. "Soon as I got back from the war."

"You said you were seventy years old. It would seem to me like you'd earned the right to sit in a rocking chair for a while."

"A fella can't make a living sitting in a rocking chair," Billy replied.

"I guess you're right about that," Falcon agreed.

Falcon stared down at the bodies. All three had their arms folded across their chests. Only Buddy Taylor had both eyes open, and Curly Latham had both eyes closed, his eyelid muscles having been destroyed by the bullet that hit him right between the eyes.

Another man came up to stand near Falcon and Billy Puckett. This man was also wearing a badge. He was younger, taller, and slimmer than Billy. He was wearing a big, black handlebar moustache.

"Falcon, this here is my deputy, Walter Merrill," Billy said.

Falcon and the deputy nodded at each other.

"Walter's been with me for five years now. He's goin' to make a good sheriff someday. Fact is, he'd be a good sheriff now if I'd step out of the way."

Merrill shook his head. "I ain't ready for you to step out of the way yet, Sheriff," he said. "I'm still learnin' a lot from you."

"See why I like this man?" Billy teased. "He knows how to suck up."

Falcon and Merril both laughed.

Sheriff Billy Puckett lit a cigar and took several puffs before he spoke again.

"Falcon, folks are talkin' about the big man, a passenger on the train, who took these outlaws on. I've got a strong feelin' you are the one they are talking about."

"I reckon I am," Falcon replied.

"I understand they got away with the money."

"Not they. One man," Falcon said.

Hearing a sound, Falcon looked toward the stock car and saw that they were leading a big, black horse down a ramp.

"Excuse me, I've got to see to my horse."

"That's yours?"

"Yes."

"He's a good-looking horse."

"Diablo is a good horse," Falcon said. "He'll probably live longer than I will."

Puckett chuckled. "Yes, well, to be honest with you, Falcon, from all I've heard, I don't know how the hell you've stayed alive this long," he said.

"Lucky, I guess," Falcon said.

"Uh-huh. Listen, Judge Heckemeyer is in town. Just to be on the safe side, why don't you come on down to my office so we can get an official ruling of justifiable homicide on these three? There's no sense in taking a chance on getting some more bad paper out there."

"Heckemeyer? Did you say Judge Heckemeyer?"

"Yes, why? Do you know him?"

"No, I don't think I've ever met him," Falcon said. "But the name seems familiar to me."

"You will come talk to him, though?"

"All right. But if you don't mind, can I come down after breakfast?" Falcon asked. "I'm a little hungry."

"Sure, no hurry," Puckett said. "I've got to figure out what to do about these three anyway." He sighed. "Damn, Falcon, I invited you up to do a little elk hunting, not cause me all this paperwork," he said.

Falcon chuckled. "Sorry 'bout that. Where's a good place for breakfast?"

"I'd say the Dunn Hotel is about as good as anyplace," Puckett answered.

Falcon's saddle was unloaded as well and, taking his leave of the sheriff, Falcon saddled Diablo, threw his bags across, sheathed his long gun, then mounted his horse and rode down the street looking for the Dunn Hotel.

Falcon ate so many of his meals out on the range that when he did have the chance to eat in town, he ate well. Breakfast this morning consisted of a stack of pancakes, two eggs, fried potatoes, an oversized piece of ham, and half-a-dozen biscuits. He was just washing it all down with a second cup of coffee when Sheriff Puckett came in.

"Join me for a cup of coffee, Billy?" Falcon invited.

Puckett shook his head. "Wish I could," he said. "But the judge is over at my office now, and he wants to see you."

"All right," Falcon said. He stood up, took a last swallow, then left fifty cents on the table, which not only paid for his meal, but left a generous tip.

Judge Heckemeyer was a relatively large man, bald, with a round face and bulldog jaws. He was sitting at Sheriff Puckett's desk reading a newspaper when Puckett led MacCallister in.

"Judge, this is Falcon MacCallister, the fella I was telling you about," Puckett said.

"Your Honor," Falcon said with a slight nod of his head.

"I understand that you killed all three of them?" Heckemeyer said by way of reply.

"Yes," Falcon said, not elaborating on his answer.

"Was it really necessary to kill all three of them?"

"Yes," he said again.

"Not one of them offered to surrender, or made an effort to get away without creating danger to you or any of the passengers?"

"Not one."

Judge Heckemeyer drummed his fingers on the desk for a moment as he looked up at Falcon, studying him over the top of his glasses.

"Judge, I've already interviewed half-a-dozen people on the train," Puckett said. "They tell me that Falcon wasn't only defending his own life, but was defending them as well. Two of the passengers were shot, you know. Micah Peters was killed and Harley Jones was shot in the shoulder. Harley, he's over to the doctor's office now, if you would like to talk to him."

"I don't need to talk to him," Judge Heckemeyer replied. He continued his questioning of Falcon. "There were four train robbers, you killed three. Odd, isn't it, that the one who got away got away with the money?" Heckemeyer asked.

"What is so odd about it?" Falcon asked.

"Well, perhaps odd isn't quite the word I wanted. Perhaps ironic would be better. How did it happen, by the way, that the one man who did make good his escape, did so with the money?"

"I had to make a choice between retrieving the

money, or keeping the outlaws who were on the train from shooting any more passengers," Falcon said.

"I have heard of you, sir. I have also heard of your prowess with a gun. And I don't like what I hear."

"I have always tried, to the best of my ability, to obey the law," Falcon said.

"So you say. On the other hand, you always seem to be walking very close to the edge. I know for a fact that there have been wanted dodgers posted for you. And on more than one occasion."

"And they have been withdrawn every time," Billy Puckett said.

"Ah, yes, they have been withdrawn. But the question remains, how is it that so many of them have been issued in the first place, only to be withdrawn?"

"I can't explain that."

"Well, perhaps I can," Heckemeyer said. "This is what I think, Mr. MacCallister. I think that you are a murder case waiting to happen. You are like a moth, flying close to the flame. So far you have avoided the flame . . . you have managed to stay on the right side of the law. Though, I think that even you will agree with me, you have barely managed to do so."

"Yes, sir."

"Mr. MacCallister, it has been my experience that wanted posters are not frivolously issued. In every case, a law enforcement authority somewhere has been convinced that you were guilty of one felony or another. Then, no sooner are the circulars issued than something turns up that temporarily exonerates you.

"But your luck cannot continue, Mr. MacCallister. Where there is smoke, there is fire, and I feel certain that one day that fire is going to flare up and . . . like the moth, you will be consumed by it."

"Your ruling, Judge?" Sheriff Puckett asked.

Heckemeyer nodded. "Yes, my ruling," he said. "I'm going to rule that these three men died by the hand of Falcon MacCallister—"

"Judge?" Puckett interjected quickly, but before he could go any further, Judge Heckemeyer held up a finger.

"By the hand of Falcon MacCallister," Heckemeyer continued, "in an act of justifiable homicide. I have no choice, the facts compel me to do this." He wagged the finger that he was holding up. "But I shall be keeping an eye on you, Mr. MacCallister. Yes, sir, I will be keeping an eye on you."

Chapter 4

It had rained earlier in the day, and when Thad Howard rode into the little town of Sheffield, the street was a quagmire. The mud, worked into the consistency of quicksand by the horses' hooves, had mixed with the droppings to become one long, stinking, sucking pool of ooze. When the rain stopped, the sun, yellow and hot in its late-afternoon transit, had begun the process of evaporation. The result was a foul miasma, rising from the offal of the street.

The saloon wasn't hard to find. It was the biggest and grandest building in the entire town. Because of the shadows, there was an illusion of coolness inside the saloon, but it was an illusion only. The dozen-and-a-half customers who were drinking had to keep their bandannas handy to wipe the sweat from their faces.

Thad looked over everyone in the room. No one was wearing a badge, and none of the drinkers seemed to pose a problem. From all he could tell, there were only cowboys and drifters here, and less than half of them were even wearing guns. A couple of the cowboys were wearing their guns low and kicked-out gunfighter-style, but Thad could tell at a glance that it was all for show. He was certain they had never used their guns for anything but target practice, and probably were not very successful at it.

The bartender stood at the end of the bar, wiping the used glasses with his stained apron, then setting them among the unused glasses. When he saw Thad step up to the bar, he moved down toward him.

"What'll it be?"

"I'm supposed to meet my brothers in here," he said.

"Your name Thad?"

"Yes."

"They're here. You owe me six dollars."

"Six dollars? What the hell for?"

"That's how much a tab they've already run up," the bartender said.

"Get me a beer."

"I ain't getting' nothin' till you pay up the six dollars," the bartender said. "You got it or not?"

Although Thad had buried most of the money just outside of town, he had brought over a hundred dollars with him.

"Yeah, I got it," he said, taking out a roll of money. He counted out six dollars and gave it to the bartender. "I'll have that beer now," he said.

The bartender drew the beer and gave it to him.

"Now, where are my brothers?"

"Upstairs in their room."

"You rent rooms here?"

"I do."

"For sleepin' or sportin'."

"Either way you want."

"What room is my brothers in?"

"Number twenty-three, just at the top of the stairs."

Thad climbed up the stairs, then opened the door.

"Hey, what the hell?" a man's voice called out angrily.

In the bed, he saw two men and a woman. The woman scrambled to cover her nakedness.

"I got it," Thad said, smiling broadly. He waved the money in front of them.

With shouts of excitement, Creed and Bob Howard jumped out of bed and started toward him.

"What's going on here?" the woman asked.

"This here is our brother," Creed said.

"If you expect me to take him on too, it's going to cost more," the woman said.

"Oh, yeah, hey, you want to join in?" Creed asked.

Thad shook his head. "No, to hell with that." He held up a wad of money. "We've got enough for each one of us to have our own whore."

Billy Puckett showed Falcon around town, introducing him to the mayor, the banker, the newspaper publisher, and the saloon owner. He walked him to the hotel and made certain that he got the best room in the house, then that night he invited Falcon to have dinner with him.

The Dunn Hotel proudly advertised bathing rooms on every floor, and Falcon took a bath and changed clothes so that when he stepped into the hotel dining room that night, he felt like a new man.

"You would be Mr. MacCallister?" the maître d' asked.

The maître d' somewhat surprised Falcon, because he hadn't been there for breakfast.

"Yes, I'm MacCallister."

"Sheriff Puckett is waiting for you."

Falcon followed the maître d' through the crowded dining room to a table in the far back corner. There were no windows near the table and, because the table was in the corner, both Falcon and the sheriff would be able to sit with their backs to the wall.

Sheriff Puckett stood as Falcon approached, reached out again to shake his hand, and then the two men sat.

"Would you like some wine, sir?" the maître d' asked.

Falcon shook his head. "I'd prefer some sippin' whiskey."

"I'll have the same," Puckett said.

"Very good, sir."

Both men ordered beefsteak and fried potatoes. Not until the waiter returned to the kitchen with their order did Puckett resume the conversation.

"Falcon, I want to apologize for the way the judge behaved this morning. Actually, he is a fine and principled man."

"Oh, I don't have any trouble with his principles," Falcon said as he cut a piece of bread and spread some butter on it. "It's the fact that he has prejudged me that I don't like."

"I can see how you'd be a mite upset over that. But like I say, he is an honest man. I have to tell you, Falcon, I'm very happy you accepted my invitation," Puckett said. "And a little surprised as well."

"Well, I had holed up long enough. I figured it was about time for me to get out again," Falcon said. "And I confess that I have thought about you from time to time, wondering whatever happened to that fella Pa brought in more dead than alive."

"Your pa was a good man," Puckett said. "And your ma was a saint, nursing me the way she did."

"You know, I don't think I ever asked you, but how did you happen to wind up in Indian territory in the first place?"

Puckett laughed. "I had a bad winter once, went to the Rendezvous with some of the sorriest plews you ever seen. I heard a bunch of folks talkin' about a stream where the beaver were as thick as flies. Only thing was, it was Indian territory and everyone was afraid to go there."

"Let me guess. You figured if everyone else was afraid to go there, it would just make the pickings that much better for you," Falcon said.

"Boy, you read my mind," Puckett replied. "And it was a good plan too. I was halfway through the season, had more pelts than I'd taken in the previous two years. And they was good pelts too. Then, one day when I was runnin' my traps, a party of Indians showed up. I tried to parley with them, but they weren't in a talkin' mood. Next thing you know they was orderin' me out . . . without my beaver skins. Well, I wasn't going to have that, so I pointed my rifle at them and ordered them to get."

"I take it they didn't get."

"They rode out about fifty yards from me, then turned back. By then they had arrows in their bows, and they meant business. I shot one of them, but I took a couple of arrows before I could reload. Don't know why they didn't take my scalp, but when I come to, your pa was over me. Don't know what he was doing there, or how he found me."

"Pa had a lot friends among the Indians," Falcon said. "He never told me flat out, but I would guess that they told him about you."

"Well, I'm glad for that. Like I said, I wouldn't be here now if your pa hadn't found me, and your ma hadn't nursed me through."

"Billy, there was something else in your letter that got my attention. You said you had something you needed to get off your chest."

"Yes. It's something that has been bothering me for many years now. I need to talk to someone about it and, since it involves you, I've chosen you."

"It involves me? Are you talking about something that happened thirty-four years ago?"

Puckett shook his head. "No. This was more like twenty years ago."

"Twenty years ago and it involves me? How can it? I didn't know you twenty years ago."

"You were in the war," Puckett said. It was more in the form of a statement than a question.

"Yes," Falcon said.

"You were at Chattanooga." Again, the comment was more along the lines of a statement than a question.

"Yes, I was at Chattanooga."

"So was I."

"You were? I don't remember seeing you there."

"I saw you."

"Why didn't you say something to me?"

"I was wearing blue, you were wearing gray."

"Billy, that's not what you're trying to get off your chest, is it? I mean, the fact that you wore blue and I wore gray? You may not know this, but some of my brothers fought for the Union."

"It's more than that. I want to tell you a story," Puckett said.

"All right, I'm listening."

The sheriff was a skilled raconteur, and as he began telling the story, Falcon found himself slipping back in time, reliving those days when, as a young man, barely in his twenties, he fought for the Confederacy, riding as a scout for Morgan's Raiders.

The shock waves of the explosion moved across the field and hit Falcon, making his stomach shake. The blasts were set off by long fuses, but were timed to go together, starting as bursts of white-hot flame, then erupting black smoke from the points where the charges were laid. The underpinnings of the trestle were carried away by the torpedoes, but the superstructure remained intact for several more seconds, stretching across the creek with no visible means of support, as if defying the laws of gravity. Then, slowly, the tracks began to sag and the ties started snapping, popping with a series of loud reports like pistol shots, until finally, with a resounding crash and a splash of water, the whole bridge collapsed into the river.

"Now, that's the way to do it," Falcon said exuberantly. "We dropped her into the water just as neat as a pin!"

"I suppose so," Captain Ward said.

"What's wrong, Captain?" Falcon asked. "You don't sound very enthused about it. It was a good job, and it'll delay the Yankees for at least a week."

"A week," Captain Ward said. "Don't forget, Mac-Callister, I live here. I watched them build that trestle before the war. Do you know how long it took?"

"No, sir, I don't."

"It took seven weeks. We blow it up in seven seconds, and the most we can hope to get out of it is that it will delay the Yankees by seven days. And it was our bridge in the first place. The tracks, the bridges, the roads, everything we are destroying down here belongs to the South. What kind of war is it when we strike at the enemy by destroying the property of our own people?"

"It's a terrible war, Captain, but that's the kind we've got," Falcon said. "On the other hand, look at it this way. Better to give them one bridge than a whole town."

"I guess you're right," Ward replied.

Sergeant Haverkost, who had been on lookout, came riding up. "Cap'n, beggin' your pardon, sir, but they's Yankee cavalry a-comin'."

"*Very good, Sergeant. Get the men mounted,*" Captain Ward replied.

"*Whoa,*" Falcon said. "*Captain, we aren't turning tail, are we? Shouldn't we stay and fight them?*"

"*How are your shoes holding out, Lieutenant?*" Captain Ward asked.

"*My shoes?*"

"*Aren't the soles getting a little thin?*"

"*Now that you mention it, I reckon they are.*"

"*If the Yankee cavalry is here, that means their supply depot isn't guarded.*" Captain Ward smiled. "*I say we do a little shoppin', then burn what we can't carry away with us. It's about time we destroyed some Yankee property.*"

"*Right!*" Falcon said happily.

Captain Ward led his men into the supply depot, thinking it would be almost totally unguarded. But to his surprise, there was an infantry company waiting for them. Ward fell with the first volley.

Falcon leaped from his horse to try to rescue his captain, but bullets were whizzing all around him.

"*Go!*" Captain Ward shouted. "*Get out of here! Take the men and go!*"

One minié ball took off Falcon's hat, and another penetrated the loose flap of his sleeve.

"*Lieutenant, let's not lose both of us here!*" Captain Ward shouted. "*I order you to get the men out now!*"

Falcon nodded, then remounted. He shouted to the others.

"*Fall back! Fall back!*"

Two other men were hit and unseated. Another one slumped forward, and stayed mounted only because his friend held him in the saddle.

The Confederates withdrew, riding hard until they were well out of range. Then Falcon stopped them.

"What do we do now, Lieutenant?" Sergeant Haverkost asked.

"We wait until nightfall," Falcon said. "Then we go back and get them."

The wounded man who rode away from the ambush died late that afternoon. His death, and the capture of three of their own, kept the men's blood running hot until that night. After sunset, Falcon led them back to the supply depot. Dismounting, they counted off every fourth man, designating him to be a horse holder. Then, advancing on foot, Falcon led the rest down to the clearing where the ambush had taken place earlier in the day.

What they saw stopped them in their tracks. The rage Falcon felt was so overpowering that he let out a scream of anger and defiance.

"I hung 'em," Puckett said, concluding the story.

"I beg your pardon?"

"It was me that hung 'em, Falcon. Captain Ward, Private Higgins, and Private Morrison. I was in command of the Union Infantry troops that were guarding the depot."

Falcon was quiet for a long moment. The rage he had felt at the time he discovered the bodies of his captain and two of his men hanging from a tree limb had long since subsided.

"Why?" he asked.

"Rebels had destroyed three bridges, knocked down more than a hundred telegraph poles, and robbed two supply wagons. I had orders to make an example of anyone we caught who was engaged in that activity."

"So you killed your prisoners," Falcon said.

Puckett stared at the untouched steak on his plate. He was silent for a long moment. Then sighing, he nodded and said, "Yes, God help me, I killed them. At the time, I thought it was a legitimate act of war," he continued. "But I know now, and have known for many years, that what I did was wrong. It has haunted me ever since."

"Why are you telling me this now, after all these years?"

"I was there when you attacked the depot. I saw you jump down from your horse and try to save Ward. At first, I thought you were your father, you looked so much like him. But then I saw that you were too young to be Jamie. I asked Ward, and he confirmed who you were."

"Captain Ward had a wife and two kids," Falcon said.

"I . . . I didn't know that."

"He didn't tell you?"

"Other than confirming who you were, he never said a word. He didn't even say anything when we put the noose around his neck."

"Would it have made any difference to you if you had known he had a wife and two children?"

"At the time, I don't think it would have. Now, it just adds to my burden."

"Why did you tell me, Billy?"

"I don't rightly know," Puckett replied. "I reckon what I'm doing is asking for your forgiveness."

"I can't do that," Falcon replied. "It's not that I won't . . . it's that I can't. I don't think I have that right. If it's forgiveness you're wanting, I reckon you're going to have to get that from the families of the men you hanged."

Billy stared at his steak for a moment, then pushed his plate away, totally untouched.

"I can't do that," he said. "I can't ask them for forgiveness until I can forgive myself."

Seeing the pain in Sheriff Puckett's face, Falcon

sighed. "Billy, I expect that if truth were known, there's no one who fought in that war that doesn't have something they'd just as soon forget. I know that I have my own ghosts chasing me. It's something that we all have to live with. You didn't do what you did out of malice of heart, but because you deemed it your duty. But if it's any consolation to you, I want you to know that I'm not holding what you did against you. That was then, and this is now." He offered his hand in friendship. "As far as I'm concerned, you're still the same brave, strong man who once fascinated a young boy with stories of your adventures in the mountains."

A look of relief came across Billy's face then, and he smiled as he took Falcon's hand in his own.

"Thanks, Falcon," he said. "You've just taken a huge load off my heart."

Sheffield, Dakota Territory

The Howard brothers had been in Sheffield for almost two weeks now, and during that time they had spent money like water. All three were wearing new clothes. Thad had a new hat, and Creed was wearing new boots.

They had bought drinks for everyone in the saloon several times now, and had lost money in poker games without complaint. If there was any complaint, it was that whores of the town, anxious to get their share of the money, were paying so much attention to the three Howard brothers that the other men felt left out.

They had established a habit of having their breakfast in bed every morning . . . though because they were staying up so late each night, "morning" for them occurred at around one-thirty or two o'clock in the afternoon.

When Thad came down this morning, the bartender smiled and called out to him.

"Mr. Howard, it come in this morning."

"What come in this morning?" Thad asked.

"Why, your champagne, of course," the bartender said. "Don't you remember the other day when you asked me to order you some? Well, I did, and it come up from MacCallister."

"Champagne, yes!" Thad said. "I ain't never tasted it before, and I figured that if I didn't do it now, I never would do it."

Thad's brothers came down a few minutes later and Thad told them the news.

"Boys, we're goin' to drink some champagne!" he said proudly.

"What for?" Creed asked.

"Because of the way folks talk about it all the time. I want to see what it is they're carryin' on about."

By now several others in the saloon, none of whom had ever tasted champagne either, had gathered around the three brothers, and their hanger-on whores, to watch the proceedings.

Thad bit down on the cork to pull it off.

"Lord, no, don't do it that way!" the bartender warned, sticking his hand out to stop him.

"Why not?"

"You try and take it off that way and it will knock your teeth out," the bartender said. "Here, let me do it."

The bartender reached for the bottle, but Thad jerked it back from him.

"The hell you say. This is my bottle, I done bought and paid for it. Just tell me how to open it is all I ask."

The bartender demonstrated how to do it by putting

his thumbs under the cork and pushing up. Thad began following the bartender's directions and, slowly, the cork began easing its way up the neck of the bottle.

"Damn, what's wrong with it?" Creed asked. "It don't seem to want to—"

POP!

The cork popped up out of the bottle and flew three-quarters of the way across the room.

There were loud guffaws of laughter and squeals of delight as the champagne started spewing up from the bottle. Thad stuck the bottle in his mouth and tried to drink, but wound up coughing and choking instead.

Finally, when the fizz had died down a little, Thad and his brothers Creed and Bob passed the bottle around until it was gone.

Thad knew that several of the others in the saloon wanted a taste as well. They didn't want to help drink it, they knew that wasn't possible, but they did hope that the Howards, who had been so generous in buying drinks for everyone, would share in this as well.

But the Howards shared with no one, including the three whores who were so bold as to come right out and ask for a taste.

"Hell, no," Thad said. "You think I'm going to let a whore have some of this?"

When the last of the champagne was gone, Thad wiped his lips with the sleeve of his shirt, belched, then looked at his two brothers.

"I hope you enjoyed it, boys, 'cause it's all gone," he said.

"Well, it wasn't all that good anyway, if you ask me," Bob said. "I'd as soon drink horse piss. Let's just get us another bottle of whiskey."

"We can't," Thad said.

"What do you mean?"

"It ain't just the champagne that's all gone. It's the money. We done spent ever' dime we got."

"You mean you ain't got no more money?" one of the whores asked.

Thad turned his pockets inside out by way of demonstration.

"In that case, I guess you won't be needing us anymore," the whore said. "Come on, girls."

"Wait a minute," Creed called to them. "You mean after all the money we done spent on you, you ain't goin' to stay with us anymore? I thought we might go back up to our rooms for a little more fun."

"No money, no fun," the whore said.

"No money, no rooms," the bartender added. "I reckon you boys better be movin' on."

"The hell you say!" Bob said angrily. "After all the money we've spent here, you owe us. Now, give us a bottle of whiskey."

The bartender reached under the bar, but when he brought his hands up again they were wrapped around a double-barrel Greener.

"I expect you boys had better get on out of town," he said.

"Why, you low-assed bastard," Thad said, reaching for his pistol.

The sound of both barrels being cocked filled the room. "You want to try it, mister?" the bartender asked.

"Come on, Thad, let's go," Bob said.

Thad glared at the bartender for a while longer. Then, with a shrug, he turned and started toward the door with his two brothers following him.

"Bye, boys," one of the whores called to them. "Come back when you have money again."

"Yeah. Lots of money," one of the other whores

added, and their laughter and the laughter of the bar patrons followed the Howards outside.

At the livery, the three brothers saddled and mounted their horses. When they started to ride away, though, Thad went one way, while Bob and Creed went another.

"Hey, Thad, ain't you a-comin' with us?" Creed called.

"No, I ain't goin' with you," Thad called back. He neither looked around, nor gave any explanation as to why he'd decided to go off by himself.

"What are you goin' to do?" Bob asked.

Thad waved his arm as if dismissing the question.

"What are we going to do?" Bob asked. "We don't have no money."

This time, Thad didn't even give them the benefit of the dismissive wave of his arm. He just continued to ride, looking straight ahead.

Chapter 5

The angle of the late-afternoon sun brought out a kaleidoscope of colors in the buttes and hills, the coulees and ravines of western North Dakota: pinks, reds, blacks, greens, yellows, and rich browns. The rider, a well-muscled man with wide shoulders and a short, bull-like neck, paused for a moment to enjoy the dancing light and changing hues before he sloped down a long hill toward a ford in the river ahead. Teddy Roosevelt was sitting in a fine, silver-studded saddle and mounted on a superb bay horse, wearing a new Stetson hat and glasses that, now and then, flashed in the setting sun. A full canteen, bedroll, and saddle-rifle showed that he was either planning to spend the night on the range, or would be able to do so should the need arise.

To Roosevelt's right was a long, rather magnificent escarpment, which looked for all the world like a shelf of books in his library. The difference was that the cliff was here in the Dakota Territory, whereas his library was back in New York.

As owner of Elkhorn Ranch, Roosevelt could've sent any of his hands out to search for straying cattle, but he preferred to do it himself because these long, lonely rides gave him just the solitude he was looking for.

He had come to Dakota shortly after the Republican National Convention nominated James G. Blaine as candidate for President in the upcoming election. As Roosevelt had promised, he remained true to Senator John Edmonds until the last ballot.

Once Blaine received the nomination, Theodore Roosevelt, as a good Republican, pledged his support for the campaign. But true to Joe Murray's warning, Blaine shut Roosevelt out. He was not offered any position whatever in the campaign.

Politically, that was not good for Roosevelt. But personally, he welcomed it. It allowed him the freedom of coming to Dakota and spending time on his ranch, healing from the pain that he still felt.

The bawling of a calf caught his attention, snapping him out of his reverie. He slapped his legs against the side of his horse and started toward the sound.

"Hold steady there, little fellow," he called. "Be of stout heart, I'm coming to your rescue."

Roosevelt found the calf hung up in a briar patch. Dismounting, he helped the animal free itself, then set it to running.

"Go now," he said. "Join your mother and tell her of your great adventure."

Roosevelt remounted, then continued with his ride.

Thad Howard's horse went lame and, though the creature tried gamely to continue to carry his rider, he finally went down and was unable to get back up.

"You worthless son of a bitch!" Thad said, kicking his horse hard in its side. "What are you doing? You are leaving me stranded out here!" He kicked the horse again, trying to make it get up. The horse tried one more time and fell again. This time he didn't even lift his head.

"I'll tell you this, you sorry bag of bones. I'll not be

wasting a bullet on you. You can just lie there and die in your own good time. I'm through with you."

With one more kick of frustration, Thad removed the saddle and saddlebags. Throwing the saddle on his shoulder, he started walking, but after a few yards tossed the saddle away in disgust.

He continued on with the saddlebags, but after less than a mile threw them away too.

Two miles later, he took the last swallow of water from his canteen and tossed it aside as well.

Falcon had spent only one night in Belfield. He and Billy Puckett had stayed at the dinner table, talking long after the other diners had cleared out. It wasn't that they were reminiscing about old times. The time they'd shared had been a period of no more than three months, and that had been a little over thirty years ago. But they did catch each other up on their lives, and they shared stories of their adventures during the war. As it turned out, they had faced each other several times during the war, though it wasn't until the incident at Chattanooga that they had come in direct, or nearly direct, contact with each other.

Falcon left the next morning just after sunrise. When he'd left MacCallister to come up here for a visit with Billy Puckett, he'd planned to take the train back. In fact, he'd bought a two-way ticket. But the more he thought about it, the less interest he had in going back home. The old wanderlust that had pulled at him for so many years had grabbed hold of him again. He left Belfield on horseback, with no clear idea as to where he was going.

Falcon wandered around with no particular destination in mind for about two weeks. He was heading back to Belfield for some more supplies when he came across someone on the trail.

The man looked exhausted, sunburned, and very thirsty. Stopping, Falcon tossed his canteen to the man.

"You look like you could use a drink," he said.

"Yeah, thanks," Thad said, taking several Adam's-apple-bobbing swallows from the canteen.

"Been walking long?" Falcon asked.

"My horse stepped in a prairie-dog hole three days ago," Thad lied. "Broke his leg and I had to put him down. I been afoot ever since."

"Sorry to hear about that," Falcon said. He pointed just over a ridgeline. "But there's a town just over the ridge-line, not more'n five miles from here. It's called Belfield. If you cut through that pass, you can make it by noon."

"Thanks," Thad said. He handed the canteen back, and as Falcon was distracted while hooking it onto his pommel, Thad drew his gun. "You don't recognize me, do you, mister?"

"Should I?"

"Well, there's no reason you should. It was pretty dark that night, and I was wearin' a mask. I sure as hell recognize you, though."

"You're the train robber that got away," Falcon said. "You're the one that got away."

"With the money, yeah," Thad said. He giggled. "Too bad I ain't got none of it left, but me'n my brothers had a fine old time, I'll tell you that. Say, whatever happened to them boys that robbed the train with me? Did they go back to jail?"

"I killed them," Falcon said matter-of-factly.

Thad nodded. "Yeah, I figured you did. I just wanted to see if you would admit it."

"You don't seem all that broken up over it," Falcon said.

"Why the hell should I be? With them dead, me'n my brothers just had more money to spend. Now, climb down off that horse."

"Now, why would I want to do that?" Falcon replied calmly.

"Because if you don't, I'm going to put a bullet in your gizzard," Thad said. He reinforced his comment by pulling back the hammer of his pistol. The double clicking sound of the sear engaging the cylinder was cold and deadly.

"All right, you've convinced me," Falcon replied. He dismounted and handed over the reins.

"Hah, looks like maybe you're smarter'n I thought you was," Thad said. He pointed to the same pass Falcon had indicated earlier. "But, like you say, if you walk though that pass, it won't take you 'ny more'n an hour or so to reach that little town you was a-tellin' me about. Only thing is, you're goin' to have to go alone."

"How about leaving me my canteen?" Falcon asked.

Thad started to reach for it, then smiled and shook his head. "You think I'm fool enough to fall for my own trick?" he asked.

Falcon smiled back. "You're a smart one, all right," he said. "His name is Diablo."

"What?"

"The horse," Falcon explained. "His name is Diablo."

"Hell, mister, I don't give a damn what your horse's name is," Thad said gruffly. "I am to ride 'im, not make a pet out of him."

Thad jerked Diablo's head around. "Come on, horse," he growled.

Diablo didn't move.

"Come on, horse, giddyup," he said again, speaking more loudly this time. He slapped his legs against the side of the horse.

Diablo remained still.

"What the hell's wrong with this horse?" Howard asked.

"I don't know. He works fine for me."

"Say something to him."

"Now, Diablo," Falcon said.

Suddenly, and without warning, Diablo bucked hard, and Thad was thrown off.

With a shout of alarm and surprise, Thad tossed his gun aside as he was flying through the air. He hit the ground hard, then lay there for a long moment trying to collect his senses and get his breath. Finally, he got up onto his hands and knees, shook his head a few times, then stood.

"Are you in one piece?" Falcon asked.

"Yeah, I—" Thad started to say. Then, looking up, he noticed that Falcon had not only remounted his horse, he was holding a gun. And the gun was pointing directly at Howard.

"What the—?" Thad stuttered. "How the hell did you do that?"

"Pick up the canteen and take another drink of water," Falcon said. "You've got a pretty good walk in front of you."

"Falcon," Billy Puckett said. "I didn't expect to see you again so soon." He smiled broadly when he saw the man Falcon was bringing in. "I'll be damned! That's Thad Howard."

"I ran across him about five miles out of town," Falcon said. "He's the other train robber."

"He's also a murderer," Billy said. "Turns out he killed a sheriff over in Blue Springs. Was tried and convicted for it too, but escaped jail before they could hang him."

"He ain't goin' to get out of our jail," Deputy Merrill said. "Come along, you, in the jail with you."

"There's a reward for him," Billy said. He opened his desk drawer and pulled out a voucher, then made it out to Falcon MacCallister. "Take this over to the bank," he said. "It's good for five hundred dollars."

"The hell you say," Falcon said, smiling broadly. "Well, that more than pays for my trip up here, doesn't it?"

"I reckon so. What are you going to do with all that money?" Billy asked. "As if that is a lot of money to you. Your pa was one of the richest men in Colorado before he died, and you don't strike me as the kind of man that spends a lot. If I had to guess, I'd say you had just about every penny your pa left."

"Maybe a little more," Falcon said. He held up the voucher. "But found money is always good. And as to what I plan to do with it, well, I thought I'd go down to the saloon, have myself a good lunch, a few drinks, and maybe get into a friendly game of cards."

Billy laughed. "Must be good to be a man of leisure."

Falcon started toward the door, then stopped and turned back toward Billy.

"I've been thinking about Judge Heckemeyer," Falcon said.

"You don't want to go thinking too much about him, Falcon. Like I told you, he's a fair and honest man, but he ain't someone you want to be against you."

"No, it's not that. It's the name. I told you I had heard that name before, and now I remember where it was. Does he have a daughter, oh, I'd say about twenty or twenty-one now?"

"Yes, he does. Her name is—"

"Anna," Falcon said.

Billy looked surprised. "Now, how could you possibly know that? She's been away to school for four years now."

"In New York," Falcon said.

"Yes, in New York. Falcon, you want to tell me what's goin' on?"

"I met her," Falcon said.

"Where?"

"In New York. You may recall from our conversation the other night, my brother, Andrew, and my sister, Rosanna, live in New York."

"Yes, they are actors of some note, you said."

"Actors, musicians, composers," Falcon said. "It's clear they got all the talent in the family. Anyway, about two or three years ago I went up to New York to visit them, and I saw one of their plays. There were three young girls . . ." He paused in mid-sentence, then remembered Anna's comment that, biologically speaking, they were beyond girlhood. "Make that three young women, who needed tickets to the play. I let them sit in the box with me."

"And you say one of them was Anna Heckemeyer?"

"Yes. From Medora, Dakota Territory, she said."

Billy Puckett nodded. "That would be her, all right. I'll be damned. This is a small world, ain't it?"

Deputy Merrill came back to the main office. "I got him all locked up back there. So, what do we do next?"

"How would you like to spend a day or two in Bismarck?" Billy asked.

Merrill smiled broadly. "That would be great," he said. "My sister lives there."

"Go to the Territorial Attorney's office and get a warrant transfer for Thad Howard," he said. "And tell them to send the hangman."

"We goin' to hang him here?" Merrill asked.

"That's the instructions we received," Billy said. "They don't want to take a chance on his escaping in transit again. So, whoever takes him into custody will have a warrant transfer that will authorize execution of the court findings. In this case, a hanging."

Merrill looked up at the clock. "If I hurry, I can catch the twelve-fifteen," he said.

"Are you going to stay around for the proceedings?" Billy asked.

"What? You mean the hanging?" Falcon asked. He shook his head. "Watching a man's neck stretch isn't my idea of a good time."

"Damn," Billy said, pinching the bridge of his nose. "Oh, damn, I'm sorry, Falcon, I wasn't thinking. You would be thinking about Captain Ward and your men, wouldn't you?"

Falcon shook his head. "Well, now that you mention it, I guess I was. But truth to tell, I'd as soon see them come up with some other way of executing folks."

"Like what?"

"I don't know. Shooting them, I suppose. They say the French have a guillotine, a big blade that whacks the head off. Folks die quick that way. It's got to be better than hanging."

"Yeah, well, if somebody does murder, then I'm not all that particular about how they die," Billy said. "Maybe if a few more people would stop and think about what it's like to get hung, wouldn't be so many of 'em committin' crimes that lead 'em to the gallows."

Chapter 6

The little town of Belfield sat baking in the late summer sun. To the six riders approaching from the east, the collection of sun-bleached wooden buildings were so much a part of the land that the town could've been the result of nature, rather than man.

Percy Shaw, the youngest of the riders, slipped his canteen off the pommel and took a drink. The water was sour and tepid, but his tongue was dry and swollen. He ran the back of his hand across his mouth, then recorked the canteen and hooked it back onto his saddle.

"Hey, Aaron, what do you say we stop in to the saloon and get us a few beers? I gotta have me somethin' to wet this here dust we been chewin' on for the last ten days."

"You just had a drink of water," Aaron answered. Aaron Childers was the oldest, and the acknowledged leader of the six riders, which also included his two brothers, Frank and Corey, and their cousins, Dalton and Ethan Yerby.

"Yeah, but the water in this here canteen is beginnin' to taste like piss," Percy complained.

Frank Childers laughed. "Well, now, just how the hell would you know what piss tastes like, Percy? You been drinkin' a lot of it lately, have you?"

"Well, I ain't exactly drunk no piss, but I can guess

what it tastes like. It tastes just like this water. What do you say, Aaron? Can we get us a couple of beers afore we take care of our business?"

"We ain't a-goin' into no saloons in this town," Aaron said. "Iffen we was to start drinkin' with the locals, the next thing you know, ever'one's goin' to have a good description of us."

"Hell, you think they ain't goin' to have a description of us anyway?" Percy asked. "The moment we rob the bank, ever'one there's goin' to know what we look like."

"They ain't goin' to recognize us if we do the job right," Aaron said. "You just do what I tell you. We'll be in that bank, have the money, and then be out of there again before anyone in town knows what hit 'em. Then when we ride into the next town, we can go in style. Why, we'll have enough money to swim in beer if we want to. Women, hotels, restaurants, gamblin' money. We'll have enough to do anything we want."

"Yeah," Percy said, smiling broadly. "Yeah, that sounds good."

"You're through bellyachin' about beer then, are you?"

"Yeah, I'm through," Percy said.

"Good. Now, let's get on with it. You boys check your pistols."

The men pulled their pistols and checked the cylinders to see that all the chambers were properly charged. Then they slipped their guns back into their holsters.

"Ready?" Aaron asked.

"Ready," Percy replied.

"Yeah, me too," Corey said.

"We're ready," Ethan said, speaking for himself and his brother.

* * *

Falcon MacCallister was sitting at a small table in the back of the Blue Dog Saloon. On the table in front of him was a meal of vegetable soup and biscuits. Admittedly it wasn't the best fare, but at least it wasn't trail-cooked.

As Billy had instructed, Falcon had taken his voucher to the bank and now in his pocket was five hundred dollars in cash. This was the reward money paid for the capture of Thad Howard.

Falcon hadn't even known about the reward when he turned Howard over to Sheriff Puckett. It was Puckett who'd brought it up, and Puckett who'd authorized immediate payment.

Because it was midday, the saloon was nearly empty. As a result, Cait Smathers was the only bar girl working. The others would come tonight, when the saloon was busier.

Cait was standing at the end of the bar, nursing a sarsaparilla.

"Sure is quiet in here," she said.

"Yeah," the bartender replied. He was washing and wiping glasses. He nodded toward the table where Falcon was having his lunch. "That fella over there is Falcon MacCallister. Why don't you go talk to him?"

"Why? Looks like all he is interested in is eatin'. I'm not likely to make any money from him."

"Maybe you will and maybe you won't," the bartender said. "But I do know that he is flush right now."

Cait's interest perked up. "Oh? And how do you know that?"

"He brought in Thad Howard this morning," the bartender said. "Sheriff Puckett paid him the reward money."

"He already paid the reward?"

"Yes."

"How come him to pay so fast?"

"Turns out the sheriff and MacCallister are old friends," the bartender said.

Cait looked over toward Falcon. What she saw was a big man concentrating on his meal. His long hair was the color of winter straw.

The bartender drew a beer and handed it to Cait. "He's already paid for this," he said.

Cait took the glass over to Falcon's table, then sat down without being invited. She pasted a big smile, on her face, but when he looked up at her, his eyes, like blue steel, were hard and cold. For a moment she felt a twinge of fear . . . she had infringed upon his privacy and the expression on his face indicated that he did not appreciate that.

Then he relaxed and the coldness fell away, to be replaced by a face that was, at a minimum, interesting and could even be considered handsome. It was at least inviting, and her smile returned.

"Frank said you ordered this," she said, putting the beer in front of him.

"Thanks."

"He also said you brought in Thad Howard."

Falcon nodded. "I did," he said. He took a drink of the new beer.

"And you already got your reward?"

"Yes."

Falcon was proving to be a man of few words, and that was making it difficult for Cait. Falcon used the back of his hand to wipe the foam away from his lips.

"So, what are you going to do with all that money?" Cait asked.

"Spend it," Falcon said.

* * *

The boardwalks were filled with men and women, moving from store to store in Belfield, attending to their daily commerce. A farmer parked his wagon in front of the mercantile, and his wife and two children jumped down to run inside the store, even as six men rode by in the street out front.

The six men, all of whom were wearing long white dusters, continued on into the town until they reached the Bank of Belfield. There, Aaron, Percy, Ethan, and Dalton dismounted, and handed their reins to Corey.

Corey and Frank remained in the saddle and kept their eyes open on the street out front. The other four looked up and down the street once, then pulled their kerchiefs up over the bottom halves of their faces and, drawing their guns, pushed open the door and barged inside.

There were six customers in the bank when the four men rushed in. Because of the masks on their faces and the guns in their hands, the customers and the bank teller knew immediately what was going on.

"You men, get your hands up and stand over against the wall!" Aaron shouted.

The customers complied with the orders.

While the other three kept everyone covered, Aaron hopped over the railing to go behind the teller cage. Pulling a cloth bag from his pocket, he held it out toward the teller. "Put all your money into this here bag," he ordered.

Trembling, the teller emptied his cash drawer.

Across the street from the bank, young Marcus Wise was standing at the window of the mercantile store. He had come into town to go shopping with his mother and, as a reward for "being a good boy," she had bought him a licorice whip. Eating the licorice, he was staring at the bank across the street.

Marcus saw the men pull kerchiefs up over their faces, then go inside. Then he saw the people inside put up their hands. He laughed.

"Mama, look across the street at those funny men," Marcus said. "They sure are funny."

"You look, dear, I'm busy right now," his mother answered. She picked up an apple peeler. "Mr. Dunnigan, are you telling me this will peel an apple?"

"It will indeed, Mrs. Wise," Dunnigan answered. "It will automatically peel and core an apple just as slick as a whistle."

"My, my," Mrs. Wise said, studying the mechanical marvel. "What will they think of next?"

Marcus laughed again. "Now everyone is holding their hands up in the air."

This time, Marcus got the grocer's attention. "What did you say, Marcus?" Dunnigan, the store owner, asked. "Something about people in the bank with their arms up?"

"Look over there. See? All those people in the bank are holding their arms in the air," Marcus said.

Dunnigan walked over to the window and looked across the street toward the bank.

"The boy is right," he said. "Oh, my God! They are robbing the bank!"

Another customer was in the store and when he heard Dunnigan, he ran outside and started shouting.

"They are robbing the bank! They are robbing the bank!"

"Mrs. Wise, grab Marcus and get to the back of the store. Get down behind the counter," Dunnigan warned. Even as he spoke, he grabbed a double-barrel shotgun from beneath his store counter and broke it open to slip two shells into the chambers.

Inside the bank, the teller's hands trembled as he took money from the teller's drawer to drop into the sack Percy Shaw was waiting for. In a surprisingly short time, he handed the bag to Percy.

Percy looked down into the bag and saw just a few bills and some change.

"What the hell?" he said. He handed the bag back. "What are you trying to pull, mister? Put it all in there!" he demanded.

The teller nodded, and pointed to his empty drawer. "It is all in there," he said. "Do you see? The drawer is empty."

"Why, there's not enough here to have a good drunk," Percy said gruffly. He handed the sack back to the teller. "If you know what's good for you, you'll put more money in here."

"Please, mister, you see the drawer," the teller said. "I've put everything in there."

"Hurry up, Percy! What the hell's the holdup?" Aaron asked anxiously.

"This son of a bitch is holding out on us," Percy said. He showed the sack to Aaron. "This is all we got."

"The hell with that," Aaron said angrily. He came around behind the teller's counter and stuck the end of his pistol into the bank teller's nose, pushing so hard that it began to bleed.

"Are you telling me this is all the money there is in this bank?"

"N-no," the teller stammered. "There's more money in the safe."

Aaron looked over at Percy. "Can't you do a damn

thing right?" he asked. "Do I have to do everything myself?" Then, looking back at the teller, he demanded, "All right, mister, get the money out of the safe."

"I can't," the teller answered.

"What do you mean you can't? I'm the one holding the gun here, and I say you can."

The teller shook his head desperately. "No, sir, I can't. I can't open the safe. I don't know the combination."

"Don't tell me you don't know the combination. You work here, don't you?"

"Ye-yes, sir," the teller replied. "But Mr. Harkins owns the bank and he's the only one who knows the combination."

"All right, get him."

"He's out of town for the day," the teller replied. "He won't be back till late this evening."

Suddenly the front door opened and Frank, who didn't have the bottom half of his face masked, stuck his head in.

"Aaron, you better come quick!" he shouted. "Somebody seen these fellas with their hands up and went runnin' down the street yellin' that the bank was bein' robbed. We got to get out of here!"

"I ain't goin' nowhere till I get the rest of the money," Aaron replied. He pointed his pistol toward the teller and cocked it. "Open the damn safe!"

The teller began to shake uncontrollably. "Mister, don't you think I would if I could? I sure as hell don't want to die! I can't open that safe."

"Ha!" Percy said, pointing to the teller. "Lookee there. He just pissed in his pants. You know what, Aaron? I believe him."

Shouting in frustrated rage, Aaron brought his pistol

down on the teller's head. With a groan, the teller dropped to the floor.

"What are we going to do now?" Percy asked.

Aaron looked around the bank, and at the terrified faces of the customers, all of whom were standing against the wall with their hands still raised. Then, with the sack of money clutched firmly in his hand, Aaron vaulted back over the teller's counter.

"Let's go!" he shouted.

Dunnigan came running out onto the front porch of his store, his shotgun loaded and raised. As soon as he saw the men emerging from the bank, he let go with both barrels. The gunshot was as loud as a thunderclap, and the recoil of both barrels being fired kicked back so hard that the gun went almost straight up.

He missed, but saw the result of his double-aught buckshot as it hit the front window of the bank, bringing it down with a loud crash.

"You son of a bitch!" Frank shouted. He fired back at Dunnigan, and the bullet hit the pillar that was supporting the porch overhang. Dunnigan's face was peppered with the splinters of wood that were raised by the impact of the bullet, but he wasn't injured.

Realizing then that he had fired both rounds and had nothing left to shoot with, Dunnigan darted quickly back into the store, just as another bullet slammed into the wall close by.

As he reached the front door of the bank, Aaron saw someone from across the street shoot at them with a heavy-gauge shotgun. The charge of double-aught buckshot missed him and the others, but it did hit the front window, bringing it down with a loud crash. Aaron shot back, and though he missed the man with the shotgun, he at least drove him back inside.

"Come on! Come on! Get mounted! Get mounted!" Corey shouted, trying to hand the others the reins to their horses. Corey's own horse started twisting around with him.

Aaron and the others leaped into their saddles, then started at a gallop down the street.

There had been several citizens out on the street and the sidewalks when the shooting erupted, and now they stood there watching in shock as the men who had just robbed their bank were getting away. They were too shocked by the suddenness of the event to dive for cover. On the other hand, either none of them were armed, or else none of them wanted to be a hero, because no one attempted to engage the bank robbers.

Falcon heard the roar of the shotgun first, then the shout of the man who was running down the street.

"They are robbing the bank! They are robbing the bank!" the man shouted.

Quickly, Falcon got up from the table and, gun in hand, hurried to the door, arriving just as the six mounted men thundered past him. It was strange. They were at a full gallop, and yet he could see each of them with such crystal clarity that it was as if they were on stage, performing a tableau.

He could see their jaws set, the muscles in their necks standing out, the raw, wind-burned brown of their skin, the flared nostrils, and their eyes, desperate eyes, staring straight ahead.

The hooves of the horses were throwing up large clods of dirt from the street as they passed by in full gallop.

* * *

It looked to Aaron as if they were about to get away cleanly. Other than the one attempt with a shotgun when they first emerged from the bank, no one made any attempt to stop them.

Then, ahead of them, a man stepped down off the boardwalk and out into the street. A flash of sunlight revealed the fact that a star was fastened to his vest.

"It's the sheriff!" Aaron shouted.

Falcon watched as the retreating bank robbers raised their pistols toward Billy.

"Billy, look out!" Falcon shouted, even as the sheriff raised his own pistol.

There was a ripple of gunfire and a cloud of smoke as the bank robbers fired a volley toward the sheriff.

After the first volley Billy grabbed his shoulder, then staggered back a step. Aaron followed up with a second shot, as did the others, and the sheriff went down under the fusillade of bullets.

With a shout of rage, Falcon fired at the bank robbers. He saw a puff of dust rise from the impact of his bullet.

"Dalton, I'm hit! I'm hit!" Ethan shouted. He grew unsteady in the saddle, then tumbled to the ground.

Corey went down next.

"Corey! Corey!" Frank shouted. Turning his horse, he headed back toward Ethan.

"Frank, keep up!" Aaron shouted.

"I ain't a-goin' to leave Corey and Ethan."

Frank rode back toward the two wounded men, but the others continued on out of town.

"Come back here!" Frank shouted in desperation. "Aaron, come back here! We can't leave them like this!"

Frank leaped from his saddle, then knelt beside the two wounded men.

The man who had shot them came running up with his gun drawn and pointed directly at Frank.

"Stand up," the big man shouted, illustrating his command with vigorous motions of his pistol.

"Who would you be, mister?" Frank asked.

"The name is MacCallister. Falcon MacCallister."

"What did you take a hand in this for? You ain't no lawman."

"You interrupted my lunch," Falcon said sarcastically.

"They're hurt pretty bad," Frank said, pointing to his brother and his cousin. "They need a doctor."

"If the sheriff dies, they won't be needing a doctor, they'll be needing an undertaker," Falcon growled as he came closer. "All three of you will."

Frank dropped his gun, then stood with his hands raised.

By now the three remaining robbers were well out of town and pushing their horses into a lather to put as much distance between them and the town as they could.

"Is anyone comin' after us?" Aaron shouted.

Percy, who was bringing up the rear, looked back over his shoulder at the receding town. He saw no one in pursuit.

"No," he answered. "They ain't no one mounted. We got away clean!" He laughed out loud, whooping into the wind. "We got away clean!"

"All except Ethan, Frank, and Corey," Dalton said. "They're still back there."

"What the hell got into Frank to go back like that?" Aaron asked.

"We should'a gone back for them our ownselves," Dalton said.

"The hell you say. If we had, we'd be right there with them now."

"Nevertheless, we shouldn't of just left 'em like that," Dalton said. "They're our kin."

"What could we do for them if got captured too?" Aaron asked.

"Nothin', I reckon. Why? Are you planning on somethin'?"

"Maybe," Aaron said without being specific.

By now others from the town were moving, cautiously, out into the middle of the street where Falcon was standing with his three prisoners, Ethan Yerby and Frank and Corey Childers. Ethan had a bullet in his thigh, and Corey had one in his shoulder. Frank wasn't wounded.

"You got 'em," one of the townspeople said.

"How's Billy?" Falcon asked.

A couple of men were standing over the sheriff, and one of them looked back toward Falcon and shook his head slowly. "The sheriff's dead," he said.

"Looks like we've got you boys for murder," Falcon said to his prisoners.

"Hey! There's another one!" someone shouted, pointing to a body lying in the alley between the sheriff's office and the apothecary that was next door.

Quickly, several men ran to the other body.

"It's Eames!" someone called. "Gerald Eames! He's dead, shot clear through the heart."

"I need a doctor," Ethan said.

"Is there a doctor in town?" Falcon asked.

"We got Doc Gill, if he ain't drunk yet," someone said.

"He ain't normally drunk this time of day."

"Get 'im," Falcon said. "Bring 'im down to the jail to have a look at this man."

Falcon waved his pistol toward the sheriff's office, and the three prisoners responded.

When Falcon took them inside the building, Thad Howard was standing in his cell, his hands wrapped around the bars.

"What happened out there?" he asked. "Where's the sheriff?"

"The sheriff's dead," Falcon said. "These two killed him. It looks like you're going to have company on the gallows."

When Falcon went back outside, he saw several people standing over Billy, looking down at his body. He joined them, then looked up as Emil Prufrock arrived. Prufrock was the undertaker, and Falcon recognized him because he had seen him at the depot after the shootout on the train.

"Oh, my," Prufrock said, removing his hat as he looked down at Billy. "Oh, my, it's the sheriff."

"I want you to do right by him, Prufrock," Falcon said.

"Oh, yes indeed, I will," Prufrock promised.

"Give him the best coffin you have."

"You would be talking about the Eternal Cloud," Prufrock said. "That is a lovely coffin, but I'm afraid the county can't afford that."

"I'll pay for it," Falcon said.

"Yes, sir!" Prufrock said. "Oh, I'm sure Sheriff Puckett would be so pleased to know that he had such a dear friend. What a wonderful thing you are doing."

"Yeah," Falcon said dryly. "Wonderful."

Chapter 7

Walter Merrill was appointed to the office of sheriff of Belfield, replacing Billy Puckett. Shortly after the new sheriff was appointed, the Honorable Judge Andrew J. Heckemeyer came to Belfield for two days of trials. On the first day he tried Thad Howard. Howard was found guilty of train robbery, and as an accessory in the murder of the train engineer and the passenger. For that crime he was sentenced to forty years in prison. That sentence was meaningless, however, because the execution warrant for his conviction for murder in the first degree had been already been transferred for implementation.

On the second day, the Childers brothers, Frank and Corey, and Ethan Yerby were tried. The trial had lasted less than an hour, and the jury had gone out for deliberation.

A few minutes ago, the bailiff had announced that the jury had reached a verdict and Falcon and the others had filed back into the courtroom to await both the verdict and the judge's sentencing.

The bailiff came out first.

"All rise!" he called.

There was a sound of rustling cloth and creaking seats as the gallery responded to the bailiff's order.

"Oyez, oyez, oyez, this court in and for the county

of Stark is now in session, the Honorable Andrew J. Heckemeyer presiding."

Wearing a black robe, Judge Heckemeyer entered the courtroom from a door in front, stood behind the bench for a moment, then sat down.

"Be seated," he said.

The gallery sat.

There were four people at the defendants' table: Dan Gilmore, the court-appointed defense counsel, as well as Frank Childers, Corey Childers, and Ethan Yerby. Corey and Ethan were still showing the effects of their gunshot wounds. However, both had recovered sufficiently to stand trial.

The three men were being tried, not only for the murder of Sheriff Billy Puckett, but also for the murder of Gerald Eames.

Heckemeyer picked up a gavel and banged it once. "This court is now in session. Before we bring in the jury, I would like to address a few remarks to Mr. Falcon MacCallister. Mr. MacCallister, would you stand, please?"

Falcon, who was sitting about halfway toward the back of the court, was surprised by the judge's request, which, because he was a judge, was actually an order. Falcon stood.

"Mr. MacCallister, there are those who might want to congratulate you for capturing three of the men who robbed the bank and killed Sheriff Billy Puckett. Some might even call you a hero.

"But I do not share that opinion. Although a comparison of the caliber of the bullet that killed Mr. Eames showed that it was not from your gun, I believe you were indirectly, if not directly, responsible for his demise. By engaging the outlaws as you did, you showed reckless disregard for the safety of the citizens of Belfield. For that, sir, I feel that you should not be commended for your action, rather you should be chastised. You may sit down."

Falcon, barely able to hold his anger in check after being publicly berated by the judge, sat back down. He could feel the eyes of everyone in the room staring at him.

"Now, Mr. Bailiff, if you would, please bring the jury into the courtroom."

The bailiff left the room for a moment, then returned, leading the twelve men who had served on the jury. They were a disparate group consisting of cowboys, farmers, store clerks, draymen, and businessmen. Without a word, and without a glance right or left, which might tip off the verdict, they took their seats.

"Mr. Foreman, has the jury reached a verdict?" Judge Heckemeyer asked.

The foreman of the jury, who also owned the gunsmith shop, stood.

"We have, Your Honor."

Heckemeyer turned toward the defense table. "Would the attorney for the defense and the three defendants please stand?"

Gilmore, the lawyer for the defendants, and his three clients stood.

Heckemeyer turned back toward the foreman of the jury.

"Publish the verdict, Mr. Foreman."

"Your Honor, on the first charge, the murder of Sheriff Billy Puckett, we, the jury, find the defendants Corey Childers and Ethan Yerby coequally guilty of murder.

"On the second charge, the murder of Mr. Gerald Eames, we, the jury, find the defendants Cory Childers and Ethan Yerby coequally guilty."

"We find Frank Childers, on both counts, guilty of bank robbery and reckless endangerment."

"So say you all?" the judge asked.

"So say we all," the foreman replied.

"Thank you, you may be seated."

Heckemeyer turned toward the defendants, who were still standing.

"Mr. Gilmore, please bring the prisoners before the bench."

Gilmore instructed his three clients to approach the bench. Corey strolled up defiantly, arrogantly. Frank was a bit more contrite. Childers, because of the bullet wound in his thigh, limped up to the bench.

"Before I pass sentence, do any of you have anything to say?"

"Do what you have to do, you fat-assed son of a bitch," Corey said.

There was a gasp of surprise from the gallery.

"Corey, you son of a bitch, you have condemned us all," Frank said angrily. "I should have left your ass in the dirt."

"Oh, believe me, Mr. Childers, when I tell you that I will do what I have to do," Heckemeyer said. He cleared his throat.

"Frank Childers, you could have gotten away with the others," Judge Heckemeyer said. "But you came back to aid your brother and your cousin. Even though you have chosen a life of dishonor, there is some honor in what you did. Also, you were carrying a thirty-six-caliber pistol. None of the bullets taken from Sheriff Puckett's body were thirty-six caliber. The bullet that killed Mr. Eames was a forty-five caliber. That means that you did not kill either one.

"The jury could not find you guilty of murder, but you are guilty of armed bank robbery and by the discharge of your weapon, the reckless endangerment of innocent civilians."

Judge Heckemeyer looked out into the galley and fixed a steely and telling gaze upon Falcon, though he didn't address him. Then he returned his attention to Frank Childers.

"Therefore, it is the decision of this court that you will be taken to the territorial prison in Bismarck, there to serve a twenty-year sentence."

Realizing that his life had been spared, Frank gave a sigh of relief.

Heckemeyer then turned his attention to Corey and Ethan. The expression on his face grew more stern.

"Man is put upon this earth but a short time, and we are obligated by God to spend that short time in such a way as to make the world a better place by our having been here. Some do this by helping others, some do this by being a faithful steward to the bounty God has bestowed upon us.

"In your case, Corey Childers, and in your case, Ethan Yerby, the world will be a better place simply by being rid of you. Therefore, the jury having found you guilty of the murders of Sheriff Billy Puckett and Mr. Gerald Eames, it is my obligation, and, though I don't often say this, it is also my satisfaction, to make the world a better place by taking you from it.

"I hereby order, command, and direct that a contrivance be built of sufficient height and strength to elevate you from the ground, and from which you will be hanged by the neck.

"And there, hanging from the aforementioned gallows, you both shall remain suspended until all breath has left your bodies, your hearts have ceased to beat, and your blood stops its course. I further order, command, and direct that your bodies shall not be cut down until a doctor ascertains that you are both dead . . . dead . . . dead.

"Unfortunately, my power ends with the termination of your worthless lives, for if I could, I would not only hang you, I would send you to hell. However, I have every faith and confidence that the Judge of all men awaits you just on the other side of death's portal. And there is no doubt in my mind but that this Judge will take care of that situation for me."

Heckemeyer slammed the gavel against its pad.

"This court is adjourned."

There were at least one hundred people gathered in the town square, with more arriving by the minute. The gallows stood in the center of the square, its grisly shadow stretching under the morning sun. Judge Heckemeyer had ordered the hanging of Thad Howard to take place at exactly noon. Corey Childers and Ethan Yerby were to meet their fate exactly one half hour after the doctor declared Thad Howard dead.

The crowd, already thick and jostling for position, was awaiting the show with eager anticipation.

A few enterprising vendors passed through the crowd selling fried chicken, lemonade, beer, popcorn, and sweet rolls. A black-frocked preacher climbed up onto the gallows, even as the carpenters were making last-minute adjustments behind him. Taking advantage of the gathered audience, he began delivering a fiery sermon. He had a long, narrow face, sunken cheeks, and eyes as black as coal.

"In a short time, three men are going to be hung. Men like you and me, men who woke up this morning to the sweetness of God's own earth, will, by the time night rolls around, be six hours into their eternal damnation!

The never-ending fires of hell will burn their souls, and the pain they feel tonight will be just as severe ten thousand years from now.

"It is too late for them. Already, the devil is making room for them, for they are unrepentant sinners. But what about you?" He shouted the last word and pointed to a young boy who was standing in the front row, eating popcorn. "Do you want to go to hell?"

The boy turned white as a sheet, and began shaking so badly that he spilled popcorn from the bag.

"Repent now! Repent, you sinners, before it is too late!"

Thad Howard, Corey Childers, and Ethan Yerby were in two jail cells some 150 feet away from the gallows. Howard was in one, Corey and Ethan were sharing the other one.

"It ain't fair," Corey said.

"What ain't fair?" Ethan asked.

"It ain't fair that the judge sentenced me'n you to hang, but he let Frank go free."

"He didn't let Frank go," Ethan said. "He put him in prison for twenty years."

"Yeah? Well, that ain't hangin' him, is it?"

"He come back for us," Ethan said. "He didn't have to, but he did. He's your own brother. A body would think it would make you happy, knowin' he isn't goin' to hang."

"You know what would make me happy? Knowin' *I* wasn't goin' to hang."

Although they couldn't see the gallows because the window of their cell looked out onto the alley behind the jail, they could hear the preacher's harangue, even from there.

"That fella does preach one ripsnorter of a sermon, don't he?" Corey said.

"Don't that bother you none?" Ethan asked.

"What?"

"Thinkin' about burnin' in hell for ten thousand years."

"If it bothered me, I never would'a chose this here life," Corey replied. "Why do you ask? Does it bother you?"

"I confess I been thinkin' about it some."

"Yeah, well, think about it like this. Most of the folks we know that's dead is prob'ly in hell already. So it'll just be like an ole-time get-together."

"Yeah," Ethan said. He forced a laugh. "Yeah, I guess you could kind'a look at it like that."

"Hey, you, Howard," Corey said.

"Yeah?"

"Looks like you're going to get there about half an hour before us. Find us a good, cool spot, will you?"

"Go to hell," Thad said, growling.

Ethan laughed. "Go to hell? That's a good one!" he said. "Why, you dumb son of a bitch, what do you think we are talking about? That's exactly what we are all just about to do. Go to hell," he said again, still chuckling. "That's a good one."

The door to the jailhouse opened and Walter Merrill stepped inside.

"Howard, we're ready for you," he said.

Thad, who had been sitting on the bunk, got up and shuffled over to the door of his cell. He had to shuffle because there were shackles on his legs and his arms.

"I'll be back for you boys in a little bit," the sheriff said, glancing over at Corey and Ethan.

"That's all right, Sheriff, don't you be hurrying none

on our account now," Cory said. "Just take your time." He laughed out loud.

"Corey, you've gone stark raving mad," Ethan said, shaking his head.

The new sheriff took Thad outside then, and led him through the crowd to the gallows.

"Get back, get back," the sheriff said, waving his arms at the people as they crowded closer in order to get a good look. "Get back out of the way and give us some room. Ain't you got no decency? This here man is about to meet his Maker."

One little boy suddenly darted out of the crowd, reached out to touch Thad, then darted back into the crowd.

"I touched him!" the boy shouted proudly. "I touched a fella that's about to hang! I just retched right out and touched him."

"Jimmy, you get back over here and behave yourself," a woman's voice ordered.

Thad was led up the steps, then out onto the gallows platform. He stood there for a moment, looking out over the crowd. In his entire life, he had never seen so many people gathered in one place before.

"Thad?" the sheriff said.

Thad didn't reply.

"Thad, pay attention here," the sheriff said. "We want to do this right."

"Sorry," Thad said. "What was it you was sayin' to me?"

"I was sayin' that we got us two traps here," the sheriff explained, " 'cause we're goin' to hang the next two together. But since you're first, you can take your choice of which one."

"This here'n will do," Thad said, nodding toward the first one.

"Come over here and stand on the trapdoor," the sheriff said.

Thad complied, and as he stood there, they removed the chains, but tied his feet together with rope, then tied his arms down by his side.

"You want some time with the preacher?" the sheriff asked.

Thad looked over at the man who, but moments ago, had been haranguing the crowd.

"No. I'd rather go straight to hell than have that son of a bitch prayin' over my soul," Thad said. "I don't even want him standin' up here on the scaffold with me."

The crowd gasped in shock at his words.

"Repent," the preacher shouted, pointing a long bony finger at Thad. "Repent, you sinner, before it's too late."

"Get that son of a bitch away from me," Thad growled.

"You heard him, Preacher," the sheriff said. "Step on down now."

The preacher left the scaffold, but halfway down the thirteen steps, he turned and pointed back toward Thad. "You have just condemned you soul to eternal torment!" he shouted.

"You go to hell!" Thad called back, and a few of the men in the front row chuckled nervously, though many mouthed quick, silent prayers.

"You got 'ny last words? Anything you want to say?" the sheriff asked.

Thad looked out into the faces of the men, women, and children who were gathered to watch him hang.

"I see a great many people here," Thad said. "But not one I could call a friend."

"Hell, you killed ever'one that ever called themselves your friend," someone from the front shouted out, and the laughter over his comment moved through the crowd like a wave as his words were repeated.

The hood was placed over Thad's face, and everything went dark. As the hangman dropped the noose around his neck, Thad tensed up, lifting his shoulders and shortening his neck.

"Don't tense up, Mr. Howard," the hangman said. "It'll go easier for you if you're relaxed."

"How the hell does a body relax when you are about to break his neck?" Thad asked, through the hood.

"I'm just tellin' you for your own good," the hangman said. "Whether you are tense or not, you're goin' to die. It'll just be easier on you if you don't try an' fight it. Just let it happen."

"Stop your palaverin' and get this over with," Thad said.

"Whatever you say, Mr. Howard," the hangman replied. "I figure you got about thirty seconds left in this world."

The hangman stepped back to the edge of the gallows platform, put his hands on the lever, then looked over at the sheriff.

Sheriff Merrill nodded, and the hangman pulled the lever.

Inside the jail, Corey and Ethan heard the snap of the trapdoor falling open; then they heard the gasps and shouts from the crowd.

"Looks like ole Howard is gone," Ethan said.

"Yeah," Corey replied, his voice sounding tight now.

Strangely, Corey wasn't as defiant as he had been earlier, Ethan thought.

"Corey, you think it's going to hurt?"

"Hell, yes, it's going to hurt, you dumb son of a

bitch!" Corey replied. All bravado was gone now as he was on the edge of panic.

"Hey," someone whispered from outside the jail. "Frank, Corey, Ethan, you in there?"

Corey and Ethan looked at each other in surprise. Then Corey got up from the bunk and walked over to look through the window.

Aaron was standing in the alley just behind the jail building, a big smile on his face.

"Howdy, boys," Aaron said.

"Aaron, what are you doing here?" Corey asked.

"Me'n the boys have come to get you out," Aaron replied. "Where's Frank?"

"That lucky son of a bitch ain't a-goin' to hang," Corey said. "They sent him back to the territorial prison in Bismarck."

"You're the lucky ones," Aaron said. "He's in prison. But I'm about to get you boys out. You got somethin' you can get under? Like maybe a mattress or somethin'?"

"They's straw mattresses on these here cots," Corey replied. "What'd you ask that for?"

"Well, my advice to you two boys is get over in the corner and cover up with them mattresses," Dalton said. "'Cause I'm about to blow up this here wall."

"Wait, do you think that's wise? We could be killed," Ethan said.

Aaron chuckled. "Hell, you goin' to be killed anyway, ain't you?" he asked. "If you're goin' to die, you may as well die tryin' to escape."

"He's right," Corey said, grabbing one of the mattresses. "Come on, let's cover up."

"Get back, I'm lightin' the fuse right now," Aaron called.

The blast went off with devastating effect, blowing

out the back wall and filling the jail, now hollowed out, with dust and gun smoke.

"Are you still alive?" Aaron shouted.

Coughing and wheezing, Corey and Ethan threw aside the mattress that had provided them with protection and stood up.

"Barely," Corey said.

"Get mounted," Aaron said. "Let's get out of here."

Chapter 8

When the dynamite went off, it was so loud that it broke windows out on the street. The preacher, who had returned to the scaffold after Thad Howard's body was cut down, had started preaching again. At the explosion, he leaped down from the gallows and fell to the ground, covering his head with his arms. The crowd that had been waiting for the second act of the hanging screamed and scattered.

For several moments, nobody got around their fear quickly enough to figure out what was going on. It wasn't until someone saw smoke rising from the alley behind the jail that anyone got suspicious.

"The jail!" he shouted. "It looks like there was an explosion over at the jail!"

"My prisoners!" Merrill shouted, starting toward the jail on the run.

A half dozen of those nearest the sheriff ran along with him to see what happened. When they threw the front door open, all their questions were answered. The entire back wall of the jail building was gone, destroyed by a blast of some sort. The cell that had housed Corey Childers and Ethan Yerby was empty.

"Son of a bitch!" the sheriff shouted in anger. "They got away!"

* * *

The escaped prisoners were little more than five miles away when Corey's horse went lame.

"Hold it up! Hold it up, fellas!" he called to the others.

Aaron halted the group, then looked back at his brother. "What is it? What's wrong?"

"You give me a lame horse," Corey said. "This here animal can't go another mile."

"We can't stop now," Ethan said anxiously.

"Look behind you, Ethan. Do you see anyone comin'?" Corey asked.

"No."

"No, and you ain't likely too neither. They got 'em a new sheriff in that town, and he don't know whether to pick his nose or scratch his ass. And I don't see him gettin' a bunch of citizens together to form a posse to run us down neither. More'n likely, he'll just wait 'n see what the U.S. Marshals do about it."

"So, what are you sayin', Corey? That we can just stay here?" Percy asked.

"No, I ain't saying nothin' of the kind. All I'm sayin' is, we don't have to run around like chickens with our heads cut off. We got time to find me a horse that ain't broke down."

"Looks like they's a farm or a ranch or some such place up ahead a piece," Dalton said.

"All right, let's head for there," Aaron suggested.

Mary Douglass opened the oven to check on her biscuits. The nineteen-year-old woman was a mail-order bride, married but three months to a man she had never met until he came to St. Louis to claim her, after she answered an ad in a magazine.

She was a very pretty woman, hardly the kind of person one would think would be a mail-order bride. But when she suffered a miscarriage, the result of an affair with the son of a local banker, her reputation in St. Louis had been ruined.

Mary had been advised not to tell her husband-to-be of her past, but she felt that would be dishonest, so she told him within an hour after meeting him.

"Hell, darlin', you ain't exactly gettin' yourself a Sunday School teacher," Luke had replied. "What's past is past."

The biscuits were a golden brown and she smiled, pleased with herself at the outcome. Luke loved her biscuits.

She heard the door to the kitchen open behind her.

"Luke, what are you doing in so early? It's . . ." she began, but turning, she saw three strange men.

"Well, now, lookee here, will you?" Aaron exclaimed. "I believe this little lady has dinner all ready for us."

"Who . . . who are you?" Mary asked in a frightened voice.

"We're just some friendly neighbors, dropped by for dinner," Aaron said. He walked over to the stove, picked up a biscuit, and took a bite.

"Neighbors? Are you friends of Luke's?" Mary asked.

"Luke's, yeah, we're friends of Luke's."

"I'm Mary. I'm Luke's wife," Mary said. "Uh, Luke didn't say anything about having guests for lunch. I'm not sure I cooked enough."

"What you got here is fine," Aaron said. He, Percy, and Ethan helped themselves to biscuits and bacon.

Mary watched in shock, and not a little fear, as they tore open biscuits and layered bacon onto them.

"What the hell, Aaron, you takin' all the bacon?"

"They ain't that much," Aaron replied. "Just dip your biscuit in the bacon grease."

"I'll just put some of these fried taters on mine," Percy said, scooping up a handful of fried potatoes and laying them on his biscuit.

"What . . . what are you doing?" Mary asked, shocked by the sight of the three men standing around the stove, eating with their hands.

At that moment Corey and Dalton came in.

"Better get some of this grub while you got a chance," Aaron said, speaking with a mouthful of food. "Did you find a horse?"

"Yeah, they was a good-lookin' mare in the barn. I done got her saddled."

"You saddled Rhoda?"

"That the horse's name? Good. They always ride a little better when you know their name."

"You're not friends of Luke at all, are you?" Mary asked, putting her hand to her throat as she began to realize the truth.

Aaron looked at her, then smiled, an evil smile. "Never even heard of him," he said.

"Then I must ask you to get out of my house," Mary said.

Percy laughed. "Listen to her. She's got spunk, you got to give her that."

"Aaron, look out!" Dalton suddenly shouted.

Unnoticed by all but Dalton, Mary had picked up a poker. She swung it at Aaron but, thanks to Dalton's timely warning, Aaron was able to jump out of the way. The poker hit the stove with a loud clang.

"Get out of my house!" Mary shouted angrily. She

raised the poker for another swing, but a gunshot rang out and Mary gasped in pain and surprise as she was knocked back by the impact of the bullet. She looked down to see a dark, ugly wound in her left breast. Blood was spreading quickly over her dress. Luke had bought her this dress and, irrationally, she thought of how upset he would be to see it stained.

Then she felt her head spinning and she went down. Her body got cold as everything went dark around her.

Corey Childers stood there looking at her, holding a smoking gun in his hand.

"What the hell did you shoot her for?" Aaron asked.

"What do you mean what did I shoot her for?" Corey replied. "The bitch was trying to kill you. Or didn't you notice?"

"Hell, couldn't you have stopped her without killing her? As long as she was alive, we could've had a little fun with her."

"Is she dead?" Percy asked.

Dalton got down to look at her, putting her hand on his neck.

"What about it?" Ethan asked. "Is she dead?"

Dalton nodded. "Yeah," he said.

"What do we do now?" Percy asked.

"Look around, take anything we can use, then burn the house," Aaron said.

Luke Douglass had been clearing land, and he was walking home for lunch when he heard the shot. He had no idea what it was, but it frightened him, and he broke into a run.

Just as he reached the clearing where his house stood, he saw five men standing outside. At first he was confused as to who they were, and why they were here.

Then he noticed that one of the saddled horses was a golden palomino. It was Rhoda!

"Who are you men?" he called. "What are you doing here, and why is Rhoda saddled?"

At that moment the first flames burst through the windows of the house.

"My God! The house is on fire!" he shouted. "Where is Mary?"

"Was that your woman's name?" Aaron asked.

"Was?" Luke asked in a tight voice.

"Whatever her name was, you'll find her dead inside."

With a shout of anger and grief, Luke ran toward the house. He tried to go inside, but by now the flames were so high that he couldn't get through the door.

"You bastards!" Luke shouted.

To the surprise of everyone, Luke launched himself from the porch, knocking Corey from the saddle as he did so. The two men fell to the ground and, in the struggle, Luke managed to get Corey's gun. Sticking the gun in Corey's belly, he pulled the trigger.

"Son of a bitch! He just shot Corey!" Aaron shouted.

Rolling away from Corey, with Corey's gun in his hand, Luke shot a second time, knocking Ethan from his saddle.

By now Aaron, Dalton, and Percy had all drawn their own guns, and all three shot at the same time, killing Luke.

Aaron got down to check on his brother, Corey, while Dalton checked on Ethan.

"Ethan's dead," Dalton said.

"Yeah, so is Corey."

Dalton walked over to look at Luke. "What the hell got into you, you crazy son of a bitch?" Dalton shouted in anger. He kicked Luke's body.

"Come on," Aaron said, mounting his horse. "Let's get out of here before the fire starts bringing neighbors."

"What about Corey and Ethan?" Dalton asked.

"What about 'em?" Aaron replied, looking down now from his saddle.

"Well, are we just going to leave 'em here?"

"Yes."

Dalton shook his head. "No," he said. "No way am I going to just leave my brother here."

"Dalton, Aaron's right," Percy said.

"What the hell do you have to do with this?" Dalton snapped. "Ain't neither one of them your brother."

"No, but they was both my friends," Percy said. "And if we leave 'em here, folks will think they kilt each other."

Dalton was quiet for a moment, then he nodded. "All right," he said. "All right, I reckon I can see that. But it don't seem right to just leave 'em lyin' here without doin' somethin'. I mean, shouldn't we say some words over 'em or somethin'?"

"Whatever words you wanna say, you can say from the saddle," Aaron said. He jerked his horse around. "Let's get the hell out of here."

Falcon MacCallister was about two miles away when he saw the smoke. He knew that only one thing could make that kind of smoke out here. Someone's house was on fire.

Falcon slapped his legs against the side of his horse, urging the animal into a gallop. He didn't know whether he could get there in time or not to help save the house, but from the looks of the smoke, he probably could not. He did know, though, that whoever owned the house would welcome any kind of help, no matter how little good it might do.

By the time Falcon reached the location, the structure of the house had collapsed in on itself so that only flames and smoke remained. Through the smoke, he saw three bodies lying on the ground and, dismounting, he hurried to them.

Two of the men he recognized immediately. They were the two men who had been tried and convicted for the murder of Billy Puckett. He had not stayed around for the hanging, and was surprised to see them here.

He went over to check the third man, and saw that he was still alive, though barely. Falcon knelt beside him.

"Who are you?" Falcon asked.

"Douglass," the man said, barely able to say the word. "Luke Douglass."

"What happened here?"

"My wife!" Douglass suddenly said. He tried to sit up, but fell back down. "She's in the house!"

Falcon looked toward what had been the house, but was now so much kindling wood.

"I'll see what I can do," said, saying the words to comfort Douglass because he knew there was nothing he could really do.

"They took Rhoda," Douglass said.

"Rhoda?"

"She's a palomino. I bought her for Mary."

"I'll get her back for you," Falcon said, but his words fell on deaf ears. Douglass was dead.

Shaking his head sadly, Falcon began looking around. On first sight it appeared as if Cory Childers and Ethan Yerby had fought it out with Luke Douglass. But as he examined the evidence, he saw that things weren't as they initially appeared.

Corey Childers didn't have a gun, not in his hand, not

in his holster. Ethan Yerby did have a gun, but it was in his holster, and hadn't been fired.

Two bullets had been fired from the gun in Douglass's hand. Oddly, he was not wearing a holster, which led Falcon to believe that, somehow, he must have gotten Corey's gun.

On the other hand, Luke Douglass had three bullet wounds, so somebody shot him. The question was, who?

Making a wider examination of the area, Falcon saw that five horses had left the farm. However, from the depth of the hoof marks, it was obvious that two of the horses were not being ridden.

It was also obvious by the tracks that one of the horses had come from the barn.

When Falcon found the tracks approaching the farm, he saw that there were only four horses, though one of them was carrying double. Evidently they had come to steal a horse, and anything else they could find. The farmer and his wife had resisted them, resulting in both being killed.

Falcon walked out to the barn and found a spade. Then he dug two graves in the soft dirt of the woman's garden. By the time he was finished, the fire was burned down and, looking through the ash, he found what was left of Douglass's woman. He turned his head aside when he saw the blackened, twisted body.

"I'm glad you didn't have to see this, Mr. Douglass," he said quietly.

Finding a piece of tarpaulin in the barn, he got her body onto it, and dragged it out to one of the graves. He put Luke Douglass in another piece he found, then closed both of them and stood there for a long moment, his hat in his hand, as the wind blew through his hair.

"Lord," he said. "Take care of these two, put them

back together. And if you need any help in seeing to them, why, I reckon my Marie would be glad to give you a hand.

"And if you've a mind to, you might help me track down the murderin' bastards who did this. It doesn't look like there's anyone else around to settle the score, so I'm goin' to do it. Amen."

Falcon put his hat back on. He didn't know how reverent the prayer he just said was, but if saying words from the heart counted for anything, then he was pretty sure the Lord had heard him.

The buzzards had been circling around all afternoon. They'd never been too far away while Falcon went about the grizzly business of pulling Mrs. Douglass from the smoldering remains. He buried her and her husband, then rode off, noticing that the birds had come closer, emboldened by the fact that Falcon was leaving.

"You boys have yourselves a feast," Falcon said as the buzzards settled on the two bodies he left unburied.

Falcon had not stayed in town for the hanging. He had seen hangings before, and he didn't care for them, not even for people who deserved to die. A firing squad was better.

Although Falcon wouldn't admit it, even to himself, one reason he didn't like hangings was because it wasn't all that unreasonable to think that he might wind up on the gallows someday.

Falcon lived life on his own terms, never looking for trouble, but never backing away from it either. He had killed before, and sometimes the difference between killing in self-defense and murder was a very fine line. Falcon had never crossed that line, but he had crowded it so closely that a wrong perception from an eyewitness could make him a wanted man.

Although all the wanted posters that had been put out

on him had been officially rescinded, there might still be some around, faded yellow on some sheriff's bulletin board somewhere.

WANTED

DEAD OR ALIVE

FOR MURDER

FALCON MacCALLISTER

REWARD

$5,000

It was the size of the reward and the "Dead or Alive" part that made the posters dangerous. That meant that some well-meaning, law-abiding citizen could shoot Falcon first, and ask questions later. If put into that position, Falcon would have no choice but to shoot back. If his adversary happened to be a lawman, then he would have a difficult time making a case of self-defense.

Chapter 9

When Aaron, Dalton, and Percy reached the top of the pass, they stopped to give their horses a breather.

"Here," Aaron said, handing the reins of his horse to Dalton.

"What are you handin' those to me for? I'm already leadin' one horse beside my own."

"Hold him," Aaron said. "I want to see if the son of a bitch is still back there."

"What? What son of a bitch back where?"

"If you didn't have your head stuck up your ass, you would know that we're being followed, and have been for the last two hours."

"Damn, no. I didn't know that," Percy said.

"Hold my horses too," Dalton said, handing the reins of the horse he was riding, plus the one he was leading, to Percy.

"What the hell? Do I look like a hitching rail?" Percy asked.

"Nah. Every hitching rail I've ever seen is better-lookin' than you are," Dalton replied with a hoarse chuckle. He stepped over to the side of the trail and began urinating on a bush. "Hah!" he said. "I just pissed that grasshopper off his limb."

Aaron lay on his stomach on a flat rock and looked back down the trail. He saw a lone rider coming slowly and, from the way he was acting, Aaron knew he was trailing them.

"Hand me my long gun," Aaron said.

Dalton, finished with his own business now, pulled Aaron's rifle from the saddle sheath and handed it to him.

"He's too far away," Dalton said. "Even with a rifle."

Aaron jacked a round into the chamber. "I just want the son of a bitch to know he ain't foolin' nobody," he said.

Raising the rifle to his shoulder, Aaron pulled the trigger.

Falcon happened to look up just as Aaron fired. He saw the muzzle flash, then the puff of smoke, followed three seconds later by the sound of the report. The bullet wasn't even close enough for Falcon to determine where it struck.

Falcon smiled, not so much because the gunman had missed widely, but because it told him that he was on the right track. Of course, that also told the people ahead that they were being followed. And he knew that he would not be able to go through the pass as long as they held it. For the time being, he was stopped.

Falcon dismounted and led his horse over to a clump of rocks to get him out of the way of any lucky shot. That was when he heard the sound of thunder for the first time, rolling deep in the hills. He had been so busy trailing the three men that he had not paid any attention to the sky. Now, as he looked up, he saw heavy black clouds building up in the west.

Within minutes it began to rain, just a few drops at first, but they were large, heavy drops. Then the intensity increased and the rain started coming down in a deluge. Falcon took his poncho from saddle roll, put it on, then hunkered down under an overhang, trying to find some shelter from the rain. His horse stood nearby with large, soulful eyes, clearly miserable in the downpour.

"Sorry, Diablo," Falcon said to the big, black horse he was riding.

Diablo whickered and shook his head in protest.

"I know you're not liking it much, but I've got no place to put you to get you out of this." Falcon pulled the poncho around himself more tightly. "But then, I don't have anyplace to get myself out of it either."

As the rain continued, the water started pouring down the mountainside, turning the trail into a sluice. Brown, muddy water, sometimes as much as a foot deep, cascaded down the mountain path. Not only did it prevent Falcon from going up the trail, but he knew that it would also erase all tracks, making it more difficult to follow.

"Come on," Aaron said. "Let's go."

"Let's go? What, are you crazy?" Dalton asked. "In case you ain't noticed, it's rainin' like pourin' piss out of a boot."

"Yeah," Aaron said, as he mounted his horse. "And in case *you* ain't noticed, the rain is washin' out all the tracks. If we go now, we can be well out of here before the fella that's followin' us knows we're gone."

"Why don't we just wait here and kill the son of a bitch?" Percy asked.

"I don't believe he's going to be all that easy to kill," Aaron said. "I think I've figured out who he is."

"Who?"

"Falcon MacCallister."

"Son of a bitch! You sure?"

"Yeah, I'm sure."

"Who is Falcon MacCallister?" Percy asked.

"He's the one come out shootin' back in Belfield when we held up the bank. You might remember, he shot Ethan and Cory, and when Frank went back after them, why, he got caught too."

"I ain't never heard of him. What kind of a fella is he?" Percy asked.

"Who he is depends on who is doin' the tellin'," Aaron said. "Some call him a gunfighter, some say he's just a drifter. One thing is sure, he is a dead shot, he's good with a knife, and he can track a buzzard's shadow."

"Seems to me that a fella like that would make a lot of enemies," Dalton said. "I mean, you seen the way he butted into our business back there."

"Oh, he's made a lot of enemies all right," Aaron said.

"And there ain't nobody ever gone after him yet?"

"Oh, yes."

"What happened?"

"The lucky ones didn't find him," Aaron answered. Without waiting for the others, he rode off into the rain. Dalton and Percy had to scramble, quickly, to get mounted and follow him.

Falcon forded the Little Missouri River, then crossed the railroad track. The depot was a small red-painted wooden building, surrounded by a wide plank platform. A white sign with the black letters MEDORA identified the little town. Three freight cars sat on one of the sidings, and a large-wheeled baggage cart was tucked up against the side of the depot.

A couple of young boys were playing mumblety-peg on one corner of the platform. One of them did a "spank-the-baby" move, but the knife got away from him and flew through the air, landing at the feet of Diablo.

"Jimmy, what are you trying to—" one of the boys began, but he interrupted his question when he saw Falcon dismount to pick up the knife.

"I'm sorry, mister, I didn't mean nothin'," Jimmy said, obviously frightened.

Falcon held the knife for a second, then flipped it around so he could grasp it by the point. Then, in a sharp, snapping motion, he threw at a narrow post near the two boys, sticking the knife in at the very center.

"Wow!" Jimmy said in awe, looking at the knife. "Did you see that?"

Remounting, Falcon crossed Third Avenue, then, seeing a livery down at the corner of Third Avenue and Sixth Street, turned south. When he stopped in front of the livery, he was greeted by Chance Ingram, the owner of the business.

"That's a good-looking horse you have there, mister," Ingram said, patting the horse's neck.

"Thanks."

"You lookin' to board him?"

"Yeah. Give him some oats tonight. And a good rubdown. Clean straw in his stable."

"I'll do it," Ingram said. "A horse like this one needs good treatment. Glad to see you do right by him. This your first time in Medora?"

"Yes. Where can a man get a good meal?"

"Well, ordinarily, I'd say Bessie's Café," Ingram said. "But she went over to Posey to help her sister birth a baby, so her place is closed for a few days. Only other places to eat are Ma Perkins's boardin' house and the Golden Spur Saloon. But Ma Perkins only sets one table for supper and, like as not, she's done fed."

"Well, then the Golden Spur it is," Falcon said.

"Ed cooked up a ham yesterday. I think he's still feedin' offen it. It ain't bad, I had some myself for lunch."

"Thanks," Falcon said. He snaked the rifle from the saddle holster, then tossed his saddlebags over his shoulder. He didn't have to ask where the Golden Spur was; he had ridden past it as he was coming in. It was the largest and most brightly lit building in town.

He could hear the sounds of the saloon from half a block away. A piano player was banging away, and the slightly out-of-tune music could be heard above the loud guffaws of the men, the high-pitched, trilling laughter of the women, the steady drone of conversation, and the tinkling of glasses.

Pushing through the batwing doors, Falcon stepped to one side, placing his back against the wall and taking himself out of silhouette from the street. He wasn't on the run from the law, nor did he have any known enemies at the moment, but a lifetime of caution governed his behavior.

With his saddlebags draped over one shoulder, the butt of his rifle on the floor, and his left hand holding it just behind the sight so that it was kicked out a little way, Falcon studied the saloon. Such establishments had become a part and parcel of his being, and his life was defined by the saloons, liveries, and false-fronted streets of the dusty cow towns he had been in over the years. He could not deny these places without denying his own existence. He had already put the last town out of his mind, and he had no idea where he would go next. He was here, now, and that was all that mattered.

The saloon was full, but no more than half a dozen of the patrons looked up at him. Most looked toward him only to see if they knew him and, seeing that they did not, returned to their conversations at hand.

Several bar girls flitted about the room like bees going from flower to flower. Heavily made-up and garishly dressed, they were using their charms to push drinks. Falcon always enjoyed watching the reaction of the men to such girls. A few were shy, and some actually even blushed when the women stopped to flirt with them. Others were more brazen, and many would reach out to try and grab the girls, but the girls were not only used to such behavior, they knew who to avoid and what to do, and they managed to dance, adroitly, out of the way while maintaining some composure.

Toward the back of the room, Falcon saw a table so small that it could accommodate only two chairs. The table was empty, perhaps because it made no allowances for socializing. But since Falcon was more interested in getting something to eat than in socializing, the table was ideal for him.

Shortly after he sat down, a young woman came over to his table. Although she was a very pretty girl, her modest dress, the hair pulled back into a severe bun, and the lack of makeup told Falcon that she wasn't one of the bar girls. And indeed, as she wiped the table with the towel she had draped across her shoulder, she asked what he wanted.

"The livery man told me you had a pretty good ham. Any of it left?"

"Yes, sir, there's a mite left," the girl said shyly.

"Good. Bring me some ham . . . you got 'ny beans?"

"Yes, sir," the girl said. "Ham, beans, greens, and cornbread."

"The cornbread any good?"

The young girl smiled broadly. "I hope to say it is," she said. "I made it myself."

"You made it yourself, huh? And just who would you be?"

"My name is Ella," the girl said shyly.

"All right then, Ella, fix me up a plate. And two beers, one now to kill the thirst, and the other to enjoy with my dinner."

"Yes, sir," Ella replied, hurrying back to the kitchen to prepare his order. As she passed the bar, she said something to the bartender. He nodded, drew a beer, then held the mug up toward Falcon.

Falcon walked over to get it.

"You just visitin' Medora, or passin' through?" the bartender asked.

"I haven't made up my mind yet," Falcon answered as he blew away some of the head. He took the beer back to his table and drank it slowly as he waited for his dinner.

"Well, now, if you ain't the dandy," someone said in a loud, obnoxious voice.

"Leave 'im alone, Muley," another voice said. "He ain't done nothin' to bother you."

"The way he looks bothers me," Muley replied. "Tell me, Mr. Easterner. How come you didn't buy yourself a whole pair of glasses?"

Looking toward the commotion, Falcon saw a couple of rough-looking cowboys accosting someone. The recipient of the gibes was a young man wearing an Eastern-style suit, complete with jacket and vest. He was standing at the bar, staring straight ahead, trying to avoid his antagonists.

"Look at them funny-lookin' little glasses, Zeb," the one called Muley said to his partner. "They ain't got nothin' to wrap around the ears. How the hell you think he keeps 'em on?"

"You'd think a man what owned a ranch—" Zeb started, but Muley interrupted him.

"Mr. Teddy Roosevelt owns two ranches, from what I've heard," Muley said.

"Two ranches," Zeb continued. "You'd think a man what owned two ranches could afford a whole pair of glasses, 'stead of them things that's just pinchin' the end of his nose like that."

"Interesting you would make that observation," Roosevelt said, turning away from the bar and speaking for the first time. He took the glasses from his nose and held them out. "Because, you see, that is exactly how they are held on. That's why these are called pince-nez glasses, which means 'pinched nose.' I guess you aren't as dumb as you look after all."

The others laughed at Roosevelt's observation, but Muley and Zeb scowled at him.

"Don't get funny with me, tenderfoot. I'll knock them stupid-looking glasses offen your ugly face," Muley said.

"You fellas got no call to be raggin' Mr. Roosevelt like that," Josh Andrews, one of Roosevelt's cowboys, said. "Lay off him."

"Who do you fellows ride for?" Roosevelt asked.

"Ain't none of your business who we ride for, Four-eyes," Muley replied.

"They ride for Mr. Montgomery, over at Two Rivers Ranch," Josh said.

"Well, I know Don Montgomery. He's a decent and upright man," Roosevelt said. "I can't imagine he would have anyone working for him who wasn't of good stuff. I'm sorry we seem to have gotten off on the wrong foot. Suppose you two lads go down to the end of the corner and have a few drinks on me? Barman, if you would, provide these gentlemen with libations of their choice. I will pay. Oh, and you can set up another round for my cowboys as well."

"Thank you, Mr. Roosevelt," Josh said. "Come on, boys, belly up," he called to the others. "Muley, you and Zeb too. Have a drink."

"What about you, Mr. Roosevelt? Another lemonade?"

"Yes, thank you," Roosevelt said.

Muley and Zeb walked down to the end of the bar to have their drink, and the situation was eased. Within a moment, Roosevelt's cowboys were laughing and talking among themselves.

"Here is your supper," the young woman said, bringing Falcon's food.

"Thanks, Ella," Falcon said. He nodded toward Roosevelt. "What did they call him? Roosevelt?"

"Yes."

"He's from the East?"

"Yes," Ella answered. "From New York."

"What's he doing out here?"

"Well, he owns a ranch out here. But that's not why he's here. He's here 'cause his mama and his wife both died on the same day, and he needed to just get away from it all. Isn't that just about the saddest thing you ever heard?"

"Yes, it is," Falcon agreed, remembering how it felt when his own wife was murdered.

Falcon looked at Roosevelt and realized that, even from the back, he could see the young man's grief. Roosevelt stood at the bar, looking neither left nor right, and not participating in conversation with his men.

"He's out of place out here," Falcon said. "A dandy like that is going to be eaten alive by men like those two down there." He nodded toward Muley and Zeb.

"They are a bad sort, all right," Ella agreed. She rubbed her hands on her apron and smiled shyly at Falcon. "I hope you like the cornbread," she said.

Falcon took a bite, then closed his eyes and smacked his lips appreciatively. "Uhmm, uhm," he said. He held up the piece of cornbread. "This might just about be the best cornbread I've ever tasted."

Ella laughed and waved her hand dismissively, though it was obvious she was pleased by his compliment. She went back into the kitchen.

Falcon began eating then, and had just cut a piece of ham when he saw Muley and Zeb moving back up the bar. Both had menacing scowls on their faces, and one of them was carrying a bar stool. It was plain to see that they intended to repay their benefactor for his generosity in buying them drinks with a violent attack.

Normally, Falcon did not like to mix into other people's fights . . . especially a barroom brawl. But he knew that the Eastern dude wouldn't stand a chance against these two. And as far as Falcon could tell, he had done nothing to deserve such treatment.

Quietly, Falcon pushed his chair back from the table and stood up. He started toward the bar.

"I aim to bash in your head and have me them funny-lookin' glasses!" Muley shouted, closing the remaining distance to Roosevelt in a few, quick steps.

Falcon hadn't started soon enough. Muley was going to be to Roosevelt before he could get there to lend a hand.

To Falcon's surprise, Roosevelt made no effort to avoid the charge. Instead he turned to meet it head-on and, from nowhere, it seemed, Roosevelt's left arm jabbed out and his fist caught Muley right on the tip of his chin.

Muley went down, just as Zeb, who was carrying the bar stool, raised it over his own head, intending to bring it crashing down on Roosevelt. Roosevelt sent two quick left jabs into Zeb, snapping his head back and causing him to drop the stool. Roosevelt followed with a hard right to Zeb's jaw, and Zeb wound up on the floor with Muley.

Sensing Falcon's approach, Roosevelt whirled to meet him, taking up the stance of a boxer, with his fists raised.

"Whoa! Hold on there, Mr. Roosevelt!" Falcon said, holding his hand out to stop Roosevelt. "I'm not attacking, I was coming over to help." He looked down at Muley and Zeb, then chuckled. "Although it's pretty clear that you don't need any help."

"Let's hear it for Mr. Roosevelt," one of his cowboys said, and the others in the saloon cheered loudly.

"You were coming to defend me?" Roosevelt asked Falcon.

"Well, that was what I had in mind," Falcon said. "Sort of foolish of me, huh?" he added sheepishly.

"I was a boxer in college," Roosevelt explained. "Perhaps I should have mentioned that to these two gentlemen before they undertook their little adventure. Had I told them, they may not have been so incautious."

"Oh, I think they had it in their mind to take you on no matter what," Falcon said.

"You called me by name. Do I know you?" Roosevelt asked.

"No, my name is MacCallister. Falcon MacCallister." Falcon extended his hand, and Roosevelt gripped it firmly.

"MacCallister? There are a couple of actors in New York named MacCallister."

"Andrew and Rosanna," Falcon said.

"Yes, I believe that is their names. I'm not much for the theater but they are so popular, everyone in the city knows of them, even those of us who do not follow the theater. I'm not sure if they are husband and wife or . . ."

"They are brother and sister," Falcon said. "Twins actually."

"You seem to know a good deal about them."

Falcon smiled. "I should. They are my brother and sister," he said.

"You don't say. My, what an interesting coincidence. Won't you join my friends and me, Mr. MacCallister?" Roosevelt invited.

"Thank you very much for the invitation," Falcon said. He nodded toward his table. "But I'm just having my supper."

"Then enjoy your dinner, my friend," Roosevelt said.

Muley and Zeb got up then and, rubbing their jaws, slunk out of the saloon, aware of the sniggering comments of the other customers.

Falcon returned to the table and finished his dinner. When he asked for the bill, he learned that Roosevelt had already paid for it. He was also told that any drinks he ordered for the rest of the night would be paid for by Roosevelt.

Glancing up, he saw that Roosevelt was looking toward him. Smiling, Roosevelt touched his eyebrow in a salute. Falcon nodded his thanks back to him.

At that moment, Muley and Zeb stepped back into the saloon. Both men were holding pistols.

"Say your prayers, you four-eyed son of a bitch!" Muley shouted, raising his pistol.

Neither Muley nor Zeb had seen Falcon rise from the table, his own gun in hand. Before either of the belligerent cowboys could fire, the room was filled with the sound of two quick explosions. Muley went down with a bullet in his shoulder; Zeb had a bullet through his hand. Though neither wound was life-threatening, they caused both men to drop their guns.

It had all happened so fast that, for the first several

seconds, only Muley, Zeb, and Falcon knew what *had* happened. Everyone else in the saloon spun around in surprise at the sound of the guns. It didn't take long for them to piece it together, though, as they saw Falcon standing there with smoke curling up from his gun, while Muley and Zeb's pistols were both on the floor.

Muley stood there for a moment, holding his hand over his shoulder wound, while Zeb held one hand over the wound in his hand.

Sheriff John Dennis came into the saloon then, drawn to the saloon by the sound of gunfire. As it happened, he arrived even before the smoke from the discharges had rolled away.

"What happened here?" the sheriff asked gruffly.

"I'll tell you what happened," Muley said, glaring at Falcon. "This here son of a bitch shot me 'n Zeb for no reason a'tall."

"That's right, Sheriff," Zeb added. "He didn't have no call to do what he done."

"Why are your guns on the floor instead of in your holster?" the sheriff asked.

"They're on the floor because . . . because . . . well, he started in a-shootin' at us," Muley replied. "What was we supposed to do, just stand here an' let him do it?"

"Yeah, what was we supposed to do? Just stand here with our thumb up our ass and let him do it?" Zeb added.

So far, Falcon hadn't said a word, but he had put his pistol back in his holster. Now he sat down and, using a piece of cornbread, raked some beans onto the tines of the fork. It was this, his almost studied indifference to what was going on, that both fascinated and frustrated the sheriff.

"You got 'nything to say, mister?" Sheriff Dennis asked.

"Yeah," Falcon said, holding up a piece of cornbread. "This is good cornbread."

The others in the saloon laughed.

"You know what I'm talkin' about, mister," the sheriff said. "This here shootin'. Did you do it?"

"I did it front of the whole saloon," Falcon replied. "It would be kind of hard for me to say I didn't do it now, wouldn't it?"

"So you're sayin' it happened just like Muley said?"

"Sort of like he said. There's a few differences."

"Like what?"

"Like, I didn't just open up on 'em like they said. They both had their guns drawn, and they were about to shoot Mr. Roosevelt."

"Is that your story? That they was about to shoot Mr. Roosevelt?"

"That's my story," Falcon said.

"Well, it looks to me like we've got us a little situation here," the sheriff said. "Two of you are telling one story, one is telling another. So, that's two to one against you, mister."

"Sheriff Dennis, I would like to make that two to two," Ella said, speaking for the first time.

"I beg your pardon?" the sheriff replied.

"It happened just the way this gentleman said it did," Ella said, pointing to Falcon. "I saw it all. Those two men there were going to kill Mr. Roosevelt. And they would've too, if this gentleman hadn't stopped 'em."

"Make that three to two, John," the bartender said. "'Cause I also seen it."

"You seen it too, did you, Ed?"

"I did," Ed answered.

"You want to tell me what it is that you saw?" the sheriff asked.

Ed nodded toward Falcon. "The big fella there is tellin' the truth. These two was about to shoot Mr. Roosevelt. Would've too, if he hadn't stopped 'em. And the thing is, he could'a killed them both. Instead, he just nicked 'em up a bit."

"Well, now, boys, looks like things has turned a mite against you," the sheriff said to Muley and Zeb.

"Yeah, well, we wasn't aimin' to kill Roosevelt or anything like that," Muley said. "All we was goin' to do was have a little fun with him. We wasn't really goin' to shoot him, was we, Zeb?"

Zeb shook his head furiously. "That's right. We wasn't really goin' to shoot him. We was just goin' to scare 'im."

"So, you see, that fella had no right to shoot us like he done. So I demand that you arrest him."

"I'm not goin' to do any such thing," the sheriff said. "You admit that you two was comin' after Mr. Roosevelt with your guns drawn. How was anyone to know that you didn't plan to kill him? Fact is, I believe you did intend to kill him, but was stopped by bein' shot."

The sheriff paused for a moment and stroked his chin as he studied the two men.

"The problem is, I can't prove what you planned to do, only what you done. And you didn't do anything 'cause that man stopped you before you could do it. So, I got no choice but to let you go."

"We're purt' near bleedin' to death here," Muley protested. "And you ain't doin' nothin' to the man who shot us."

"That's right," the sheriff said. "So my advice to you is to get yourself down to the doc and let him patch you up."

Muley reached down to pick up his gun. "Come on, Zeb," he said with a growl. "Let's get out of here."

"Yeah," Zeb agreed.

The saloon had been relatively quiet following the gunfight, but as soon as the two men left, it erupted once more into laughter and loud talk.

"Well, gentlemen," Roosevelt said. "Once more I am obliged to buy a round of libation, this time in celebration of my rescue from certain death."

The men laughed and cheered as they rushed to belly up to the bar.

Belfield

Emil Prufrock looked up from his work when two men came into the embalming room of his establishment. On the embalming table in front of him was the body of an elderly woman.

"Oh, gentlemen, visitors aren't allowed back here," Prufrock said. Quickly, he pulled a sheet up over the woman's body.

"Why not?" one of the men asked.

"Out of respect for the deceased."

"Hell, she's dead. She don't know we're here."

"Then, let us say out of respect for the bereaved. Please, if you have business with me, let's conduct it in the front."

Prufrock ushered them from the embalming room to the front parlor.

"Now, what can I do for you?"

"My name is Creed Howard, this here is Bob Howard. Where-at is our brother?"

"Your brother?"

"Thad Howard. He got hisself hung here a few weeks

ago. By the time me'n Bob found out about it, it was too late. So, where-at have you put him?"

"Oh, yes. Well, your brother was an indigent."

"He was a what?"

"An indigent . . . a person without means. He was buried at public expense," Prufrock said. "So that means he is in potter's field."

"Where is that?"

"The cemetery is at the south end of town. Potter's field is at the back of the cemetery," Prufrock said.

"I hope you spelled his name right on the marker."

"Oh, I'm afraid there is no marker," Prufrock said.

"What do you mean there ain't no marker? How can you bury a man without puttin' a marker over his grave? How can anyone find 'im?"

"As I explained to you, your brother was an indigent. The county will pay to have the body interred, but that is as far as it goes. No marker."

"It ain't right that he don't have a marker," Bob insisted.

"If you would like to pay for a marker, I will put one up for you," Prufrock offered.

"Yeah," Bob said.

"How much does a marker cost?" Creed asked.

"You can get a very nice marker for ten dollars."

"Ten dollars?" Creed replied.

"Yes, that would be a very nice one, with a rose carved into the marker and a nice sentiment."

"Yeah, well, we don't need all that. What's the cheapest one got on it?"

"It has nothing but his name, date of birth, and the date of his death."

"I don't know the date of his birth," Creed said. "Do you, Bob?"

Bob shook his head.

"So, don't put nothin' on it but his name. How much would that cost?" Creed asked.

"Two dollars."

Creed and Bob stepped over into a corner to discuss it between themselves for a moment; then they came back.

"So," Prufrock said, smiling and rubbing his hands together. "Have you gentlemen decided what you want on your brother's grave marker?"

"Yeah, we decided he don't need one," Creed said. "Tell us where his grave is at and we'll just go look at it."

"Yes, well, here is a chart of the cemetery," Prufrock said, pointing to a chart on the wall. He put his finger on one of the spots. "Your brother is buried here, in the last row, third from the end."

Without so much as a word of thanks, Creed and Bob left the undertaker's parlor, then rode out to the grave-yard.

"You think we should'a paid to get a marker put up?" Creed asked as he and Bob walked through the cemetery, looking for their brother's plot.

"What for?" Bob replied. "Hell, he's dead, ain't he? He won't know, one way or the other. And I can think of a lot of better ways to spend two dollars."

"Yeah," Creed said. Reaching Thad's grave, they stood there for a moment, looking down at it.

"Think we ought to say some words?" Bob asked.

"Nah, I can't think of nothin' to say."

"Then let's go have a few beers."

As they rode back into town, looking for the saloon, they passed the jailhouse. There was a lot of construction going on at the back of the jail, and they asked about it at the saloon.

"You mean you didn't hear about all the excitement

we had here a few weeks ago?" the bartender answered as he set a couple of beers in front of Bob and Creed.

"All we heard was that you hung a fella named Howard here."

"Oh, yes, that would be Thad Howard. Well, he was hung on the same day the jail got dynamited."

The bartender began telling the story, aided by a couple of nearby patrons. That was when they heard Falcon MacCallister's name for the first time.

"You say MacCallister fought off the train robbers, brought in Thad to be hung, and took on the bank robbers besides? What is he, a one-man army?" Creed asked.

"Some might say that he is," the bartender answered. "Others might think he is just a man who seems to find himself in areas where trouble breaks out."

"Where is he now?" Creed asked. "This MacCallister fella, I mean."

"Oh, I don't know. When he left here, I don't think he had any particular place in mind," the bartender said.

"He's in Medora," one of the bar patrons said.

"Medora? How do you know that?"

"I was there myself a couple of days ago, and I seen him shoot the guns out of the hands of two men who were about to shoot Mr. Roosevelt."

"Roosevelt? Who is Roosevelt?"

"He's some fella from the East who owns a ranch over near Medora."

"And you say that MacCallister is over there?" Bob asked.

"He was when I left."

Bob nodded. Then he and Creed took their beers over to a table where they could talk more privately.

"What you got in mind, Bob?" Creed asked.

"Maybe a little revenge," Bob said.

"Whoa, wait a minute. You plannin' on goin' after this MacCallister fella, are you?"

"Yes," Bob said.

"You heard what they said about him. And we know for a fact that he single-handed took out Rufus, Buddy, and Curly. Thad told us that, remember? Only thing is, he didn't know the fella's name at the time."

"Yeah, he sounds like a one-man army all right."

"Knowin' all that, you still plan to go after him?" Creed asked.

"Maybe we can get some help," Bob suggested.

"Get some help? From who? What are you talkin' about?"

"You heard what the man said about MacCallister shooting the guns out of the hands of two men over in Medora."

"Yeah, well, I don't know that I believe him about that. Shooting a gun out of someone's hand? That's pretty much of a tall tale."

"Maybe, but somethin' must've happened. And if we could find the fellas it happened to, they might be interested in a little revenge of their own," Bob said.

Chapter 10

Zeb Kingsley and Muley Simpson, the two men Bob was talking about, were nursing drinks and their anger in a little ramshackle saloon in the tiny settlement of Puxico.

"Mr. Montgomery didn't have no right to fire us like he done," Zeb said. "I mean, when Deekus got all stoved up when he got throwed while he was breakin' horses, why, Montgomery didn't fire him. So, maybe we can't work for a few days while we're on the mend. He didn't have no right firin' us."

"Yeah, well, he didn't fire us 'cause we got hurt," Muley said. "He fired us 'cause we jerked a cinch into that Eastern dude. And all the ranch owners stick together, you know that. They all stick together so the cowboys have to work for practically nothin'."

"Practically nothin' is better'n nothin' at all," Zeb said. "And nothin' at all is what we got now."

At that very moment, Aaron Childers, Dalton Yerby, and Percy Shaw were approaching Puxico. What they saw in front of them was a small settlement of no more than a handful of low-built, chinked-log buildings. A sign out front of one of them read WHISKEY, BEER, FOOD, GOODS. Tying their horses to the hitching rail out front, the three men pushed through a canvas hanging that acted as the door, then went inside.

The inside of the building was dimly lit, and cross-shot with sun bars of gleaming dust motes that pushed in through the dirty window and the cracks between the logs. There were six customers inside the building, two leaning on their elbows and nursing rotgut whiskey, the other four sitting around a rough-hewn table.

A young woman was on her hands and knees with a bucket of soapy water and a brush, scrubbing the floor. She looked up when Aaron and the other two came in and, smiling at them, brushed an errant tendril of hair back from her face. Her smile showed the gap produced by two or three missing teeth.

The bartender, who had been talking to the two men at the other end of the room, moved down to greet Aaron, Dalton, and Percy when they stepped up to the bar.

"Somethin' I can do for you gents?" the bartender asked, making a halfhearted swipe at the bar with a foul-smelling damp cloth.

"A beer," Percy said. "And somethin' to eat."

"You got money to pay for it?" the bartender asked.

"Yeah, we got money," Percy said, as if irritated by the question. "You get a lot of folks come in here buyin' things without money, do you?"

"Not a lot," the bartender said. "But we do get 'em from time to time. Often enough that I like to see the color of the money before I put anything in front of any-one"

"By God, mister, you got some sand treatin' your customers like that," Percy said.

"You ain't my customers till you spend money," the bartender replied. "And I ain't seen no money."

"Why, you—" Percy started angrily, but Aaron held his hand out to stop him.

"Hold on," he said. "The man is runnin' a business here. He has every right to ask whether or not we got money."

This rather accommodating position was something new for Aaron, and both Percy and Dalton looked at him curiously.

"The truth is, mister, me 'n my partners has run into a bit of bad luck," Aaron said. "We got money, but we ain't got a lot of what you call cash money."

"Well, then, your luck ain't gettin' no better," the bartender said. "'Cause cash money is the only kind of money there is."

"But we've got a couple of fine horses out front we'd be willin' to sell."

"This ain't a livery."

"Two good horses, with saddles," Aaron said.

"With saddles?"

"Yes."

The bartender stroked his chin for a moment. "Are these horses stolen horses?"

"They ain't stole. One of 'em belonged to my brother, the other'n belonged to his brother," Aaron said, pointing to Dalton. "They was killed, both of 'em."

"How?"

"I don't reckon that's none of your business how they was killed," Aaron said. "The point is, these here horses ain't stole. So if you'd like to buy 'em, we can make you a good price."

"I'll take a look at 'em," the bartender said.

"While you're lookin', we'll be drinkin'," Aaron said. He put fifteen cents on the bar. "Give us three beers."

The bartender took the money, then drew the beers and set them before the three. When he went outside, Aaron turned his back to the bar and, drinking his beer, listened in on the conversation of the men at the table.

"What'd you say his name was?" one of the men at the table asked. The man who asked was a big man, with long hair and a full, bushy beard.

"His name is Roosevelt. Theodore Roosevelt, but the dandified son of a bitch calls hisself Teddy." The man who answered had a soiled bandage on his right hand, and he seemed to be favoring it as he held his beer glass.

"Dandified?" the bushy-bearded man asked.

"Yeah, he wears fancy clothes, and these funny-loookin' little glasses that sort of just set on his nose. He's from back East somewhere."

"Yes, well, he may be some dandy from the East, but I hear tell he handled you and Muley pretty good."

"Me 'n Muley was caught by surprise. Wasn't we, Muley?"

"Yeah," the one called Muley answered. "An' by the time me'n Zeb figured out what was happenin', why, he had some hired gun shootin' at us. He shot me through the shoulder and shot Zeb there through the hand." He put his hand to his shoulder to emphasize his point, though as the wound he described was covered by his shirt, there was no visible evidence to support his claim.

"This here fella Roosevelt has him a hired gun, does he?" the bearded man asked.

"That's what it looked like to me. The fella that shot us is a big fella, with sandy hair and blue eys," Zeb said.

Up until that point, Aaron had been listening with only half an interest, but the man Muley described sounded a lot like Falcon MacCallister, the man who had been hounding them. He wondered if it was the same person.

Percy interrupted Aaron's musing.

"Hey, Aaron, what do you say that after we sell them horses we get us a whore?" Percy asked.

"Yeah," Dalton said. "Let's get us a whore."

"You see any whores around?" Aaron asked.

"What about her?" Percy said, pointing to the woman who was still on her hands and knees, scrubbing the floor.

"She don't look like no whore to me," Aaron said. "Looks like a cleaning woman to me."

"Yeah, well, she's a woman, though, ain't she?" Percy said. He smiled at the woman, who, all the while she was scrubbing, had been glancing up toward the three.

At that moment the bartender came back into the saloon. "I'll give you twenty dollars apiece for the horses," he said.

"How much for the saddles?"

"That includes the saddles."

"The saddles are worth that much without the horses," Aaron complained.

"You think you can get more for 'em, ask someone else," the bartender said, indicating the others in the saloon.

Aaron cleared his throat. "Any you gents want to buy a horse and saddle?"

"Not me," the bearded man at the table said. The other three shook their heads as well.

"What about you two?" Aaron asked the men standing at the end of the bar. "You want to buy a couple of horses and saddles? Sixty dollars will get you both horses and saddles."

Everyone in the saloon laughed.

"What is it?" Aaron asked. "What's so damned funny?"

"I doubt that either one of these boys has ever even seen sixty dollars," the bartender said.

Aaron sighed in disgust. "All right," he said. "I'll take your damn forty dollars."

"I thought you might come around to seein' things

my way," the bartender said. He smiled. "Now you are my customers. What can I get for you?"

"What you got to eat?"

"Biscuits, bacon, beans."

"That'll do. We'll be over there," Aaron said, pointing to the only other table.

"Hey, bartender, what about that woman over there?" Percy asked.

"What do you mean what about her?" the bartender answered.

"Is she your wife or somethin'?"

"She's just a woman that works here."

"Is all she does is scrub the floors and such?" Percy asked.

"She does a little more'n that," the bartender replied.

"Does she whore?"

"She whores some."

"How much?"

"You have to take that up with her," the bartender said.

Percy went over to talk to the woman while Aaron and Dalton found a table next to the table where the four men were talking.

"What's your name?" Percy asked the scrubwoman.

"Millie," the woman answered. She raised up on her knees and looked up at Percy, again brushing a strand of hair back from her face. There was dirty water on her hand, and it left a smear. She smiled, showing a mouth empty of teeth; then obviously self-conscious about it, she covered her mouth with her hand.

"Well, Millie, the bartender said you whore some. Is that true?"

Millie nodded. "I'll whore, if the price is right, and if I happen to take a fancy to the man," she answered.

Percy preened himself a little. "What about me?" he asked. "Do you take a fancy to me?"

"You'll do," Millie replied.

"Look at ole Percy over there, struttin' his stuff," Dalton said. "If he ain't the little rooster in the henhouse, though."

"Shh," Aaron said. "I want to listen in on what these folks over at the next table is talkin' about."

"What for?"

"You can pick up a lot of information by keepin' your ears open and your mouth shut," Aaron said.

Percy, wearing a broad grin, sauntered back over to the table.

"She said she'll do it for a dollar," Percy said.

"Is that a dollar apiece? Or will she do us both for one dollar?" Dalton asked.

"I don't know, I didn't ask," Percy said.

"Well, go find out."

"What the hell? You go find out," Percy said.

Dalton shook his head. "Huh-uh," he said. "You're the one she likes. If she's going to do it, it will be because she's taken a shine to you."

"Yeah," Percy said. "Yeah, she does like me. You could tell, huh?"

"I could tell."

Percy looked back toward the young woman. "All right, I'll go ask her."

Percy walked back over to the woman. "Will you do me 'an my friend for a dollar?" he asked.

"What? You mean at the same time?" Millie asked in surprise.

Percy thought about the question for a moment, as if

actually intrigued by the idea; then he smiled and shook his head.

"No," he said. "Not at the same time. I'll be first, then my friend."

"Why should I do both of you for one dollar?"

"Well, come on, Millie, look at yourself. Without them teeth, you ain't exactly what someone would call a pretty woman. You'd think you'd be grateful for any man that paid any attention to you a'tall. So, what the hell happened to them teeth anyway?"

"A drunken cowboy knocked them out," Millie said, hanging her head.

"Yeah, well, me'n Dalton wouldn't do nothin' like that. All we want is a little poke, that's all. But we don't want to pay no more'n a dollar for it. Think about it, it's more'n you got now. And it's got to be better'n bein' on your hands and knees, scrubbin' the floor."

Millie looked over toward the table toward Aaron and Dalton.

"I'll do two of you for a dollar. I won't do all three of you."

"That's all right. Aaron, he don't want to do it anyhow. It'll just be me 'n ole Dalton."

"I've got a room in the back," Millie said, standing up and brushing her hands together.

"I'll get Dalton."

As Millie began taking off her apron, Percy hurried back to the table. "She'll do us both for a dollar," he said.

"Really? Why would she do that?"

"'Cause I told her that, with them teeth knocked out, she wasn't goin' to be able to do no better."

Dalton laughed. "You do know how to talk pretty to a girl."

"Yeah, I always did have me a way with women," Percy said. "Come on, let's go."

"What about our food?" Dalton asked.

"I had me some food just yesterday," Percy said. "But I ain't had me no woman since I can't remember when."

"Yeah," Dalton agreed. "You got a point. The food will still be here when we get back. What about you, Aaron?"

"You boys have your fun," Aaron said. "I ain't interested."

As Percy and Dalton followed Millie into the back of the saloon, Aaron turned his attention to the conversation of the men at the adjoining table.

"What's this fella Roosevelt doin' out here anyway?" the bearded man asked.

"He owns Elkhorn," Muley answered.

"Elkhorn. That's a ranch?"

"It ain't just a ranch. It's a big ranch," Zeb said. "The biggest in the county."

"Owns a ranch, huh? Well, they say most of the ranches now is owned by rich men from the East who never even see the land. At least this Roosevelt fella has come out here to run his ranch," the bearded man said.

"Maybe he ain't as rich as all them other ranch owners," the fourth man at the table suggested.

"The hell he ain't," Zeb said. "He's rich all right. And they say that he carries more money on him than most folks will ever see in a lifetime."

"Why would he do that? Carry so much money, I mean?" the bearded man asked.

"Ahh, he likes to be the big man," Muley put in with a dismissive wave of his hand. "He comes into town, pays cash for all his supplies, then he goes over to the saloon and starts buyin' drinks for ever'one. He's got ever'one eatin' sugar cubes from his hand. If you want to know the truth, I think that's why the son of a bitch pisses me off."

The bearded man laughed. "Why is that, Muley? Did you miss out on your turn at the sugar tit?"

The others laughed as well.

"You can laugh if you want. I just don't care for the son of a bitch," Muley said.

"Me neither," Zeb said.

The men at the table turned to another subject then, but Aaron was no longer interested in following their conversation. He was beginning to develop a plan.

Percy and Dalton came back to the table then, their faces flushed, each of them wearing a smile.

"You should'a been with us, Aaron," Percy said. "It was good. It was real good."

"Come on," Aaron said, standing. "We've got to go."

"Go? What do you mean we've got to go?" Dalton said. "Me'n Percy ain't even et yet."

"You had your chance. You chose to go with the washerwoman. Now, we've got things to do. Let's go."

"Just what is it we've got to do that's so damn important we can't even eat?" Percy asked.

"I just figured out an easy way for us to get a lot of money," Aaron said, starting toward the door.

"Yeah, well, I hope it works out better'n it did the last time," Dalton said. He grabbed a biscuit, opened it up, and put the bacon inside. By the time he had made his sandwich, Aaron was outside.

Percy had no choice but to follow suit and, biscuits in hand, he and Dalton hurried after their leader.

Chapter 11

Grand Central Station, New York

Misses Anna Heckemeyer, Gail Thorndike, and Emma Lou Patterson were sitting on a bench in Grand Central Station. As the trains rumbled in and out of the great shed, they could feel the building shake.

"Oh, my train is here!" Anna said when she saw the flag go up by the announcement board. Standing, she reached for her small train case.

"It is another hour before my train leaves," Emma Lou said.

"Do you have everything, Anna?" Gail asked. Because Gail lived in New York, she wasn't going anywhere, but she had come to the station to see her two friends off, Anna to the Dakota Territory and Emma Lou to Richmond.

"Yes, my luggage has already been checked through," she said.

As the three girls looked at each other, their eyes welled with tears.

"I don't know how I would have gotten through the last four years without you two," Anna said. "You have been such wonderful friends."

"You are my best friends," Gail said.

"Oh, and to think that we will never see each other again," Emma Lou said.

"Don't say that," Anna said. "We will write letters, and we will visit again. I'm sure of it."

"Yes, I am too," Gail said.

The three girls embraced warmly; then Anna started toward the door under the sign that said TO TRACKS.

"Bye, Anna!" Gail called.

"Bye, Anna!" Emma Lou echoed.

As she reached the door, Anna turned for one last look at her two friends. She smiled through her tears, waved, then turned and quickly stepped through the door and out into the train shed.

Here, the noise of the trains was much louder than had been the subdued rumble one could hear inside the station itself. Here also was the smell of coal smoke and steam. She hurried down the platform, against which three dozen trains were backed. As she passed each train, she looked down the walkway between them where she saw passengers getting on and off. Each train, she knew, was an adventure within itself, and she wondered about all the people and what stories they might have to tell.

Finally she reached Track 29. The sign read EMPIRE STATE LIMITED—CHICAGO—DEPARTS AT 4:30 P.M.

Several porters were standing out on the walk alongside the train. One of them approached Anna.

"May I help you, ma'am?" he asked, reaching for the train case.

"Yes, thank you. I believe this is my train," she said, showing her ticket.

"Yes, ma'am," the porter answered. "And I see you got a parlor car. You goin' have youself a fine trip, miss," he said.

The porter led Anna up the stairs and into the train,

where he showed her to a comfortable, overstuffed chair. "Soon's we're out of the station, I'll come take your reservation for the dining car," he promised.

"Thank you."

It was early morning when the Empire State Limited from New York backed into Chicago's Union Station, and even the squealing of the train as it came to a stop didn't awaken Anna Heckemeyer.

"Miss Heckemeyer? Miss Heckemeyer, ma'am, the train has arrived at the station," a voice called. The call was accompanied by a knock on the compartment door.

Anna opened one eye as the knock sounded again, harder this time, and the persistent voice, which the young woman now recognized as the porter's voice, repeated, "Miss Heckemeyer?"

Awakening slowly, Anna raised herself up on her elbow and pulled the shade aside to look through the window. Another train was just a few feet away, separated from hers by a narrow, brick-paved walkway that was crowded with detraining passengers. The passengers were walking swiftly toward the main station through wisps of steam that drifted out to tease them.

"Miss Heckemeyer?" the porter called again, rapping on the door so loudly that Anna was certain he could be heard all up and down the car.

"Yes, yes," Anna said. "I'm awake."

"You have only thirty minutes to change trains, Miss Heckemeyer," the porter said. "If you'd like, I'll get a station porter to take your luggage for you now."

"Wait," Anna said. "Give me about ten minutes to get dressed."

"Yes, ma'am. But you'd best not tarry none," the

porter said. "The train you be wantin' will leave at eight o'clock sharp."

"I'll be ready," Anna promised.

Getting up from her bunk, Anna walked over to the little lavatory and ran water into the basin. As she washed her face and brushed her teeth, her image stared back at her from the mirror.

"Arrogantly beautiful" was the way Gail had once described her, and when Anna asked what arrogantly beautiful meant, Gail told her that she was "beautiful as if it is your right to be beautiful, and as if you can't understand why everyone else isn't as beautiful."

Anna had just completed four years of schooling at the New York Conservatory for Young Women. During the previous summer vacation, she had gone to Europe on a "Continental Tour" as part of her overall education. She was headed back home now for the first time in over two years, and she was anxious to see her father again.

Anna's mother had died when she was five years old, so long ago that Anna's memories of her were manifested in bits and pieces . . . the smell of cinnamon and flour . . . the feel of her skin when she embraced Anna, and the look of the sun in her hair.

Anna's father, Judge Andrew Heckemeyer, had not remarried, so he had taken on the responsibility of being both mother and father to his daughter. For that reason, Anna had missed him even more than might be normally expected, so she was very anxious to get back home.

By hurrying, Anna was dressed within ten minutes after the first call. She opened the door to her compartment and looked out into the aisle. She saw the porter standing out on the vestibule, looking out over the station.

"Porter?" she said.

"Yes, ma'am?"

"I'm ready now. Would you see to my luggage, please?"

With a nod of assent, the porter looked back out over the crowded depot platform.

"You!" the porter shouted authoritatively, pointing to one of the many station porters scurrying about on the platform. "Come quickly. Miss Heckemeyer needs you."

"Yes, sir, I be right there," the man responded, recognizing the elevated position of the train porter.

Twenty minutes later, Anna was on the Northwest Flyer, leaving Chicago for points west. She would not have to change trains again until she got off in Medora, Dakota Territory.

Settled into her new compartment, Anna took out the last letter she had received from her father, and began to read.

> *I am most anxious for you to meet Mr. Theodore Roosevelt of New York. Mr. Roosevelt owns Elkhorn Ranch near here, and is a man of considerable wealth and, so I am told, political influence back in New York.*
>
> *But all the wealth and influence in the world could not prevent a terrible tragedy from befalling him, for his wife and mother died on the same day.*
>
> *He is an engaging man, and we have enjoyed many interesting conversations, but it is clear to see that the sorrow of his loss is just beneath the surface. I think you might be just the one to cheer him up. At least, I hope so. It is not good that a man like Mr. Roosevelt be so immersed in sorrow.*

Anna had inquired among her friends to see if any of them were familiar with Theodore Roosevelt. She was surprised by just how many people did know of him, and even more surprised to hear that no one had anything bad to say about him.

That, more than anything else, intrigued her. What sort of man could be so well known, yet not have developed enemies, if not from some event, then from jealousy? And yet this man, Theodore Roosevelt, seemed to be just such a man.

She found herself looking forward to meeting him.

Falcon MacCallister was in Medora because he had lost the trail of the three men he was following, due to the torrential downpour that had washed away their tracks. He wasn't too concerned, though. There weren't that many places a person could go out here, so all he had to do was bide his time until they crossed paths again. And he knew, without the slightest doubt, that they would cross paths again.

Falcon was both the hunter and the hunted, though at the moment, he had no idea anyone was looking for him. It would not have shocked him to learn that Thad Howard's two brothers were after him, though. He had dealt with men bent upon revenge before, and there was no doubt in his mind that he would have to deal with such people again.

Actually, it was just as unlikely that he was the hunter now too. He had no official capacity as far as law enforcement was concerned. And despite the fact that he'd accepted reward money for bringing in Thad Howard, Falcon was not a bounty hunter.

It wasn't reward money that had put him on these men's trail. He was trailing them to avenge the senseless slaughter of Luke and Mary Douglass. He knew in a real sense, though, that these three men were merely surrogates for the outlaws who had killed his wife.

Marie Gentle Breeze was killed by renegade Cheyennes. She was already dead by the time he learned of it, and he didn't even have the satisfaction of settling scores himself. The ones who did it were dealt with by others.

Falcon learned a lot about loss and grief from that experience. He learned that grief never really goes away. Time can dull the ache, but it doesn't heal it. He left home after that, drifting from place to place as if in that way he could run away from the ghosts that trailed him.

Falcon developed a mixed reputation during those years of wandering. Because he was a man who gave no quarter when put in a life-and-death situation, there were some who thought he was a cold-blooded killer. Others claimed he was an outlaw, though those who knew him also knew that the dodgers once circulated had been withdrawn. Falcon paid no attention to what others thought of him. They could think whatever they damn well chose to think.

Some of the stories were true. He was called a gunfighter, a gambler, and a bad man to crowd. He was all of these things. He was also called a skilled tracker, a solitary hunter, and a formidable foe, and he was these things as well.

But the stories of him being a desperado, like the stories that he was a highwayman and a mercenary assassin, were not true. If he sometimes rode the owlhoot trail, it was not by choice.

There were many men who wanted to find Falcon MacCallister, some for the reward that had been offered for his capture, not realizing that the reward, like the wanted posters, had been withdrawn. Some sought revenge, meaning to pay Falcon back for an alleged wrong, generally because Falcon had killed some close relative of theirs in a gunfight. Their lust for revenge made no allowances for the fact that every man Falcon had killed had been in face-to-face combat with him.

There were also those who sought him so that they might test themselves against him, especially as time passed and his reputation grew. And as Aaron Childers had observed, the unlucky ones found him.

After a few days' rest in Medora, enjoying a real bed to sleep in, and meals he didn't have to cook for himself, Falcon went out again in search of the men who had killed the Douglasses. The recent rains had washed away any of the original tracks, but when he ran across a fresh set, he got down from Diablo for a closer examination.

He smiled, because this was what he had been looking for.

When Falcon followed them from the Douglass Ranch, he had been trailing five horses, three carrying riders, two with empty saddles. What he saw now was the track of three horses, all of which were carrying riders. He didn't know what happened to the other two horses, but he was certain that at least two of these horses were the ones he had originally been tracking.

One of the horses had a nicked shoe on the right hind foot. One of the other horses led with his left forefoot. These tracks fit that pattern. In addition, a nearby horse dropping was still fresh.

He was close. He was very close. Stroking his chin, Falcon mounted Diablo and looked ahead. The trail led into a low-lying range of mountains. That was good, because the mountains established a limit as to the number of directions they could go. They could only go where the mountains would let them go.

* * *

Falcon was even closer than he thought, for less that three miles ahead, Childers, Yerby, and Shaw were discussing their upcoming operation.

"What makes you think this here Roosevelt fella will be carryin' a lot of money on him?" Shaw asked.

" 'Cause he's rich. Not just flush, I mean really rich. And he'll be ridin' into town today to pay for supplies for his ranch," Childers replied. "Whenever he goes to town, he also goes into the saloon, where he puts on the big dog by buyin' drinks for ever'one. They say he carries a roll of money around that's big enough to choke a horse."

"How do you know all this?" Yerby asked.

"While you boys was beddin' that ugly girl back at the tradin' post, I was listenin' in on the talk at the other table. Why . . . robbin' him will be as easy as takin' money from a baby."

"Yeah, well, that bank was supposed to be easy too, and look what happened. We didn't get no money, and we wound up gettin' my brother killed."

"He didn't get killed robbin' the bank. That didn't happen until later. Besides, my brother was killed too, if you remember," Childers said.

"Yeah, but you didn't like your brothers."

"That ain't true. I liked Frank all right. Him an' me had the same ma. It was Corey I didn't like."

"Yeah, well, that don't change the fact that they was caught and was almost hung when we tried to rob that bank. And for all that, we didn't get practically nothin' at all from the bank."

"Well, let me ask you this. Did you know the clerk couldn't open the safe?"

"No," Yerby answered.

"Then how the hell was I supposed to know?"

"Let's quit jawin' about the bank and think about the

money we're goin' to take off this here dude," Shaw suggested.

"Yeah, that's what I say," Childers said. "There ain't no sense in cryin' over spilt milk."

"Where do you want to hit him?" Shaw asked.

"Well, according to what them fellas back at the tradin' post was sayin', his ranch is right on the other side of that range that's just ahead of us. That means that whenever he goes to town, he's going to have to come right through that draw there," Childers said. He pointed. "Look up there at them rocks about halfway up the wall. We'll be waitin' up there. Soon as he comes in, we'll open up on him."

"When will he come?"

"Today's Saturday, ain't it?"

"Yes."

"He comes into town ever' Saturday."

"Whoa," Roosevelt said to his horse.

The horse stopped, and Roosevelt took off his hat and wiped the sweat from his forehead with a big red bandanna. He looked at the bandanna and chuckled.

"If the people back in New York could see me now," he said. "Sweating like a dockhand, carrying this . . . this . . . tablecloth of a bandanna. I tell you, they would have a laugh."

Roosevelt knew that talking to his horse was only slightly above talking to himself, but it was a habit he had developed recently. The long, lonely rides were necessary for him to work out the grief, but often he felt the need to express himself verbally, and the only way to do that was to talk to his horse.

"Besides, you are a good listener," he said. "About the only one I've ever spoken to who wasn't just waiting patiently for his own time to talk." This time he didn't chuckle, he laughed out loud.

Putting his hat back on his head, he leaned over to retrieve his canteen.

That was when he heard it . . . the angry whine, like the buzz of a bee . . . whizzing by overhead.

Almost simultaneous with the buzz came the cracking sound of a rifle being fired.

The horse bolted in fear, and even though Roosevelt was an accomplished horseman, he was in an awkward position when the horse bolted. Because of that, he was unseated.

Even that incident, which normally would have been embarrassing, saved his life, for two more shots rang out immediately following the first. And, like the first shot, they missed.

The echo of the shots reverberated through the canyon in such a way as to make it very clear what was happening. Roosevelt was being shot at, and he knew it.

Roosevelt wasn't wearing a pistol, but he had a rifle in his saddle sheath. Even as he realized that, though, he saw his horse moving away from him.

"Whoa, horse," Roosevelt shouted.

The horse paused for a moment, and Roosevelt was nearly to him, would have made it, at least in time to recover his rifle, had there not been another shot. This one hit a rock, then ricocheted off with a loud, keening whine. Again, his horse bolted, running away as his hoofs clattered over the hard rocky surface.

For a moment, Roosevelt stood there, looking at the fleeing horse. Then, another rifle shot, so close by that he could practically feel the concussion of its passing, reminded him that he was unarmed and defenseless against whoever it was trying to shoot him. He had no choice but to run toward a nearby ridge, where he took cover just as a bullet ricocheted off the ground right by his feet.

Falcon heard the shots and, looking toward the sound, saw Roosevelt running toward the ridge as his horse galloped on up the draw. He also saw bullets kicking up around the rancher. Turning his gaze up the wall of the draw, he saw a little puff of smoke drifting away from a rock outcropping. Even as he was looking, two more rifles fired, almost simultaneously.

Falcon slapped his legs against the side of his horse, urging Diablo into a gallop. At the same time he snaked out his rifle, jacked a round into the chamber, and snapped off a shot.

Reaching the ridgeline where Roosevelt had taken cover, Falcon leaped from his horse, slapped it on the rump to get it out of danger, then fired again at the rocks halfway up the wall.

"Are you all right?" Falcon asked.

"Yes, thank you."

"I wasn't able to offer you much help the other day, but looks like you could use it this time."

"Yes, indeed," Roosevelt said. "There is something to be said for persistence. If at first you don't succeed in offering help, try, try again. I'm glad you tried again."

The shooting stopped and Falcon raised his head to look up toward the rocks. He saw three men moving quickly up a path toward the top of the cliff.

He had not yet seen the men he was trailing, so he couldn't identify them on sight, but he would have bet cash money these were the same three. He raised his rifle and aimed at one of them.

"Please don't shoot him," Roosevelt said, reaching his hand up to pull the rifle down.

Sighing, Falcon lowered his rifle. "Why the hell not?" he asked. "I've been trailing these sons of bitches for a couple of weeks now, and they just tried to kill you."

"Yes, but I'm in no danger now, thanks to you."

"Mr. Roosevelt, you don't know what these men have done," Falcon said.

"No, but if you shoot them now, I know what you would be doing. You would be acting as their judge, jury, and executioner. I don't think you really want to do that now, do you?"

Falcon eased the hammer back down. "All right," he said. "You win."

"Thank you."

"Any idea why they were after you?"

"Oh, yes. I'm quite sure they wanted to rob me," Roosevelt said.

"You carry enough money with you to tempt a robbery?"

"I have about one thousand dollars on me now," Roosevelt said, taking out a roll of money to show Falcon.

"Put that away," Falcon said sharply. "Damn, mister, don't you have any more sense than to go flashing around that much money? You're unarmed. How do you know I won't take it?"

"I may still be learning about the West," Roosevelt answered, "but I am quite skilled in reading people. I know you won't take it."

"Well, you're right. I won't. But some people can fool you, so you should be more careful."

"Oh, indeed I will be more careful from now on, thank you," Roosevelt said.

"Your horse ran away. If I can run mine down, I'll go see if I can find him for you," Falcon said.

"Thank you, but that won't be necessary," Roosevelt

said. Sticking two fingers into his mouth, Roosevelt let out a loud, ear-piercing whistle.

"What the hell? How did you do that?" Falcon asked.

"Believe me, it is a necessary skill when summoning a hack in New York."

Within moments, Roosevelt's horse came clattering back down the draw.

"If you will wait here," Roosevelt suggested, "I'll recover your horse for you."

"Thank you," Falcon said.

Roosevelt chuckled. "Under the circumstances, it is the least I can do."

"A piece of cake, you said. Some Eastern dude that carries a lot of money. All we have to do is shoot him, then take the money, you said. Well, we listen to you and that MacCallister person shows up and we damn near got ourselves killed," Yerby complained.

"Dalton, you'd bitch if you was hung with a new rope," Childers said.

Percy Shaw laughed out loud.

"What are you laughing at?" Yerby asked.

"You'd bitch if you was hung with a new rope," Percy said. "That's funny."

"There ain't nothin' funny 'bout gettin' hung, new rope or no," Yerby said. "In case you don't remember, Corey and Ethan was near 'bout hung. And if we'd'a been caught, why, we would'a all hung, 'cause there wouldn't of been anyone to get us out the way we done for Ethan and Corey."

"Why do you reckon that MacCallister fella is after us?" Shaw asked. "Is he a lawman?"

"He ain't no lawman, that's for sure," Yerby said.

"Fact is, I've heard they's paper out on him. Whoever kills him would get a reward."

"You don't say. How much of a reward?" Shaw asked.

"Believe me, whatever it is it ain't enough," Childers said.

"Yeah, well, I don't know much about him, but I'll say this. That son of a bitch can shoot," Yerby said. "From the gallop, he purt' near put a bullet through my head. And if you want to know the truth, I've had about a bellyful of him."

"So, what are we goin' to do now?" Shaw asked.

"What do you mean, what are we goin' to do now?" Childers asked.

"About money," Shaw replied. "We 'bout out of the money we got from sellin' them horses, and now we're so broke that if piss pots was a dime a dozen, all we could do is shout ain't that cheap."

"I'll come up with somethin'," Childers promised.

"Yeah? What?" Yerby asked.

"I don't know, I have to think about it for a while."

"Now there's something to look forward to," Yerby said sarcastically. "You a'thinkin'. So far, there ain't nothin' you've come up with that's worth a plugged nickel."

On board the Northwest Flyer, Anna Heckemeyer was writing in her journal.

I had nearly forgotten how lovely it is out here. As I look out toward Painted Canyon, the play of light and color across the face of this wild and beautiful country nearly makes me forget the crowded streets of New York. And as exciting as New York was, this wonderful and wild West is even more exciting.

Geologists will tell us that centuries of wind and water have shaped this magnificent land, adding depth and contrast to define its character. But as I view it through a scattering of wind-twisted cedars and junipers, ensnared by the colors and awed by the clarity of the light, I clearly see the hand of God.

"Welcome home, Miss Heckemeyer," the conductor said, stopping at her commodious and comfortable seat in the Wagner Parlor Car.

Anna smiled up at him. "Well, hello, John, when did you get on the train?"

"At Bismarck," John said. "I've missed seeing you. How long has it been now?"

"Four years," Anna replied. "Though I did get home two years ago."

"You were back East somewhere, weren't you?"

"Yes, I went to school in New York."

"And how was it?"

"It was wonderful, and I'm sure that it was all worthwhile. But I must confess that I am very happy to be back."

"What seating do you want for lunch?"

"I'm in no hurry," Anna replied. "I'll take the third seating."

"Very well, I'll take care of it," John said.

Anna watched the conductor move through the car to get the seating preferences from the other passengers. John Norton had been a conductor on the Northern Pacific for as long as Anna could remember. He had been there to provide help to Anna and her father when they traveled to Bismarck for shopping expeditions, and he had been there four years ago when Anna took the train east to finish her education in New York.

Chapter 12

"If we want to continue to elect Republicans, we are going to have get some more of the Western territories in as states," Judge Heckemeyer was saying. "It is the only way to counterbalance the Democratic South."

"That's all well and good, Andrew, but we, as a party, can't afford to just turn our back on the other states. Take my own state of New York, for example. It went Democratic for the most recent election, but I know we can get it back into our column. Though I'm not sure we have put forth the best candidate in James G. Blaine."

Roosevelt enjoyed his visits with Andrew Heckemeyer because the judge was well versed in politics and their discussions kept Roosevelt sharp.

"What about your own future, Teddy?" Heckemeyer asked. "Have you plans?"

"I don't know," Roosevelt replied. "At one time I was entertaining various plans, mayor of New York, governor, the U.S Congress or Senate maybe. But I may have burned a few bridges with my steadfast support of John Edmonds at the convention in Chicago. I was completely shut out of Blaine's campaign."

"Maybe that is not such a bad thing," Heckemeyer suggested.

"How so?"

"Well, if Blaine is as corrupt as you say he is, then

some of that corruption may rub off on some of his supporters and advisors. If you are out of the picture, you will be clean."

Roosevelt nodded. "You may have a point," he said. "At any rate, since my Alice died, it all seems inconsequential. I've rather lost interest in politics, and politics has lost interest in me."

"Nonsense," Heckemeyer said. "You are a good man, Teddy. And the nation can always use a good man."

"Speaking of a good man," Roosevelt said, "I have recently had two encounters with someone who is my idea of the true Western hero."

Heckemeyer chuckled, as he relit his cigar. "You don't say. Well, who is this man who has so captured your imagination?"

"His name is MacCallister. Falcon MacCallister," Heckemeyer said.

The smile left Heckemeyer's face and he bit down hard on the cigar. "Falcon MacCallister, you say?"

"Yes. Do you know him?"

Meckemeyer nodded. "I know him," he said.

Roosevelt studied the expression on Judge Heckemeyer's face.

"From the way you are reacting to his name, I take it that you don't agree with my assessment of the gentleman."

"Believe me, he is no gentleman," Judge Heckemeyer replied. "And you are right, I don't agree with your assessment."

"Is there something about him I should know?" Roosevelt asked.

"For one thing, he is too quick to use the gun. Let me give you two recent examples.

"He was a passenger on a train when the train was stopped and boarded by train robbers. Instead of remaining quiet like the other passengers, MacCallister engaged them in a gun battle, killing three of them. And despite all that, one of the robbers managed to get away with the money."

"You fault him for trying?"

"Yes, I fault him for trying," Heckemeyer said. "The gun battle took place inside the train, in the midst of all the passengers."

"Heavens, did he wound or kill any of the passengers?"

"In fact, one passenger was killed, though the statements of the other passengers said that he was killed by the robbers before the gun battle ensued."

"Then isn't it possible that Mr. MacCallister prevented more passengers from being killed?"

"It is possible," Heckemeyer admitted. "Though it is just sheer luck that more weren't killed in the shoot-out."

"You said you had two incidents," Roosevelt said.

"Yes, I do. I told you about the case that I tried in Belfield. The bank robbery and murder?"

"Yes."

"Falcon MacCallister happened to be in town when the bank was robbed, and he turned the town into a shooting gallery by shooting at the robbers as they were fleeing. He is reckless and irresponsible."

"Did he hit any of the bank robbers?" Roosevelt wanted to know.

Reluctantly, Heckemeyer nodded. "Yes, he shot two of them from their saddles, and when another dismounted to see to them, MacCallister subdued him as well."

"So, for resisting a bank robbery attempt, and for stopping three of them, you say he is reckless and irresponsible?"

"I do indeed."

"But wasn't he just doing his civic duty?" Roosevelt asked.

"Two men were killed as a result of that shoot-out. Sheriff Billy Puckett and an innocent bystander. As it turns out, it wasn't MacCallister's bullets that killed either of them, but I'm convinced that had he not opened fire like that, those two men would still be alive."

"I suppose there is that possibility," Roosevelt admitted. "But it would seem to me that you are stretching the possibility to reach the conclusion."

"The man is a killer," Judge Heckemeyer said.

"If by defending himself he has killed, then I could believe that. But if you are calling him a killer by nature, I do not believe that. I'm sorry, but I cannot believe ill of someone who saved my life," Roosevelt insisted.

"You say MacCallister saved your life? How did he do that?" Judge Heckemeyer asked.

"Yesterday, while I was riding into town, I was set upon by a band of outlaws. Their first shot startled my horse, he bolted, and I was unseated. I suddenly found myself dismounted without a weapon of any sort, and being shot at by three armed and desperate men."

"That's a hell of a situation to be in. What did you do?" Heckemeyer asked.

"I ran to a nearby ridge to seek cover, but I knew that wouldn't help because, once they discovered I was unarmed, there would be nothing to prevent them from just coming toward me as bold as you please, killing me, and relieving me of my money."

"Teddy, I've told you before, and I will tell you again. You shouldn't make it a practice to go about with so much money. This is a far cry from the civilized streets of New York," Heckemeyer said, scolding gently.

"I know. I really should be more careful. But I guess the Man Upstairs was looking out for me that day, because He sent someone to my rescue."

"That someone, I take it, was Falcon MacCallister?"

"Yes," Roosevelt said. "He appeared from out of the blue and, with a few well-aimed shots, soon sent my attackers on the way."

"He appeared from out of the blue, you say."

"Yes. Just when things were most desperate, there he was."

"Did he kill any of them?"

"No, he just shot at them and, evidently, came close enough to convince them that killing and robbing me wasn't going to be as easy as they thought. Why did you ask that?"

"From time to time I have warrants transmitted to me, authorizing the immediate arrest and incarceration of Falcon MacCallister for aggravated manslaughter," Judge Heckemeyer said. "Invariably, those warrants are withdrawn within a few weeks after they are issued."

"Why are they withdrawn?"

"According to the documents that request the withdrawal, it is because new information has come to light suggesting that the manslaughter incidents have all been justifiable homicides."

"If the homicides are justifiable, why are you so down on him?"

"Because I don't believe anybody can find themselves enmeshed in that many justifiable homicides, unless he is actively seeking the opportunity to, as you describe, 'suddenly appear out of the blue.' His bold and restless activity in Belfield bears me out on that. However, having said that, I must confess that I am glad that he was there to save your life."

"Even so, that hasn't changed your opinion of him, has it?" Roosevelt asked.

"I'm afraid not," Judge Heckemeyer replied. "But you do have the advantage over me in that you have seen him in one of these life-and-death situations, so you are better able to judge his actions than I am."

Roosevelt thought back to the incident in question. Falcon MacCallister had raised his rifle and aimed at one of his assailants, even as they were withdrawing. Had it not been for Roosevelt's interference, at least one of the outlaws would have been dead at Falcon's hand.

And though the death would have no doubt been ruled justifiable homicide, it was not actually needed to save his life.

"What is it?" Heckemeyer asked.

"I beg your pardon?"

"You were thinking about something just now."

"It was nothing."

"No, I think it was something. What happened when MacCallister intervened on your behalf?"

"Nothing happened, other than the fact that Mr. Mac-Callister drove away the outlaws."

Roosevelt thought of, but did not voice, the fact that he had pulled Falcon's arm down to prevent him from shooting one of the outlaws as they were leaving.

Heckemeyer chuckled. "Teddy, you are the consummate politician. Something did happen, you just don't want to tell me."

"And you are the consummate jurist," Roosevelt replied. "Always looking for more than you are told."

At that moment, Judge Heckemeyer's law clerk stuck his head into the room. "Excuse me, Judge?"

"Yes?"

"We just received a telegram from the sheriff at Sentinel Butte. They're ready to hold the trial."

"I thought the defense counsel asked for another week," Judge Heckemeyer said.

"Yes, but he withdrew the request and is now asking

that the trial be conducted immediately," the law clerk said.

"Well, you just telegraph them back and tell them," Judge Heckemeyer started to say . . . then, stroking his chin, he stared at Teddy Roosevelt for a moment.

The judge's daughter was supposed to arrive on the afternoon train. If he left this morning for Sentinel Butte, he wouldn't be here to meet her train. He had the authority to postpone the trial until the originally agreed-upon date, and that was what he'd started to do.

On the other hand, what better and more natural opportunity was there for him to arrange a meeting between Roosevelt and his daughter than this?

He smiled.

"Yes, Judge?" the clerk asked.

"I beg your pardon?"

"You asked me to telegraph them at Sentinel Butte and tell them . . . what?"

"Oh," Judge Heckemeyer replied. "Why, tell them I'll be there, of course."

"Very good, sir."

"Teddy, I wonder if you could do a favor for me?" Judge Heckemeyer asked.

"Yes, I'd be glad to. Anything you ask," Roosevelt replied.

"You know about my daughter, Anna, who has been away in school?"

"Yes, you showed me her picture. She is a lovely young woman."

"Thank you, I think so as well, though I admit that it may be a father's prejudice. At any rate, she is arriving on the three o'clock train this afternoon. Would you be so kind as to meet her and make certain that she and her luggage reach the house safely?"

"Yes, I would be delighted to do that for you," Roosevelt said. "But suppose I don't recognize her?"

"You will," Judge Heckemeyer replied. "I may be a doting father, but I can tell you without hesitation to simply look for the most beautiful woman to leave the train."

The arrival of a train in Medora was always an event. Trains brought mail and newspapers from the East, fresh produce from the South, and people from all over, and in so doing, connected the small town with the rest of the world. As a result, there were generally many more people gathered on the depot platform than there were people who had a legitimate reason for meeting the train.

As Teddy Roosevelt sat in the backseat of the carriage, waiting for the train to arrive, he stuck his hand down into a small paper bag and pulled out a piece of horehound candy. Popping a piece into his mouth, he handed the bag forward, offering some to his driver.

"Candy, Willie?" he asked.

"Thank you, Mr. Roosevelt, I don't mind if I do," the liveried and dignified-looking black man replied. He stuck his own hand down into the bag.

"Willie, have you ever heard of a man by the name of Falcon MacCallister?"

"Why, yes, sir. I reckon just about ever'one's heard of the MacCallisters."

"The MacCallisters? You mean there is more than one?"

"They's lots of them, I don't know exactly how many. I do know they one of the families that opened up the West."

"And Falcon MacCallister is one of that bunch?"

"Yes, sir. Fact is, except for maybe his pa, he's the most ripsnortin' of 'em all."

"What do you think of him?"

"I think maybe he wouldn't be a man I'd want as an enemy," Willie said.

"Is that a fact?"

"Yes, sir, that is a fact," Willie said. "On the other hand, anyone that can call him a friend is a lucky man."

"I have only met him twice, but I think I could call him a friend," Roosevelt said.

"That makes you a lucky man, Mr. Roosevelt," Willie said. "Yes, sir, it do make you a lucky man. But if you don't mind my sayin' so, that cuts both ways," Willie said.

"I beg your pardon?"

"Mr. MacCallister can call hisself a lucky man too, for havin' you as a friend," Willie said. "Anybody who can call you a friend is a lucky man."

"Why, thank you, Willie," Roosevelt said. "Thank you very much. And I hope that you include yourself in that number, for I consider you to be a friend."

"Yes, sir, I'm proud to say that I do," Willie said.

The sound of a train whistle reached them.

"Here comes the train!" someone shouted, though the announcement wasn't necessary because the train's second whistle alerted everyone. Looking east along the track, Roosevelt could see the train, small in the distance, but closing quickly.

It had been eight days since Anna Heckemeyer said good-bye to Gail and Emma Lou and stepped onto the train at New York's Grand Central Station. Eight days and three-quarters of a continent behind. She had traveled in luxury for the entire trip, enjoying a private compartment by night, and the parlor car by day. Despite that, the eight days had been exhausting, and she couldn't help but feel a sense of sympathy for those who had to make the long, tiring journey in the immigrant cars.

At least twice a day, as a matter of exercise, Anna had walked from the front of the train all the way to the end of the train, then back again. On these excursions she would have to pass through the immigrant cars.

The condition in the immigrant cars was appalling. Men, women, and children, crowded onto hard wooden seats, the smells of ethnic foods, unwashed bodies, and the odor of a privy, separated from the rest of the car only by a hanging curtain, made the air so foul that it was nearly impossible to breathe. She could barely stand it long enough to pass through, and she wondered how the passengers could put up with such conditions for so long.

Now she could feel the train slowing, and she knew that the next station would be Medora. As she sat in the overstuffed, comfortable chair in the parlor car, she smiled. It would be good to be home, and to see her father again.

Roosevelt stepped down from the carriage and walked across the wooden platform to stand next to the track. The engine approached, looming larger and getting louder as it closed the distance between it and the depot. Then it thundered by Roosevelt with its huge driver wheels being turned by the powerful connecting rod, and wisps of steam escaping from the cylinders while bits of glowing embers dripped down onto the tracks from the firebox.

The engine was so large and so heavy that, as it rolled by, the very ground tended to tremble and Roosevelt could feel its passage in his belly. The train was already slowing, even as the engine passed by, but it continued to slow with squeaks and groans until finally it stood still alongside the depot platform.

The train was motionless now, but it wasn't quiet. From the engine came the rhythmic pulse of pressurized steam escaping from the relief valve. The puffing sound reminded Roosevelt of some great beast, breathing hard from its recent labor. In addition to the sound of the puffing steam, there were the sounds of hot metal clicking and clanking as tie rods, gearboxes, and springs cooled and contracted.

To these mechanical sounds were added the shouts of joy and recognition as those who were waiting on the platform crowded forward to greet the arriving passengers. The detraining passengers returned the greetings with joyful cries of their own. There were also a few tears, as some of those present were telling their loved ones good-bye.

Roosevelt watched the joyful reunions and tearful departures with a sense of melancholy. He felt both a part of it, and apart from it, for he was himself a traveler, out of time and place, here in the West. And yet, he did not think he would be able to cope with the grief that was still just beneath the surface if he did not have this wonderful country in which to lose himself.

Anna stepped down into the cacophony of the depot platform. A cloud of smoke drifted by, caught by the wind, and swirled down to tickle her nose with its acrid odor. Nearly all steam locomotives were burning coal now, instead of wood, and the smoke had a distinct, much less pleasant smell than the aroma of burning wood from the earlier engines.

Anna fanned some of the smoke away from her face as she looked out at the crowd, anxiously trying to locate her father. A large smile of eager expectation spread across her face as she prepared for the long, anticipated reunion.

Her smile faded when a thorough perusal of the crowd disclosed the fact that her father wasn't there.

This seemed odd to her. She knew that she had informed him of the exact date and time of her arrival. Why was he not here?

An unreasonable fear began to creep over her. Had something happened to him?

It wasn't hard for Roosevelt to locate which of the departing passengers was Anna Heckemeyer. She was the only arriving passenger who was a young, unaccompanied woman. However, even if that had not been the case, he was sure he would have been able to recognize her by her father's description and the picture her father had shown him. The young woman who stood on the platform, anxiously searching through the crowd, had long, auburn hair, large brown eyes framed by full lashes, high cheekbones, and full lips. Clearly, she was an exceptionally beautiful woman.

Roosevelt started toward her, picking his way through the crowd. From the way the young girl's eyes were moving, he knew that she was looking for her father. He also detected a hint of anxiousness in her face, so he hurried his pace in order to relieve her of any unnecessary worry.

"Miss Heckemeyer?" he asked, doffing his hat as he approached.

"Yes?"

"Your father asked me to meet you when your train arrived."

"Oh! Is something wrong?"

"No, no, please, put your mind at ease," Roosevelt said quickly. "Your father has a trial in Sentinel Butte, that's all. I realize that I am a poor surrogate, but under the circumstances, I am honored and pleased to offer my services to you. My name is Theodore Roosevelt, though my friends all call me Teddy," he said with a disarming smile.

Anna returned the smile. "Oh, yes," she said. "I've heard a great deal about you, Mr. Roosevelt. A great deal indeed."

"Have you now?" Roosevelt asked, surprised by her comment. "My word, that is rather unexpected, I must say. May I inquire as to how you have heard about me?"

"I have heard of you both from my father, who speaks very highly of you, by the way, and from some of your friends back in New York."

"Is it too much for me to hope that my friends back in New York share your father's opinion?" Roosevelt asked. His voice, though rather high-pitched, was pleasant because of its tone.

"That is not at all too much for you to hope for," Anna replied. "In fact, all of the reports have been quite laudatory."

Roosevelt laughed out loud. "Bully for my friends. Bully, I say. Would you like to wait for your luggage? Or would you prefer to come with me now, and leave your luggage to be collected later?"

"I will come with you," Anna said.

"Anything Willie should know about your luggage?"

"No. I'm sure the station officials will recognize it and keep it safe until your man can call for it," Anna said.

"Very well. The carriage is over here," Roosevelt said, pointing toward the rather large and very elegant carriage that sat just off the end of the depot platform.

"Oh, my, that's quite a lovely conveyance," Anna said upon seeing the carriage. "I've seen similar conveyances in New York, but I don't believe I've ever seen one out here."

Roosevelt coughed in self-conscious embarrassment. "I must confess to being a bit of the dandy in some areas," he said. "While I love the ruggedness of this wonderful West, I do like a few of the creature comforts. And this carriage, I am afraid, is one of my vanities."

"A vanity I shall enjoy," Anna said as she climbed into the carriage and settled into the soft leather of the commodious rear seat.

Roosevelt sat in the facing seat; then, with a nod to Willie, they pulled away, leaving the crowded depot behind.

Chapter 13

It was that in-between time of day . . . after daylight, but before nightfall . . . and Falcon was some twenty miles from Medora. Although he was not acting in any official capacity, he was still on the trail of Aaron Childers, Dalton Yerby, and Percy Shaw. About an hour earlier, he had lost their trail, but he was sure he would find it again. It was just a matter of patience, and it was Falcon's experience that the hunter always had more experience than the hunted.

Falcon liked this twilight time of day best. The sun had set, but it was still light, the soft, silver kind of light that took away the glare and the heat. He had put on a pot of coffee a few minutes ago and was squatting by the fire, watching the glowing coals while waiting for the coffee to boil, when he felt a tingling on the back of his neck. He was being watched. Without being obvious about what he was doing, Falcon perused the area around him, and discovered that he was being watched by three men.

The strange thing was, the three men watching him now were not the three men he had been trailing. He knew this without knowing exactly how he knew it. He knew it from the intuition that he had developed over many years. Men who lived their lives like that took on senses that were beyond that of the normal person.

Without questioning how he knew, but merely accepting it as a part of his being, Falcon prepared himself for the danger that lay ahead. He tossed another stick of wood into the fire and paid a lot of attention to stirring the coals while, quietly, loosening the leather straps that held down the hammer of his pistol.

He waited, keeping a sideways watch and an open ear. He had a feeling they would make their play when he started to pour his cup of coffee, thinking they could catch him while he was distracted.

All right, Falcon thought. If this was the way they wanted to play, he would play their game with them, and he would even play it by their rules. But he was going to play this game on his own timing. As he took his tin cup from his saddlebag, Falcon was exceptionally keen to everything going on around him. He reached for the coffeepot.

Just as he knew they would, his adversaries took that precise moment to make their move. Turning toward them, Falcon dropped to the ground, then rolled to the right, even as the three men charging him were firing their own guns. Their bullets dug into the ground exactly where Falcon had been but a second earlier.

Falcon wound up on his stomach with his pistol in his hand.

"Shoot the son of a bitch, Zeb, shoot 'im!" Muley shouted.

Falcon recognized two of the shooters. Muley and Zeb were the men who had accosted Roosevelt in the saloon back in Medora. He didn't know who the third man was, but he didn't have time to speculate.

Falcon shot the stranger first, his bullet going in under the stranger's chin, then exiting the top of his head in a spray of blood, bone, and brain tissue. Whoever the stranger was, he was dead before he hit the ground.

Muley died almost as quickly, with a bullet to his heart. But Zeb caught two bullets in his gut, then went down, holding both hands over the wound, trying without success to stem the flow of blood.

In a matter of seconds what had started out to be a pleasant evening on the trail had turned into a blood-bath.

Although Falcon was certain that these three were the only ones threatening him, he remained on his belly, gun in hand, for a moment longer, just to make sure there were no surprises.

The gunfire had set some distant birds to calling, but now their calls were fading into the distance and the last echos of the gunshots were reverberating from the distant hills. When those sounds died, the only thing disturbing the silence was Zeb's quiet groans of pain.

"Damn, this hurts. This really hurts," Zeb grunted.

Falcon got up and, cautiously, walked over to look down at his wounded assailant.

"You're Zeb," he said.

"Yeah."

"Why'd you come after me, Zeb?" he asked.

"You know why."

"Surely you aren't talking about the business that happened back in Medora. Not even you could be that dumb, could you? That little altercation didn't seem like enough to get yourself killed over."

"We thought you was the one would get killed," Zeb said. "Besides, Rafferty paid us fifty dollars apiece to come with him."

"Rafferty?"

"That's him over there with the top of his head blow'd off."

Falcon walked over to look down at Rafferty. He had never seen him before in his life.

"Why'd he want me dead?"

When Zeb didn't answer him, Falcon looked back toward him. Zeb had fallen to one side. His head was back and his eyes were open, but unseeing. He wasn't hurting anymore.

Looking around, Falcon found the three horses the men had ridden in on. They were ground-hobbled less than one hundred yards away. Emptying their saddlebags, he examined the contents until it was too late to see, hoping by his investigation to find out who Rafferty was and why he wanted him dead.

He learned nothing.

For a moment, Falcon considered burying the three men out here where he killed them, but finally decided to take them into town. He threw the bodies across the backs of their horses. He hated to subject the horses to the ordeal of carrying the weight of a dead body through the entire night, but he was afraid that rigor mortis would set in and he would be unable to get them on the animals by morning.

When Falcon rode into Medora the next morning, he stirred the curiosity of the town. It wasn't every day that someone rode in leading three horses, each with a corpse thrown across the saddle.

The first of the curious townspeople picked him up as soon as he came into town and followed him down the street. The numbers grew as he came closer to the sheriff's office.

Sheriff John Dennis came out front to meet Falcon. He scratched a match on the pillar supporting the overhang of his porch, then held it to the end of an already half-smoked cigar. Palming the match with his hand to keep it from blowing out, he took several puffs, squinting at Falcon through the smoke. Finally, he nodded toward the men who were belly-down on the horses.

"Do you know who they are?" he asked.

Before Falcon could answer, several of the townspeople moved in and began examining the bodies more closely.

"Sheriff, this here one is Zeb Kingsley," one of the townspeople said after lifting the head of one.

"And this is Muley Simpson," another said. "Both of 'em used to ride for Don Montgomery."

"Who's the third?" Sheriff Dennis asked. "Did he ride for Mr. Montgomery as well?"

The man who was nearest the third body shook his head. "I don't know for sure," he replied. "I just know I ain't never seen him in the saloon before. Could be that he rides for Two Rivers."

"No, he don't," another said. "I ride for Two Rivers, and I've never seen this feller before either."

"Yeah, well, whoever he is, he's got the top of his head blow'd off," another said.

"His name is Rafferty," Falcon said. Falcon was still in his saddle, though he had crooked one leg across the pommel and was just sitting there, calmly watching the reaction of the town to his arrival with three dead bodies.

"Rafferty? What's his first name?"

"I don't know his first name," Falcon said. "Rafferty is all I know."

"Do you have any idea what happened to them?" the sheriff asked.

"Yes," Falcon said, though he didn't volunteer any more information.

"Well?" Sheriff Dennis asked.

"Well, what?" Falcon replied.

"What happened to them?"

"Oh, I thought you knew. I killed them," Falcon said, easily.

There were several gasps of surprise from the crowd.

"Did you hear that?"

"He said he kilt 'em, plain as day."

"Yes, well, I don't know this Rafferty fella, but if they was ever any two sons of bitches that needed killin' more'n Muley and Zeb, I'd like to know who they are. I say good riddance to the both of 'em."

"Wait a minute, I rode with them two boys," the man who rode for Two Rivers said. "From time to time they was a little high-spirited, but that don't give anyone the right to shoot 'em down. Sheriff Dennis, what are you going to do about this?"

The sheriff held up his hand to quiet the crowd, then squinted through his cigar smoke at Falcon.

"Seems to me like I recall you havin' yourself a run-in with Muley and Zeb a few days ago," Sheriff Dennis said. "Over at the saloon. You shot 'em up a little."

"Yes, I did," Falcon said.

"So, what did you decide to do? Finish the job?"

"I didn't have any choice, Sheriff. They came after me."

"They come after you, did they? All three of them?"

"That's right," Falcon said, nodding.

"Mister, you want us to believe you took these men on, three to one, and beat 'em all?" the rider from Two Rivers asked.

"No," Falcon answered.

"No? What do you mean no? Are you changing your story now?"

"I mean I don't care what you believe," Falcon said.

"Sheriff, Mr. Montgomery ain't goin' to take it too

kindly if you just let this fella get away with murderin' a couple of his men like that," the rider from Two Rivers said. "Even if they ain't ridin' for 'im no more."

Sheriff Dennis held up his hand to quiet the Two Rivers man.

"After that incident in the saloon the other day, I made some inquiries about you, Falcon MacCallister. Turns out I have a dodger on you. Did you know you got reward posters out sayin' you are wanted for murder?"

"I know about them," Falcon said. "I also know that they've all been recalled."

Sheriff Dennis nodded. "Yeah, when I inquired about them, that's what I was told. It's just as well. If you handled all three of these men by yourself, I don't think I'd want to try and serve a warrant on you."

Several in the crowd laughed at the sheriff's candid remark.

"So what are you saying, Sheriff? That you are just going to let him get away with murder?" the Two Rivers man asked.

"Take it easy, Sutton," Sheriff Dennis said. "Everyone who knew Muley and Zeb knows they was just the kind that would try a damn fool stunt like this. Besides which, if MacCallister here actually did murder them, he wouldn't have brought their bodies in, and he wouldn't have confessed to the killin', now would he? So I got no reason not to believe his story."

"Thanks," Falcon said.

"But what I want to know is, what about this third fella? What kind of beef did he have with you?" Sheriff Dennis asked.

"I don't know," Falcon said.

"Could be he was just some friend of Muley and Zeb's that they talked into helpin' 'em out," the sheriff suggested.

"Could be," Falcon agreed. He didn't tell the sheriff that it was just the other way around, that Rafferty had paid Muley and Zeb to help *him*. For the moment, he decided that information was best kept to himself.

Sheriff Dennis stepped down to look at the three bodies, then stopped to look at one of the horses.

"Say, wait a minute. This mare belongs to Chance Ingram, doesn't it?" he said, looking closely at the animal.

"You're right, it does," one of the men in the crowd said. "That's Belle. I've ridden her myself a few times. Chance rents her out."

"What's Zeb doin' on a rented horse?"

"Muley's on Zeb's horse," Sutton said. He looked at the other horse. "And the fella with his head blow'd off is on Muley's horse."

"I found the horses ground-hobbled," Falcon explained. "I didn't know who belonged to which horse and, under the circumstances, it didn't seem to matter much."

"Well, this here Rafferty fella is obviously the one that rented hisself a horse," Sheriff Dennis said. "That can only mean that he come into town some other way, either by train or by stage. Maybe if I ask around, I'll be able to find out who he is." He looked pointedly at Falcon. "I'm going to ask you again. You're sure you don't know anything about him?"

Falcon shook his head. "I never saw him before," he said.

There was one in the crowd who had more than a passing interest in the fate of the man Falcon had identified as Rafferty. Creed Howard wasn't a citizen of Medora, but had arrived on the same train as the man who had been identified as Rafferty.

Creed offered no information, but he could have told them all about Rafferty, including the fact that Rafferty wasn't his real name. His real name was Bob Howard.

Bob and Creed Howard were brothers. Only one other person in town knew that fact, and that was Isham Porter. Isham Porter, who worked at the wagon yard, and he was Creed and Bob's first cousin. It was Isham Porter who sent Creed and Bob a telegram, telling them that Falcon MacCallister, the man who was responsible for getting their youngest brother, Thad Howard, hung, was in Medora.

Creed and Bob came to town looking for revenge. Bob got impatient, and got killed. But then, Creed thought, Bob always was an impatient son of a bitch.

When Creed went after MacCallister, he would be more careful.

Chapter 14

"More wine, Teddy?" Judge Heckemeyer asked.

"Yes, thank you," Roosevelt said.

Judge Heckemeyer nodded at one of his house staff, and the young man hurried to the far end of the long table to pour wine into Roosevelt's glass.

The table, which could easily seat twenty, had only three around it now, Judge Andrew Heckemeyer, Theodore Roosevelt, and Anna Heckemeyer. Roosevelt was the Heckemeyers' dinner guest.

"It was most gracious of you to invite me over for dinner," Roosevelt said. "I have made friends with the staff at my ranch, but it is still a lonely place. Don't get me wrong, I appreciate the solitude . . . especially now that I have things to deal with."

Anna knew that Roosevelt was referring to the mourning period he was going through, grieving for both his wife and his mother.

"But sometimes that solitude can become . . ." He paused for a moment, considering the word he wanted to use. "Quite overwhelming," he concluded.

Realizing that he had changed the mood of the dinner by his melancholy, Roosevelt raised his glass. "But enough of that kind of gloomy talk," he said, smiling broadly. "I propose a toast to Miss Heckemeyer's graduation from the very fine school she attended."

"Hear! Hear!" Judge Heckemeyer replied, holding his own glass up.

"Thank you," Anna said. Then, scoldingly, to Roosevelt: "And I have told you, it is Anna, not Miss Heckemeyer."

"Of course it is. And Anna is such a beautiful name," Roosevelt said. "So I promise you, from now on, Anna it is."

"Tell us about your school, Anna," Judge Heckemeyer said. "Did you learn anything marvelous?"

"I got a glimpse into the future," Anna said.

"A glimpse into the future? Heavens, don't tell me you went to a fortune-teller."

Anna shook her head. "No, not that kind of future," she said. "I didn't have my personal future told. I mean that, in our class on modern science and its applications, I got to see what life in America will be like in the next century."

"Did you now? So, tell us about twentieth-century America," Judge Heckemeyer said.

"The twentieth century will be a century of marvelous inventions and gadgets," Anna said. "Why, we've already started."

"How so?"

"Consider my recent trip here, from New York. I sent you a telegraph message informing you of the precise day and hour I would arrive and, only eight days after leaving New York, I was here. Consider that only thirty years ago this same trip would have taken me months to complete."

"That's true."

"And back in New York there are already wondrous things that the people out here can only imagine. Well, Teddy, you know what I'm talking about," she said.

"You can reach any spot in the city within a matter of minutes by taking the cars."

"Taking the cars?" Judge Heckemeyer asked.

"That's what the New Yorkers call the commuter trains that whisk them from one end of the city to the other," she said. "Sometimes you ride on elevated railways so that, as a passenger, you feel as if you are flying amidst the rooftops."

"That is true," Roosevelt agreed. "The transportation system of the city is quite well developed."

"There are also several telephones in New York," Anna said.

"Telephone? Yes, I believe I have read about them," Heckemeyer said. "If I understand it right, it is a device that you can speak into, and someone else who is similarly equipped will be able to hear you."

"Not only hear you, but speak back to you," Anna said. "And let us not forget Mr. Edison's talking machine."

Heckemeyer laughed. "A talking machine? Now I have heard everything."

"No, it is true, Andrew," Roosevelt said. "The Edison talking machine uses a cylinder of wax and a stylus that, somehow, transfers the vibrations of the voice onto that wax. Then, when you play it back, the voice, or any sound for that matter, is reproduced."

"What will they think of next?" Heckemeyer asked.

"I've already thought of it," Anna said.

"Oh?"

"Yes, I proposed it to my professor in science class, and he said it was a good idea, though he had no idea how it could be done."

"What is your idea?" Roosevelt asked.

"I proposed that you find some way to connect Mr.

Alexander Graham's telephone with Mr. Thomas Edison's talking machine," Anna said.

"To what end?" Heckemeyer asked.

"Well, think about it, Father," Anna explained. "Suppose someone, we'll make up a person and call her Mary, was equipped with a telephone in her own house. And someone else, let's say Mary's grandmother, is similarly equipped.

"The grandmother calls, but Mary is not home. If a clever scientist could find a way to connect the talking machine to the telephone, the grandmother could leave a message."

Anna made a motion as if holding the telephone base with one hand, and the earpiece with the other, then she imitated the call.

"Hello, this is Mary. Thank you for calling me, but I am not home. However, you may leave a message for me on my talking machine."

Then, changing the tone of her voice, Anna continued the demonstration.

"Mary, this is your grandmother. Please come to dinner at my house tomorrow night."

Anna made the motion of hanging up. "What do you think?" she asked.

"I think you have a very active imagination," Judge Heckemeyer said.

"Active and fertile," Roosevelt added. "In fact, I will make the prediction right now that someday, some clever person will come up with just such a device. And whoever it is will no doubt think that he was the one who invented the answering machine, when a few of us will know that it was you."

"Answering machine," Anna said. "Oh, what a delightful name for it."

After dinner that evening, Roosevelt invited Anna to

take a walk with him and she accepted. They walked from the judge's house down to the railroad station and back. The night was clear and the sky was ablaze with stars.

"I missed seeing the stars when I was in New York," Anna said. "At first, I thought that perhaps there were just fewer stars over New York. Later, of course, I realized that it was just the brightness of the many gas lamps that made the sky seem dimmer."

"Yes, the sky is beautiful out here," Roosevelt said. "Everything seems more beautiful out here." He looked at Anna and smiled. "Everything," he said, with some emphasis.

"Please, Mr. Roosevelt," Anna said demurely. "You shall make me blush."

"I'm sorry," Roosevelt said quickly. "I've no wish to embarrass you."

"I know," Anna said. "I was teasing."

"Oh."

They walked on in silence for a few moments longer. Then Roosevelt spoke again.

"Anna, I cannot tell you how much I have enjoyed being in your company," he said.

"And I have enjoyed your company as well," Anna replied.

"Teddy."

"I beg your pardon?"

"A moment ago you called me Mr. Roosevelt. And yet you insist that I call you Anna. I'm sure you've heard the expression 'What is good for the goose is good for the gander.'"

Anna laughed. "Yes, I have heard that, Teddy," she said.

"I am glad you are my friend," Roosevelt added.

"It is not difficult being your friend. You are an interesting man, a fascinating conversationalist, and a generous soul."

"I appreciate your appraisal of me," Roosevelt said. He cleared his throat. "Especially since you are aware of my personal burden of grief."

"Yes, I know that your wife and your mother both died recently. And on the same day. I know what a tremendous grief you must be enduring."

"I'm glad that you understand it," Roosevelt said. "For I would not want to give you the wrong idea as to my intentions."

Anna chuckled. "Oh, heavens, Teddy. Please do not think me a naive young girl who believes that the friendly attentions of a man friend must inevitably lead to matrimony."

"It's not that I never want to marry again," Roosevelt said. "Indeed, someday I think I will get married again, and if I do, I hope it is to someone just like you. But for now . . ."

Laughing again, a lilting, friendly laugh, Anna put her hand on Roosevelt's arm.

"I'm sure you will find someone just for you," she said. "And as to whether or not she is like me, well, time will just have to tell, won't it? In the meantime, let us be just as you proposed. Good friends who find pleasure in each other's company."

"You are a good woman, Anna," Roosevelt said. "A good woman indeed."

"Now, perhaps you should take me back home before my father comes after us with a shotgun."

"What?" Roosevelt gasped.

Anna laughed. "I was teasing you, Teddy," she said. "Merely teasing."

* * *

It was nearly midnight, and Falcon MacCallister extinguished the lantern on the table in the hotel room he had taken for the night. His room fronted the street and as he happened to glance outside, he saw an orange glow in the darkness of the alley between two buildings across the street.

Falcon watched for a moment, and as he watched, the glow brightened and dimmed. That told Falcon that he was looking at the tip of a cigarette. Someone was standing back in the shadows of the alley, smoking as he stared up at the hotel. Falcon knew what it was, but he didn't know who it was, or why the person was watching the hotel with such intensity.

Creed Howard had spent the evening in the saloon, sitting in the back, quietly nursing his beer while he kept an eye on Falcon MacCallister.

Falcon had supper, then played a few hands of cards. Several men came over to talk to him, anxious to make friends with the man who could take on three assailants.

Creed had nothing but disgust for them. They were making a hero out of the man who had been responsible for the death of one of his brothers, and had killed the other.

Creed spoke to no one for the entire time he was in the saloon. When Falcon left, Creed left as well. He followed Falcon, staying about one block behind, until Falcon turned into the hotel.

As it happened, Creed was staying at the same hotel, but rather than going in then, he decided to wait across the street for a while. He had never met Falcon MacCallister, so there was little chance he would be recognized. On the other hand, he had spent the entire evening in the saloon and Falcon might have noticed him. It would be best for his plans if they didn't run across each other.

Creed walked across the street from the hotel and slipped into the shadows of the alley between the apothecary and the leather-goods store. A few minutes later, he saw a lantern flare up in one of the upstairs rooms. In the light, Creed saw Falcon moving about in the room.

Creed watched until the lantern was extinguished.

"Well, Mr. Falcon MacCallister, let's see how much of a hero you are tomorrow, when they find you dead in your bed," Creed said quietly. He tossed the cigarette to one side.

Loosening the gun in his holster, Creed crossed the dark street. It was quiet in the town now; the saloon was closed, so there was nothing coming from there. Out on the prairie a coyote howled, its howl answered by a dog from town. In a house down the street, a baby was crying. The swinging sign over the apothecary creaked somewhat in a freshening wind.

Creed stepped in through the front door of the hotel. The lobby was dark, except for a lantern that illuminated the stairway and another at the desk. Mr. Fillmore, the hotel clerk on duty at the front desk, was napping in his chair. Quietly, so as not to awaken him, Creed turned the registration book around so he could read the entries. He found the one he was looking for.

Falcon MacCallister . . . . Room 25

Creed reached around behind the desk and took the spare key from the hook under the number 25. As he went up the steps, he extinguished the stairway lamp, then each lantern in turn as he walked down the hallway toward Room 25.

* * *

Falcon lay in his bed listening to the hiss of the gas lanterns from the hallway. He could hear the decrease in sound as each lantern in turn was extinguished. He watched the little line of light under his door dim until it was dark. Then he got out of bed, pulled his pistol from the holster, and stepped into the far corner of his room.

He heard the key turn in the door lock; then the door was pushed open. In the ambient light from the street, Falcon could see a shadow, but nothing more. He had no idea who this would-be assailant might be.

For the next few seconds, the room was brightly lit by the muzzle blasts of Creed Howard's pistol as he fired three shots toward the bed. Feathers and dust flew from the bed as the bullets impacted.

Falcon fired back, shooting just to the left of the flame pattern. He shot only once, heard a groan, then the sound of a man falling. Quickly, Falcon lit the table lantern and turned the flame up, filling the room with light.

He stepped over to the body and turned it over. He didn't know who it was, but he remembered seeing him in the saloon, and had thought it odd then how he had sat so quietly for so long.

The man was still alive, though it was obvious he wouldn't be for long.

"Who are you?" Falcon asked. "And why did you come for me?"

"The name is Howard," Creed said in a voice strained with pain. "You killed both my brothers."

Falcon shook his head. "The law hung Thad Howard, I didn't. That's the only Howard I know of."

"What's going on in here?"

Looking toward the door, Falcon saw the hotel clerk and two of the guests, drawn to his room by the sound of the shots.

"I just come into my room and found this fella here," Creed said. "When I asked what he was doing in my room, he shot me."

"Your room is twenty-three, Mr. Howard," the clerk said. "This is room twenty-five."

Creed snorted. "Ain't that a hell of a note now?" he said. "I get myself kilt just for making a mistake on my room."

"What?" Falcon said. "What the hell are you talking about, Howard? You know that's . . ." Falcon stopped in mid-sentence. Creed Howard was dead, though Falcon was sure he could almost see a smug smile on his face.

By now the deputy sheriff, who had been making his night rounds, arrived on the scene.

"Somebody want to tell me what just happened here?" he asked.

"It looks like Mr. Howard came into this fella's room by mistake," the clerk said. "And this fella shot him."

"Mister, that's a hell of a thing to do just because a man made a mistake," the deputy sheriff said. "Couldn't you have just told him it was the wrong room?"

"He was lying," Falcon said. "He came in here to kill me."

"Now, why would a dying man lie?" the deputy asked. The deputy pulled his pistol. "You know what I think? I think maybe I should take you in until we get this all figured out."

Chapter 15

The courtroom was so full that the sheriff posted deputies at the door to prevent anyone else from coming in. Word had gotten out that Falcon MacCallister was being tried, and because he was so well known, news reporters came from as far away as MacCallister and San Francisco to cover the trial.

One of the reporters even brought a sketch artist with him, and Anna was sitting behind the illustrator, watching with fascination as he developed the drawing. On the artist's sketch pad, Falcon MacCallister sat at the defendant's table with his arms folded across his chest and an almost arrogant expression on his face as he glared at the judge, Anna's father.

The artist was exceptionally skilled in that he had captured Falcon's features so perfectly that someone seeing it would be able to recognize him immediately. But there, the similarity ended, for while the artist depicted Falcon as arrogantly defiant, Falcon was, in fact, the picture of respect. He sat at the table with an attentive expression on his face, and every time he was spoken to, he responded politely.

Teddy Roosevelt was handling Falcon's case, and Anna had teased him about doing unpaid work for one of their local indigents.

* * *

"My dear Anna," Roosevelt had replied. "By no means is Mr. MacCallister is a man without means. In fact, he is far wealthier than anyone you knew in New York's social set. And that includes me."

"MacCallister?" Anna asked.

"Yes, Falcon MacCallister."

"Would he have a brother and sister in the theater?" Anna asked.

"Yes, as a matter of fact, he does," Roosevelt replied.

"Andrew and Rosanna," both Anna and Roosevelt said at the same time.

"I met him in New York. In fact, he very graciously shared his theater box with me and a couple of my friends. And now here he is, with you as his lawyer. What a surprising turn of events."

"Yes, especially when you consider that I'm not really a lawyer," Roosevelt replied. "But when he requested my services . . . even though I told him I am not a practicing lawyer . . . he secured his request by the offer of a rather substantial advance."

"A substantial advance? What did he do, borrow money from his brother and sister in New York?"

"Hardly, since they often borrow money from Falcon."

"How is it that he has so much money?" Anna asked.

"It turns out that his father, Jamie MacCallister, was a man of considerable fame and fortune. He left Falcon several large caches of gold."

That conversation had taken place nearly a week ago. In the intervening week Falcon MacCallister had spent the entire time in jail. Roosevelt tried, without success, to get Judge Heckemeyer to set bail, but Anna's father refused, citing his belief that Falcon MacCallister would flee at the first opportunity in order to avoid the trial.

"What makes you think he would flee?"

"Think about it, Teddy," Judge Heckemeyer replied. "He has no business or family ties to keep him here. He has, by your own account, an almost unlimited supply of money. What would keep him here?"

"Honor," Roosevelt replied.

"You are convinced he is a man of honor?"

"I am."

Judge Heckemeyer stroked his chin for a moment, as if considering Roosevelt's request. Then he shook his head.

"I'm sorry, Teddy. I wish I could believe you. But the man has just killed too often, and I'm not convinced that anyone would find himself in so many situations where he must kill to survive. Your request for bail is denied."

"I think you are wrong about Mr. MacCallister, Judge, and I intend to prove it," Roosevelt said.

The courtroom was full, and both counselors were at their respective tables. The jury, which had already undergone the *voir dire* process, was in place, and the proceedings now awaited only the appearance of the judge.

"All rise!" the baliff called.

Everyone stood as Judge Heckemeyer came in and took his seat at the bench. He shuffled a few papers around, then looked up, cleared his throat, and hit a little wooden pad with his gavel.

"Baliff, are all parties in place?" he asked.

"They are, Your Honor."

"Let the record show that Mr. Ken Woodward is acting as prosecutor. Do you concur, Mr. Woodward?"

A tall, gaunt man with long-flowing white hair and equally white chin whiskers stood up. He was wearing a light brown tweed suit with a dark brown silk vest.

"I do so concur, Your Honor."

"Are you ready to present your case?"

"I am, Your Honor," Woodward replied.

"Very good. Mr. Roosevelt, it is my understanding that you will be acting as counsel for the defendant?"

"I will be, with the court's permission."

"How say you? Are you ready to present your case?"

"I am, Your Honor, but with the following caveat. Although I attended Columbia Law School, I did not take a law degree. I am not now, nor have I ever been, a practicing lawyer."

"So noted," Judge Heckemeyer said. "Mr. MacCallister, you have chosen Mr. Roosevelt as your attorney. Are you aware that he lacks the qualifications to serve you?"

"I am aware, Your Honor, but he is the one I want," Falcon replied.

"You do understand, don't you, that he serves at the pleasure of the court? It is my prerogative to allow or disallow his participation."

"Yes, sir. But it is also my understanding that if I waive all rights to appeal on the basis of incompetent representation, I may have Mr. Roosevelt as my attorney."

"That is correct. Do you now waive those rights?"

"Yes," Falcon said.

"Very well, your right to appeal is waived. Mr. Roosevelt is now your attorney of record. Mr. Woodward, you may proceed."

Woodward nodded, then walked over to face the jury. "Gentlemen of the jury, the time of the Wild West is gone now, gone with the lost Atlantis, gone tone and tint to the isle of ghosts and ancient dead memories. Men and women of culture and refinement are working hard to make gentle this wonderful land, to create a beautiful paradise where our children, and our children's children, can prosper and live in peace."

He turned away from the jury and pointed toward Falcon.

"But . . . into this wonderful time and place of enterprise and civilization comes the person of Falcon MacCallister."

He said the words with a derisive slur.

"Falcon MacCallister," he repeated. "I am sure that most if not all of you have heard of him, for he is a man whose reputation precedes him. Some . . . perhaps the writers of the dime novels . . . might find this reputation appealing. Others, with a misguided sense of hero worship, may even find him bigger than life, the stuff of legend. He is called a gunfighter, a gambler, and a bad man to crowd. He has been called a desperado, a highwayman, and a mercenary assassin.

"He is a deadly shot, a skilled fighter, and a man who, it is said, can track a buzzard's shadow.

"Who knows which of these stories are true, and which are fabricated from whole cloth?

"One thing that we do know . . . one thing that we have witnessed here, in our own town, is that he is a killer. Within the space of the past few days, four men have faced Falcon MacCallister, and four men have died.

"Mr. MacCallister has made the claim, not only for these deaths of which we have personal knowledge, but for his many other killings, that, in every case, the homicides were justifiable. Every man that he has killed, or so claims Mr. MacCallister, was killed in self-defense.

"Now, think about that for a moment. How many of

you have ever encountered someone who was so intent upon killing you that your only hope for survival was to kill them?

"None of you?

"Well, don't worry, you aren't alone. Fortunately for us all, it is an extremely rare situation when one man sets out to kill another.

"And yet, if we are to believe Falcon MacCallister, he has killed at least fifteen men who were trying to kill him. And the number may be far greater than that, we just don't know.

"All right, let's give him the benefit of the doubt. Let us say that for many, perhaps even for all of these previous killings, he is telling the truth. Even if that is true, we are not trying him for any of his previous killings. We are trying him for the aggravated manslaughter of one Creed Howard.

"Creed Howard's dying testimony, heard by no less than four witnesses, was that he had wandered into Falcon MacCallister's room by mistake. Mr. Howard's room number at the hotel was twenty-three, right next door to room twenty-five. It is easy to see how such a mistake could be made, especially in the dark of night."

He pointed to the jury. "Any one of you may have made the same mistake. Indeed, perhaps you have made such a mistake in the past . . . or perhaps you have occupied a room when someone entered it by mistake."

He turned back to glare at Falcon. "For the average man, a man of civilized society, a man of decency, such a mistake would be met by embarrassment, confusion, and I will grant you, perhaps even a degree of irritation.

"But Falcon MacCallister has killed so many times that he has become inured to the concept of killing." Woodward paused for a moment, then boomed out the next sentence. "With no more thought than the average man would have in stepping on a cockroach, Falcon MacCallister shot to death the stranger who made an innocent mistake."

With his words still ringing in the crowded courtroom, Woodward resumed his seat.

The artist in front of Anna had just completed his drawing of Woodward, casting the prosecutor in an almost heroic image.

Roosevelt got up to address the jury.

"Gentlemen of the jury, I agree with Mr. Woodward that the average man would not shoot to death a stranger who made the innocent mistake of entering the wrong room. Neither would Falcon MacCallister. We intend to prove that Creed Howard was neither innocent, nor did he make a mistake. He entered Falcon MacCallister's room knowing full well that it was MacCallister's room, and he did so with the intention of murdering Mr. MacCallister."

Roosevelt sat down then, catching the judge, the jury, and the gallery by surprise, for they had thought that his opening statement would at least equal in length, and more than likely even surpass, Woodward's remarks.

The sketch artist was the one who was most surprised, however, for he had barely begun his drawing.

Woodward began calling his witnesses. The first witness was Jason Fillmore.

"Mr. Fillmore, for the record, would you please state your full name and your occupation?"

"My name is Jason LeRoy Fillmore, and I am the night clerk of the Morning Star Hotel."

"And how long have you held that position?"

"For six years," Fillmore replied.

"Very good. Now, if you would, please give us your account of the events of the night of the twelfth," Woodward said.

Fillmore was a small man with a red face, hooked nose, and thin hair.

"Well, sir, I was at my front desk when I heard the gunshots," he said.

"How many shots did you hear?"

"I don't rightly know," Fillmore said.

"More than one?"

"Yes, sir. Three, maybe four of 'em. Like this. Bang, bang. Then, right on top of the first two shots, I heard two more. Bang, bang."

"What did you do then?"

"First thing I done is, I got down behind my desk."

The gallery laughed and, with a scowl, Judge Heckemeyer brought his gavel down once sharply.

"Then what did you do?"

"Well, when I didn't hear no more shootin', I run upstairs to see if I could find out what was goin' on."

"And what did you see?"

"I seen the door open to room twenty-five, and I seen a light shinin' out into the hall. So I went down there to look in and that's when I seen the one fella kneelin' over the other'n."

"Who, specifically, did you see kneeling?"

"Him," Fillmore said, pointing to the defendant's table. "Falcon MacCallister."

"Let the record show that the witness identified Falcon MacCallister as the man kneeling. Is that when you saw the gun in MacCallister's hand?"

"Objection, Your Honor, leading the witness," Roosevelt said.

"Sustained. Reword your question, Counselor."

"Did you see anything in the defendant's hand?"

"Yes, sir."

"What did you see?"

"I seen a gun."

Woodward walked over to the exhibit table and held up a Colt .44.

"Is this the gun you saw?"

"Yes, sir, that's it."

"Let the record reflect that the witness has identified Prosecution Exhibit One as the pistol he saw in Falcon MacCallister's hand."

Woodward turned back to the witness. "Did you recognize the man on the floor?"

"Yes, sir. It was Creed Howard."

"Was Creed Howard personally known to you?"

"I didn't know him personal-like, or nothing like that. But he was a guest of the hotel."

"What was Mr. Howard's room?"

"Room twenty-three."

"Where was his room in relation to the room where you found him?"

"His room was right next door."

"Was he still alive when you found him?"

"Yes, sir, he was."

"Did Mr. Howard say anything?"

"Yes." Fillmore looked accusingly toward Falcon MacCallister. "He said he thought he had gone into his own room and discovered MacCallister there."

"Did you correct him? What, exactly, did you say?"

"I said, 'Your room is twenty-three, Mr. Howard. This is room twenty-five.' "

"And what did Mr. Howard reply?"

"He said, 'Ain't that a hell of a note now?' he said. 'I get myself kilt just for making a mistake on my room.' "

"Thank you, no further questions."

Roosevelt stood up then, but he didn't approach the witness. Instead, he stood behind the defendant's table.

"Mr. Fillmore, have you rented room twenty-five since the incident?"

"Yes," Fillmore said. "Nobody told me I couldn't do it."

"Did you have to do anything to the room?"

"Do anything to it?"

"Yes. Clean up the blood or anything?"

"Oh, yes. I did that."

"Did you do anything else?"

"Oh, I just sewed up a couple of holes in the mattress, is all."

"What kind of holes?"

"Bullet holes. The sheriff took two bullets out of the mattress. They were .44-caliber bullets." He looked over at MacCallister. "Same caliber as the gun MacCallister was carryin'."

"Your Honor, please instruct Mr. Fillmore not to answer questions that I haven't asked. And I request that his remark be struck from the record," Roosevelt said.

"Court recorder will strike the last comment. Jury, you will disregard. Mr. Fillmore, answer only the questions that are asked," Judge Heckemeyer said.

"All right, Judge. Sorry," Fillmore replied.

"Thank you, Your Honor. No further questions at this time, but I reserve the right to recall this witness."

"Witness may step down."

Woodward's next witness was Deputy Sheriff Jerry Kelly. Jerry Kelly was the deputy on duty on the night in question, and he was making the rounds when he heard gunshots coming from the hotel.

He further stated that when he reached the scene, he saw Fillmore and two of the hotel residents standing in the hall, looking into a lighted room. In response to the question, he identified the room as room 25. He also stated that he relieved MacCallister of his weapon and placed him under arrest.

"Were you present when the undertaker dug the bullet from Mr. Howard's body?" Woodward asked.

"I was."

"What caliber was the bullet?"

"It was a .44 caliber."

Woodward picked up the gun from the table. "Is this the gun you took from the defendant?"

"It is."

"What caliber is this gun?"

"It is a .44 caliber."

"Thank you. No further questions."

Roosevelt stood up. "Deputy Kelly, did you find another gun in the room?"

"I did."

"Where did you find it?"

"It was on the floor by Howard."

"In other words, it was Howard's gun?"

"Objection, Your Honor. Calls for conclusion," Woodward said.

"Objection sustained."

"Deputy Kelly, what was the caliber of the second pistol that you found?"

"It was a .44."

"I see. And was Mr. Howard wearing a gun belt and holster?" Roosevelt asked.

"He was."

"Was there a pistol in his holster?"

"No."

"Were there any cartridges in the bullet loops on the belt?"

"Yes."

"I see. And what caliber were these bullets?" Roosevelt asked.

"They were .44-caliber bullets."

"All right, now, just so that we have this straight, his holster was empty, but you found a .44-caliber pistol on the floor next to him. And the cartridges in the bullet loops were .44-caliber?"

"Yes."

"You stated that you relieved Mr. Roosevelt of his pistol. How did you do that?"

"I beg your pardon?"

"How did you get the gun away from Falcon Mac-Callister?"

"I, uh, asked him for it."

"Suppose he had resisted."

"I beg your pardon?"

"Given the ferocious reputation that prosecution has painted for him, if he had resisted, do you think you could have disarmed him?"

Kelly squirmed in his seat and stroked his chin for a moment. Then, with a resigned sigh, he said. "No, sir, I don't think I could have."

"Thank you. No further questions."

Woodward called two other witnesses, both of whom were guests of the hotel. Their story was substantially the same . . . they heard gunshots, ran to the room, and heard Howard's dying testimony that he had wandered into the wrong room by mistake.

After questioning his last witness, Woodward turned to the jury.

"Gentlemen of the jury, as you have heard with your own ears, all four witnesses were present in time to hear Mr. Howard's last words. And those last words were a statement of surprise that he had been shot merely because he wandered into the wrong room by mistake."

"Your Honor, is prosecution giving his summation now, before I've even had the opportunity to present my case?" Roosevelt asked.

"That is a very good question, Mr. Roosevelt. Counselor, are you giving your summation?"

"No, Your Honor, I am not," Woodward replied.

"Then please call your next witness."

"I have no further witnesses, Your Honor. Prosecution rests."

"Very well, then court stands adjourned until tomorrow morning, at which time we will hear from the attorney for the defense," Judge Heckemeyer said. He brought his gavel down sharply.

As Roosevelt started putting papers away in his briefcase, Anna walked over to the defense table. She smiled at the would-be attorney.

"Teddy, you are doing wonderfully," she said.

"I thank you for your vote of confidence, but it's a little too early to make a valid judgment on my performance," Roosevelt replied. "All I have done today is parry the thrusts of the prosecution. Tomorrow will tell the tale."

"I'm sure you will do very well," Anna said.

The sheriff and his deputy came for Falcon then.

"Oh, gentlemen, before you take him away, please allow me to introduce him to my friend," Roosevelt said. "Mr. MacCallister, this is Anna Heckemeyer."

"We have met," Falcon said.

"Indeed we have. Allow me to thank you again, Mr. MacCallister, for your graciousness in sharing your theater box."

"It was my pleasure," Falcon said. He chuckled. "Under the circumstances, I wish it had been your father, rather than you. I'm afraid he doesn't like me very much."

Anna chuckled. "I think you have pegged him correctly, sir," she said. "On the other hand, I know my father to be an honest man. I can promise you that you will get fair treatment in his court."

"Come along, MacCallister," the sheriff said gruffly.

"Good luck to you, Mr. MacCallister," Anna called as he was led away.

"Thanks," Falcon called back over his shoulder. "I have a feeling I am going to need it."

Chapter 16

When word reached Aaron Childers that Falcon Mac-Callister was in jail and being tried for murder, he talked the others into going to Medora to see for themselves.

"You want to tell me why we're comin' into Medora when the fella who's been chasin' us all this time is in this town?" Yerby asked. "Seems to me like the smart thing to do would be to stay away from him."

"Don't know why you're so worried, Dalton," Childers said. "Ole MacCallister sure as hell ain't in no condition to do us any harm now. I mean, bein' as he is in jail and is being tried for his life."

"Yeah," Percy Shaw added. He chuckled. "Besides which, when it comes time for 'em to string ole Mac-Callister up by his neck, I want to be there watchin' and laughin'."

The three men looked around warily as they rode into Medora. None of them had ever committed a crime in this town, but all three of them were wanted and it could be that someone might recognize them.

They rode right up Third Avenue until they reached the saloon. The saloon was one of the larger buildings in town, false-fronted like most of the others and with its name, Golden Spur, painted in black letters outlined in gold. Between the word "Golden" and the word "Spur" was a pair of golden spurs.

Tying their horses at the hitching rail, they went inside, then stepped over to the bar. The saloon was fairly busy, with nearly all of the tables filled. In addition, there were several men standing at the bar. The bartender, who was laughing at something someone just said, tossed a towel over his shoulder, then moved down the bar to greet Childers and the others.

"Welcome, gents," he said. "What can I get for you?"

"Beer," Childers ordered. The others said the same.

"We just got some new barrels of beer from St. Louis. It's a really good beer."

"Is it your cheapest?" Childers asked.

The bartender chuckled and shook his head. "No, sir, it isn't the cheapest. But wait until you taste it."

"I ain't a-goin' to taste it if it ain't the cheapest," Childers said. "Give us the cheapest beer you got."

"Yes, sir, whatever you say," the bartender replied.

The bartender drew three beers and set them in front of the three men, then picked up the three nickels.

"Hey, is it true what they're sayin' about Falcon Mac-Callister?" Childers asked as he blew the foam off and took a drink. "Is he really bein' tried for murder?"

The bartender shook his head. "No," he said. "Not murder. He's being tried for manslaughter."

"Manslaughter? What's that?"

"The illegal killing of a human being."

"Well, hell, ain't that and murder the same thing?"

"No. It isn't the same thing at all."

"What's the difference?" Childers asked.

"For one thing, even if he's found guilty, he won't hang. The most that can happen to him is he'll wind up in territorial prison."

"Yeah, but he ain't a-goin' to be found guilty," one of the other men at the bar said.

"Who are you?" Childers asked.

"The name is Josh Andrews," the cowboy said. Smiling, he extended his hand. "What's your name?"

Instead of taking the cowboy's hand, Childers raised his glass to his lips. He didn't answer the inquiry about his name, but asked another of his own.

"Why do you say MacCallister won't be convicted?"

"Because Mr. Roosevelt's defending him."

"Hey, Aaron," Percy started. "That's . . ." Before Percy could complete his sentence, Aaron shushed him.

"You know this here Roosevelt fella, do you?"

"Know him?" Josh smiled broadly. "Why, I'm proud to say that I work for him. I ride for the Elkhorn Ranch."

"So he's your boss?"

"He is. And there's no finer boss in the land," Aaron said.

"Is he good at lawyerin'?"

"Ha," Josh replied. "Funny thing is, he ain't even a real lawyer, but he's better at it than just about any lawyer I ever seen. But the plain fact is that Mr. Roosevelt is good at just about anything he does."

"I'll say," one of the other patrons said. "He's sort of a dandified-lookin' fella, but that don't mean he can't fight."

That started a general discussion of the incident between Roosevelt and the onetime riders for Two Rivers Ranch, Zeb and Muley.

"Course, ole Zeb and Muley's both dead now," one of the others said.

"Dead? What happened to 'em?"

"MacCallister killed them."

"MacCallister?"

"Yeah. Funny, ain't it?"

"What's funny about it?"

"Well, here MacCallister's bein' tried for killin' a man that there didn't nobody in town even know. But he ain't bein' tried for killin' Zeb and Muley, and ever'one in town know'd them."

"Yeah," someone else said with a little laugh. "And it's because ever'one did know them two that MacCallister ain't bein' tried for killin' them. Hell, when you get right down to it, there ain't nobody who didn't think but that them two men needed killin'."

The others laughed.

"Look here, are you sayin' you think MacCallister is goin' to get off?" Aaron asked.

"With Mr. Roosevelt defendin', you damn right he's going to get off," Josh said.

"Yeah, but you know, don't you, that bein' good at lawyerin' ain't the only reason Roosevelt is goin' to get MacCallister off?" one of the other saloon patrons said.

"What do you mean?" Josh asked.

"Hell, ever'body knows that Roosevelt's been squirin' Miss Anna Heckemeyer around. Not only that, I hear tell he's done got her won over to his side. And if she wants her pa to find MacCallister not guilty, like as not that's the way it'll come out."

"Are you sayin' the trial don't mean nothing, that even if the jury finds MacCallister guilty, the judge would let him go?" Aaron asked.

"If Miss Anna asks him to, he will."

"I don't believe that," one of the others said. "I've known Judge Heckemeyer for a long time, and I've never known a more honest man."

"I believe it," another put in. "I agree with you that the judge is an honest man, but there don't nobody set more store with the judge than his daughter. He'd do anything in the world for that girl."

"Well, that's 'cause her mama died when she was just a young'n, and the judge had to raise her up all by his-self," the bartender said.

"That may be so, but don't none of that matter none," Josh said. "I know Mr. Roosevelt, and I know he's not the kind of man that would use the judge's daughter like that."

"I would," one of the other patrons said.

"What do you mean, you would?"

"Well, think about it. All you got to do to win the bull is bait the calf. Like you said, the judge would do anything his daughter asked him to do. If I was Roosevelt, I'd play that card like it was the ace of spades."

"Hey, court's about to start again," someone said, sticking his head across the batwing doors.

"What good does it do to tell us about it?" Josh replied. "Court's so crowded that nobody else can get in."

"Yeah, but they's some folks standin' just outside the open windows, listenin' it. They're lettin' ever'one else know what's goin' on."

"Hey, Aaron, we goin' to go over there and try to get in?" Percy asked.

Childers shook his head and slapped a nickel down on the bar, signaling for a second beer.

"If we hang around here, I reckon we'll be able to find out what's goin' on," he said.

Chapter 17

"Mr. Roosevelt, you may call your first witness," Judge Heckemeyer said when court resumed.

"Defense calls Sheriff Walter Merrill of Belfield," Roosevelt said.

"I object, Your Honor," Woodward said. "What possible connection does the sheriff of Belfield have to this case?"

"Your Honor, it goes to motive," Roosevelt answered. "Sheriff Merrill can dispute prosecution's claim that this whole incident was the result of an innocent mistake."

"Objection overruled. The witness may testify."

Sheriff Merrill was sworn; then he took the witness chair.

"Sheriff, did you know Creed Howard?"

"I didn't know him personally, but I knew who he was," Sheriff Merrill replied.

"How so?"

"A few weeks ago we hung Thad Howard. Creed Howard was Thad Howard's brother."

"And you know this because?"

"Because Creed and Bob Howard come to visit their brother, Thad, a few times before he was hung."

"Who is Bob Howard?"

"Better ask, who was Bob Howard," Sheriff Merrill replied. "He was Creed Howard's brother."

"Did he ever go by another name?"

"Yes. He sometimes went by the name of Bob Rafferty on account of he had a different mother from Thad and Creed. But he was a Howard too."

"Do you know what happened to Bob Howard?"

"Yes. He was killed a few weeks ago."

"Who killed him?"

"Falcon MacCallister."

The courtroom buzzed, and for a moment Anna wondered if perhaps Roosevelt wasn't making a mistake by calling that to everyone's attention.

"Was Falcon MacCallister responsible in any way for Thad Howard's death?"

"Yes, sir, you might say that in a way, he was," Sheriff Merrill replied. "You see, it was him what brung Thad Howard in."

"So, on the night Creed Howard went into Mr. Mac-Callister's room, both of his brothers were already dead, and Creed Howard blamed their deaths on Falcon Mac-Callister?"

"Objection, Your Honor. Calls for speculation. The witness would have to be a mind reader to answer that question."

"Sustained."

"Let me reword that," Roosevelt said. "Do you know who killed the man identified as Bob Rafferty, but whom we now know was Bob Howard?"

"The coroner's report says that he was killed by Falcon MacCallister," Sheriff Merrill answered.

"And though the hangman was ultimately responsible for the execution of Thad Howard, who brought him to justice?"

"Falcon MacCallister."

"All right, I'm not going to ask you who you think

Creed Howard believed was responsible for the deaths of his two brothers. But I am going to ask you—"

"Objection, Your Honor, we've already been through this. The question calls for speculation," Woodward protested.

"Your Honor, I'm asking the sheriff who he believes is responsible. It is a question he can answer because it goes to his own thought process."

Heckemeyer paused for a moment, considering both remarks, then he responded.

"Objection overruled. You may question the sheriff about his personal belief, but you cannot ask him to speculate on whether or not Creed Howard blamed MacCallister."

"Very well, Your Honor," Roosevelt replied. Then, to the witness, he said, "Sheriff, do you believe that Falcon MacCallister was responsible for the death of the two Howard brothers?"

"He was responsible for all three of them," Sheriff Merrill blurted out, and the gallery laughed.

"Thank you, no further questions."

Roosevelt's next witnesses were experts on Falcon's accuracy with a firearm. There were three witnesses, all of whom had participated in shooting matches with Falcon. All were expert marksmen, but all conceded that Falcon was better than they were, better, in fact, than anyone they had ever seen use a gun.

"Tell me this," Roosevelt asked the first witness. "In a twelve-by-twelve-foot hotel room, is it likely that Mr. MacCallister could discharge his weapon four times in the direction of a man, and yet manage only one hit?"

"Objection, Your Honor, calls for speculation," Woodward said.

"Your Honor, this witness and the succeeding witnesses are all experts in the field of marksmanship.

Indeed, when I began reading their qualifications, prosecution stipulated to same. As expert witnesses, they are entitled to speculate. That's what expert witnesses do."

"Objection overruled," Heckemeyer said. "Witness may answer the question."

"It is not likely that in a room of the size you describe, Falcon MacCallister could fire four shots at a man and miss three times. In fact, it is not likely that he would miss one time."

"Let us say that Mr. MacCallister and Creed Howard were both in a twelve-by-twelve room," Roosevelt said. "Let us say, also, that there are two pistols in the room, both of which are .44-caliber pistols. An examination of the cylinder in the pistol belonging to Falcon MacCallister shows only one empty cartridge. An examination of Mr. Howard's pistol shows three empty cartridges. There are two bullet holes in the mattress. Who do you think is responsible for the bullet holes in the mattress?"

"Objection, speculation beyond the scope of this witness's expertise," Woodward called.

"Hell, Counselor, you don't have to be an expert to figure that out," the witness replied. "Any six-year-old with half a brain could answer that question."

The gallery erupted into loud laughter, and Judge Heckemeyer had to bang his gavel to restore order.

"Any more outbreaks like that and I will clear this court," Heckemeyer said sternly when he had finally restored order. Then he glared at the witness. "The witness is ordered to speak only when responding to a direct question. Another spontaneous response such as you just gave will result in a citing for contempt of court. Do you understand what I'm saying to you?"

"Yes, Your Honor," the witness replied contritely. "It won't happen again."

"It had better not. Now, as regard to the objection, the objection is overruled. You may answer the question."

"Your Honor, after all this, I've forgotten the question," the witness said.

The gallery laughed, but it was a carefully controlled laugh.

"You may ask the question again," Heckemeyer said to Roosevelt.

Roosevelt chuckled. "I'm sorry, Your Honor, I've forgotten the question as well."

Again the gallery laughed, somewhat louder this time, though they did manage to keep it under control.

"Clerk will read the question," Heckemeyer said.

A thin, middle-aged man, with a prominent Adam's apple and thick glasses read from his notes.

"Let us say that Mr. MacCallister and Creed Howard were both in a twelve-by-twelve room. Let us say, also, that there are two pistols in the room, both of which are .44-caliber pistols. An examination of the cylinder in the pistol belonging to Falcon MacCallister shows only one empty cartridge. An examination of Mr. Howard's pistol shows three empty cartridges. There are two bullet holes in the mattress. Who do you think is responsible for the bullet holes in the mattress?"

"Thank you," Roosevelt said to the clerk. Then to his witness: "You may answer the question."

"I would say that Creed Howard was responsible for the bullet holes in the mattress."

"Thank you," Roosevelt said. "No further questions."

Woodward walked over from the prosecutor's table, then took off his glasses and polished them for a moment while he formed his question.

"You have testified that Falcon MacCallister is an excellent shot," he began.

"Best I ever seen," the witness replied.

"As an expert witness, would you say that some men can shoot very well at a still target, and yet those same men, as good as they might be, would have a more difficult time shooting at a man?"

"Oh, yes, sir. It happens all the time," the witness replied.

"So, such a man might hit a target four times out of four, but in a life-and-death situation, firing against an armed adversary, his accuracy might be impaired."

"His accuracy might be what?"

"He is less likely to hit an armed man four times out of four than he would be to hit a stationary target."

The witness nodded. "Yes, sir, that's true."

"Thank you, no further questions."

"But if you're a-thinkin' that MacCallister missed three shots out of four, you're dead wrong. He ain't—"

"Thank you," Woodward said again, more sharply this time. "I have no further questions."

The witness, mindful of Judge Heckemeyer's admonition to say nothing except in response to a direct question, stopped in mid-sentence.

The succeeding witnesses substantiated the testimony of the first, insisting that Falcon would not shoot four times but manage only one hit.

"Your Honor, defense recalls Mr. Elton Bowman," Roosevelt said.

Elton Bowman had been one of the guests in the hotel who had come to the room in response to hearing the shots.

"Mr. Roosevelt, from all I've heard about you, you're a good man. But I'm a-tellin' you right now, I ain't a'goin' to change my testimony none," Bowman insisted when he took his chair. "I seen what I seen, and that's it."

"Thank you, Mr. Bowman," Roosevelt said. "In fact, I don't want you to change your testimony. But I'm less interested in what you saw than I am in what you heard."

"I beg your pardon?"

"The gunshots. I want you to tell the court about the gunshots you heard."

"I heard four of 'em."

Roosevelt returned to the table and picked up a piece of paper.

"Yes," he said. "I wrote down your testimony. And, of course, so did the court clerk. But I want to read this back to you, and I would like for you to verify if it is correct."

"All right," Bowman agreed.

"I am particularly interested in the rhythm of the gunshots," Roosevelt said.

"The what?"

"The rhythm."

Bowman shook his head. "I don't know what you mean by that."

"By rhythm, I mean the pattern of the shooting, the way the sound happened. You said you heard the gunshots like this, I believe. 'Bang, bang, bang,' a short pause, then 'bang.' Is that correct?"

"Bang, bang, bang . . . bang. Yes, sir, that's exactly the way I heard it."

"Thank you. No further questions."

Two other witnesses testified that the sound pattern was exactly as Bowman had said. Bang, bang, bang . . . bang. Only Fillmore, the hotel clerk, stuck to his original story that it was bang, bang . . . bang, bang.

"Very well, Mr. Fillmore, I know that these things can

be confusing," Roosevelt said. "So, let's get on to something else, shall we?"

"All right."

"How did Creed Howard get into Falcon MacCallister's room?"

"He used the key."

"Does the key to room twenty-three also fit room twenty-five?"

"No, of course not," Fillmore answered. "If that was the case, there wouldn't be no need to lock the doors."

"So somehow . . . perhaps by mistake, Creed Howard had the key to MacCallister's room. Is that your understanding?"

"Yes."

"In fact, there was a key found in the door, was there not?"

"Yes."

"How do you suppose that key got there?"

"I don't know, unless Mr. MacCallister left it in the door when he first arrived. That happens from time to time."

"When a guest signs in, how many keys do you give him?"

"Why, I give him one key, of course."

"Do you have more than one key to a room?"

"Yes."

"If you give one key to the guest, what happens to the second key?"

"There are a bunch of hooks just behind the desk. Each hook has a number that corresponds to the room number, and the extra key is hangin' on them hooks."

Roosevelt returned to the defense table and picked up a sheet of paper. "This is the inventory of things that Falcon MacCallister had on his person when he was arrested." Roosevelt mumbled through a few items, then he read, "One room key, fitting the lock of the door to room two-five."

"Yes, the one in the door. He must've left it there," Fillmore said.

Roosevelt shook his head. "No, Mr. Fillmore. This inventory covers only those things that MacCallister had on his person. It was not until the next day that Sheriff Dennis returned the key to you. The key in the door was a second key, was it not?"

"It . . . yes . . . I suppose it was," Fillmore said.

"So much for the keys. Let's move on to something else. All the witnesses testified that the lamps in the hall were dark. Why didn't you light the lanterns that night?"

"What are you talking about? I did light them!" Fillmore declared resolutely. "I light them every night. Why, that's just as regular as windin' the clock."

"I can understand one lantern burning out. But all of them? Is that very likely?"

"Well, no, it isn't," Fillmore admitted. "But I did light them," he insisted.

"Oh, I believe you, Mr. Fillmore."

"I should hope that you believe me."

"So, if you lit them, what happened? Why were they all out?"

"I . . . I don't know."

"Is it possible that someone extinguished them?"

"Objection! Calls for speculation."

"No . . . I think I will let this one go," Judge Heckemeyer said. "Mr. Fillmore is the night clerk at the hotel. Who would be better qualified to hazard a guess as to whether or not the lanterns had been extinguished? You may answer, Mr. Fillmore."

"Yes," Fillmore said. "It is not only possible that

someone extinguished them, now that I think on it, that probably is what happened."

"Why would someone extinguish them, do you suppose?"

Fillmore shook his head. "I don't have the least idea why anyone would do that."

"Suppose all the lanterns were extinguished. Would it be possible for someone, like Creed Howard for example, to sneak into Mr. MacCallister's room, shoot him, then use the cover of the dark hallway to slip into another room without being seen?"

"Yes!" Fillmore said, seeing where Roosevelt was going with his question. "It was Creed Howard put out them lights."

"Objection! That's a conclusion not in evidence."

"Sustained. Mr. Roosevelt, you have been cautioned about this before. Jury will disregard."

"That's not enough," Woodward said. "How is the jury going to disregard what they just heard? That's like trying to unring a bell."

"That's enough, Mr. Woodward," Judge Heckemeyer said. "I have sustained your objection. Any further discourse on your part and you will be flirting with a contempt-of-court citation."

"I'm sorry, Your Honor," Woodward said contritely.

"Continue, Mr. Roosevelt," Heckemeyer said.

"Thank you, Your Honor," Roosevelt said. Then to his witness: "Mr. Fillmore, if someone wanted to see who was in the hotel, indeed, determine even the room, could they do it?"

"Yes."

"How?"

"By looking at the registration book."

"Can they see it from the customer side of the desk?"

"No, not unless . . ." Fillmore started to answer, then

he stopped in mid-sentence. "It *was* turned around," he continued. "Damn! It *was* turned around. I didn't think anything of it, but the book was turned around, toward the customer side."

"Thank you. No further questions, Your Honor."

Woodward tried hard to undo the damage Fillmore had done to his case, but Fillmore stuck by his guns. He was convinced that someone had extinguished the lanterns in the hallway, and that someone had turned the registration book around. He also insisted that there was a key in the door lock, in addition to the key the sheriff took from MacCallister.

When a frustrated Woodward took his seat, Roosevelt rested his case.

Roosevelt's summation was short and sweet. He made each point with geometric precision and clear logic.

"Gentlemen of the jury, Creed Howard came into Falcon MacCallister's room, not by mistake, but with the clear intention of murdering him in revenge for the death of his two brothers, Thad and Bob. He believed, and rightly so, that MacCallister was responsible for both of them, and it made no difference to him whether or not those deaths were justifiable.

"In order to carry out his scheme, he first had to learn which room MacCallister had taken. A perusal of the registration book . . . which Mr. Fillmore found turned around toward the customer side of the desk . . . would reveal that to him. The fact that MacCallister was in the adjoining room was a convenient coincidence.

"Next, he had to have the key. This he got by reaching across the counter and taking the key from its hook, unobserved by Mr. Fillmore.

"Then, as he climbed the stairs and walked down the hall, he extinguished all the lanterns. This would have afforded him the opportunity to slip back into his room without being seen. His plan was to shoot Falcon MacCallister, use the cover of darkness to go back into his room, from which he would have emerged a moment later to join the others as if drawn to the scene by the gunfire.

"And finally, gentlemen of the jury, I ask you to consider the rhythmic pattern of the shots fired. Three out of four witnesses report the same rhythm. Bang, bang, bang, a pause, then bang.

"I submit that Howard fired three times in quick succession, bang, bang, bang, at the bed where he thought MacCallister was sleeping. One of his shots missed entirely, but two of them hit the bed where, but moments before, Falcon MacCallister had been lying.

"Unfortunately for Creed Howard, MacCallister wasn't in his bed. When Howard began firing, MacCallister had no recourse but to return fire . . . which he did by shooting one time, and one time only. We have already heard expert testimony as to the accuracy of Falcon MacCallister's shooting. One shot was all he needed."

Woodward's summation was almost an exact duplicate of his opening remarks. He had thought that Roosevelt, not being a lawyer, would be an easy adversary. He was wrong, he had been outclassed, and the beads of sweat on his upper lip as well as his body language showed that he knew it.

With both cases rested, Judge Heckemeyer charged the jury with their responsibility.

"Gentlemen of the jury, you have now heard both sides in the case of the Dakota Territory versus Falcon MacCallister on the charge of manslaughter. And while you are not being asked to decide life or death, your decision is a weighty one because it could deprive a man of his freedom for as long as twenty years.

"Consider the arguments carefully, discuss the case among yourselves, and come to a conclusion based upon the fact that to find for the prosecution, you must be convinced, beyond a reasonable doubt, as to the guilt of the defendant."

At the conclusion of the charge from the judge, the bailiff led the jury out of the courtroom; then court was adjourned.

Chapter 18

Roosevelt and Anna were having lunch at Bessie's Café. During their lunch several came over to speak to Roosevelt, congratulating him on his job as a defense attorney.

"I tell you what, if I ever get in trouble, I'd be proud to have you represent me," one man said.

"Thank you, but you are a bit premature in your congratulations. The jury's decision isn't in yet."

"You'll win," the man said. "I ain't got me the slightest doubt but that you'll win."

Roosevelt had stopped eating during the conversation, and he waited until the man left before he continued.

He was interrupted two more times in the next few minutes.

"I think it's just awful how people won't let you alone," Anna said. "Why, they won't even let you eat your lunch in peace."

Roosevelt smiled. "I've chosen the life of a politician, Anna," he said. "This is the price one pays for that choice. In fact, if people weren't interested in talking to me, I'd be totally ineffective."

Anna shook her head. "I have no idea why anyone would choose such a life for themselves," she said.

"Some might think it's because of a streak of vanity,"

Roosevelt said. "And if I was to be honest with you, I'd have to say that there is some . . . no, there is a lot of truth to that."

"I don't consider you a vain man, Teddy. Why, I think you are very unassuming."

Roosevelt held up his index finger. "Ahh, that just means I am a skilled politician, able to cover up my streak of vanity," he teased. "But seriously, there is more to it than that. I love this country, and I feel an obligation to serve the public in whatever capacity I can."

"In whatever capacity?"

"Yes."

"What about President? Would you like to be President of the United States?"

"What politician would not want to be President?"

Anna shook her head. "I don't know, Teddy," she said. "That would be an awesome responsibility. I don't know how anyone could rise to that task."

"I know. It is not a decision I would make lightly," Roosevelt replied.

"On a more immediate subject, what do you think is going to happen in the trial?"

"I think he will be acquitted," Roosevelt said. "But I hasten to add that it isn't because of anything I did. The wonder is that he was charged in the first place. It was clearly a case of self-defense."

"I agree with you," Anna said. She sighed. "But Mr. Woodward did make a telling point, I think, when he pointed out that while the normal person is never called upon to kill another in self-defense, it has happened many times with Mr. MacCallister. Why do you suppose it has happened to Falcon MacCallister so many times?"

"Falcon MacCallister is a man who lives life on the edge," Roosevelt said. "And because of that, he is often challenged."

"I'm sure that is so. But that is also why my father does not like him. Father believes that a man chooses his path and could change his life so that there are no more challenges."

"I know," Roosevelt said. "And he does have a point."

"Is that her?" Percy Shaw asked.

Shaw, Childers, and Yerby were also at Bessie's Café, sitting at a table in the back corner of the dining room.

"That's her," Childers said. "That's Heckemeyer's daughter."

"She sure is a pretty thing," Shaw said. "If you ask me, this could turn out to be fun."

"No!" Childers said. "We'll snatch her, but we ain't goin' to do nothin' to her 'cept use her to force Judge Heckemeyer to order Frank released."

"Well, now, wait a minute here," Yerby said. "You'll get Frank back, but what do me'n Shaw get out of the deal?"

"Frank is your cousin," Childers said. "That makes him blood."

"Yeah, well, he ain't no kin to me," Shaw interjected.

"But he's your pard. Ain't that enough?" Aaron asked.

"I reckon it might be, but he's your brother, so it's more important to you than it is to either Dalton or me to get him back. But the thing is, me'n Dalton's takin' the same risk as you, and we ain't getting' nothin' in particular for it."

"Frank ain't the only reason we'll be snatchin' her up," Childers said.

"What other reason is there?"

"Well, look over there for yourself," Childers said. "Do you see the way she'n Roosevelt is sparkin' it up?

The way I figure it is, we'll grab her, then we'll send a message to Roosevelt and the judge tellin' 'em that we'll let her go when Frank is out of prison and Roosevelt pays ransom."

"What's ransom?" Shaw asked.

"It means that if Roosevelt wants her back, he's going to have to pay money for her."

"Yeah," Yerby said. "Yeah, well, if you put it that way, it sounds like a good idea."

"I hope it turns out better than your other two ideas," Shaw said. "The bank robbery didn't work out none too good, and neither did robbin' Roosevelt on his way into town."

"This one will work," Childers promised. "And as long as we've got the girl, there ain't nobody goin' to be comin' after us, on account of they won't want to see the girl hurt."

"I hope you're right."

"So, you can see why there can't nothin' happen to the girl," Childers said. Then he smiled. "Until afterward."

"Afterward?" Shaw asked, perking up a bit at the suggestion.

"After they let Frank go and pay us the money."

"What then?"

"After I'm finished with her, you two boys can have a little fun with her," Childers said.

"What do you mean after you are finished with her? Why should you be first?" Shaw asked.

"If you don't like the arrangement, you can always go back to that toothless whore you and Dalton took up with back in Puxico."

"No, no, however you want to do it is fine with me," Shaw said. "Long as I get my turn."

At that moment someone stuck his head in through

the front door of the café. "Mr. Roosevelt, the judge wants you back in the court. The jury's reached a verdict," he said.

Roosevelt thanked him, then he and Anna left. Within moments, Childers, Yerby, and Shaw were the only three customers left in the café.

"Damn," Shaw said. "Did you see that? Most of them folks just got up an' left food on their table."

"I reckon they're hurryin' to see if they can get in to hear what the jury's got to say," Yerby said.

"I hope they find the son of a bitch guilty," Childers said.

Shaw got up from the table and started wandering through the dining room, looking down at the plates left on the table.

"Lookee here, here's a whole chicken leg that didn't get et," he said, picking it up from the plate. "And lookee over there. There's half a piece of apple pie."

"The hell you say," Yerby said. He got up from the table then and, like Shaw, began wandering through the dining room, looking for uneaten leftovers.

Anna was the only one in the gallery who didn't have to fight for her seat. That was because the bailiff had kept it for her. She was in her seat, and Roosevelt and Woodward were at their respective tables, when Falcon was brought into the courtroom.

Anna found Falcon MacCallister to be a fascinating man. One of the things that had impressed her when she met him back in New York was how handsome he was. But he wasn't handsome like the drawing room dandies she had met back in New York. The best description she could think of was "ruggedly handsome." He looked like the mountain man that was his stock.

When you added that to his reputation, there was something frightening about him. And yet, beneath that rather frightening veneer, she knew that he was a man of honor and integrity. She knew also that no one who was in the right need fear him. It was hard to equate the picture that was being painted of him now, a man of danger and daring, with the gracious man who had invited her to join his theater box.

She remembered that she, Gail, and Emma Lou had discussed him after the theater that night.

"At first, I was a little frightened about sharing a box with a perfect stranger," Gail said. "One never knows what can happen."

"What do you mean? What could have happened?" Emma Lou asked.

"Why, what would have kept him from throwing us down on the floor and having his way with us?" Gail said.

"Nothing, I suppose," Emma Lou said. She laughed. "Gail, you are blushing. Why, I wouldn't be surprised if you wanted that to happen."

"Emma Lou! Why, what an awful thing to say!" Anna said, though all three had laughed at the suggestion.

"I will say this. He is much more handsome than his famous brother," Anna said.

"All rise!" the bailiff called, and the court stood as her father came into the room.

Despite the fact that Anna found herself in disagreement with her father over Falcon MacCallister, she couldn't help but feel a tremendous sense of pride in him. She could sense the honor and respect everyone in the courtroom had for him. But that honor and respect, she knew, was not limited to the courtroom. Her father's standing throughout the entire Territory of the Dakotas was impeccable. She knew that not all judges enjoyed that reputation.

"Be seated," Judge Heckemeyer said and, as one, the gallery took their seats. "Bailiff, please bring the jury in."

All eyes turned toward the door to the jury room, and a moment later the jury, twelve men good and true, trudged back into the room. One bearded gent expectorated a quid toward a spittoon as he walked by it, making it ring as he hit it perfectly.

The jury took their seats, then looked toward the judge. Anna studied their faces to see if she could detect any hint of what their decision might be, but all maintained a studied and stoic countenance.

"Gentlemen of the jury, have you reached a verdict?" Heckemeyer asked.

The foreman of the jury stood. "We have, Your Honor."

"Please publish the verdict."

With a great sense of drama, the foreman drew his glasses from his pocket, then put them on, looping them carefully over one ear at a time. He opened up a sheet of paper, then cleared his throat.

His posturing had the desired effect because every eye in the courtroom was fixed upon him.

"We the jury, after careful consideration of all facts presented, find the defendant, Falcon MacCallister . . ." Here, he paused, and stared directly at Falcon.

Falcon returned the stare with a steady, unblinking gaze.

"Not guilty," the foreman said.

"Yes!" someone shouted, and the courtroom erupted in spontaneous applause.

Once again it was necessary for Judge Heckemeyer

to use his gavel to bring the court to order. Finally, everyone grew quiet.

"Mr. MacCallister, you having been found not guilty by a jury of your peers, I order that all bonds and restraints be withdrawn. You are free to go. This court is adjourned."

Once more he brought down the gavel; then he left the courtroom, exiting by a door behind the bench.

Several in the courtroom hurried up to the defense table to extend their congratulations to Roosevelt for a job well done, and to Falcon for being found not guilty.

Anna Heckemeyer was one of the first to congratulate both Roosevelt and Falcon.

"Thank you," Falcon said. "Though I must confess that I was a little concerned for a while." He smiled disarmingly.

"You had no confidence in me? Oh, you of little faith. I am wounded to my core. To my core, sir," Roosevelt said, putting his hand over his heart.

Falcon laughed. "No, I had every confidence in you. It was the judge I was worried about."

"You shouldn't have worried. I told you that my father is a fair man. I knew he would conduct an honest trial."

"You did tell me that, that is true," Falcon said. "And I must admit that I found no fault with his conduct of the trial. But I am relieved that this is all over."

"So, my friend," Roosevelt said as he began gathering his papers from the table. "What is next for you?"

"After two weeks in jail, the first thing I want is a bath," Falcon said. "Then a good dinner, a few beers, then a hotel room for a few days."

"No need for you to stay in a hotel," Roosevelt said. "Why don't you come out to Elkhorn for a few days? You'll be a lot more comfortable in my guest room than you would in the hotel. And," he added with an amused twinkle in his eye, "I can just about guarantee you that nobody will barge into your room in the middle of the night, bent upon killing you."

Falcon nodded. "Sounds good to me," he said. "I think I just might take you up on it."

Chapter 19

"Are you a reader, Falcon?" Roosevelt asked as the two men rode out to Elkhorn. "That is, if you don't mind being addressed by your first name."

"I would consider it an act of real friendship to be addressed by my first name," Falcon replied. "And to answer your question, I do read when I get the opportunity. I often carry a book or two with me, but I'm on the trail so often that books are sometimes difficult to come by. I've been known to read and reread the same book many times."

Roosevelt laughed. "Back at Harvard, we called that study," he said. "I think you will like my house."

"I'm sure I will."

"It's a low-lying, one-story house of hewn logs. The roof is pitched so that it is higher in the middle, but the ceiling is only seven feet high at the walls. It is clean and neat, with many rooms, so that one can be alone if one wishes to."

"It sounds very nice."

"The reason I asked if you were a reader is because I have a library in the house."

"A library?"

"A library of sorts," Roosevelt said. "Rough board shelves hold a number of books. Without them, I fear some of the evenings would be long indeed."

"I'm sure they have brought you a great deal of comfort."

"Yes," Roosevelt said. He got a sad, faraway look in his eyes. "That is, to the degree that anything can bring me comfort right now."

Falcon realized that he was thinking of the double tragedy of his life. "I'm sorry," he said. "I shouldn't have stirred up old memories."

Unexpectedly, Roosevelt chuckled. "Oh, no, don't be sorry, Falcon. I appreciate your concern, and I'm a big boy now. I will get over this." He took in the mountain vista with a broad wave of his arm. "And this will help me do just that."

"I'm sure it will.

"I think you need a respite as well," Roosevelt said. "It can't have been very pleasant for you, spending several days in jail."

"I can't argue with that," Falcon said. "And the idea that I might have had to spend several years in jail was more than I wanted to deal with. If I haven't expressed my gratitude to you for defending me, then I do so now."

"You were innocent of the charge," Roosevelt said. "It is easy to defend an innocent man."

"I'm curious, how did a back-East man like you wind up with a ranch out here in the Dakotas? I know why you are here now, but you already owned the ranch, didn't you?"

"Yes," Roosevelt said. "I think, by tonight, you won't have to ask that question. We'll have a nice dinner, then come out to sit in rocking chairs on the veranda."

"Do you spend much time there?" Falcon asked.

"Yes, and you will see why once you are there. The house stands on the river brink, and from the porch, which is shaded by leafy cottonwoods, from the porch you can look across the sandbars and shallows to a strip of meadowland, behind which rises a line of sheer cliffs and grassy plateaus."

"Sounds nice," Falcon said.

"It is. And I can guarantee you this. In the summer evenings, when a cool breeze stirs along the river and blows in your face, why, this veranda is the most pleasant place in all the Dakotas. You can sit with a book in hand, and you don't even have to read. You just rock gently to and fro and gaze sleepily out at the weird-looking buttes opposite, until their sharp outlines blur and purple in the afterglow of the sunset."

Falcon chuckled. "The way you're describing it, I'm about to fall asleep in the saddle right now," he said.

Roosevelt laughed with him. "Oh, no, don't do that," he said. "We've got a way to go yet."

The two men rode on in silence after that, the only sound being the dry thud of horse hooves falling on prairie grass and the distant cry of an eagle.

Over dinner that night, Roosevelt began talking of his love for politics.

"I've never been much for politics," Falcon said as he spread butter onto a biscuit. "Truth is, I've never even cast a vote."

"You have never voted?" Roosevelt asked, surprised by Falcon's pronouncement.

"No."

"Why not?"

"I've always figured that I can take care of myself without any interference from the government," Falcon replied. "And regardless of who is in office, it has never made that much of a difference in my own life."

"Ah, but that is not true, my friend," Roosevelt insisted. "The bulk of government is not legislation but administration. That means you can never escape being governed. We must either govern ourselves or we must submit to being governed by others."

"That's a noble thought," Falcon said. "And I can see how, for someone like you who lives and works in a big city, that would be important. But my life is the mountains and the open spaces. I visited New York a few years ago, and I couldn't wait to get out of there. I've always figured to just let the rest of the country take care of itself. Things are plenty good enough for me just the way they are."

"And nothing the government has ever done has concerned you?"

"No. Well, I take that back. I reckon the War Between the States was over political differences, and a lot of good men died, on both sides, because politicians couldn't work things out. Seems to me like the politicians might have failed us then."

"I can see why you would have that attitude, and I must say that, in that instance, I agree with you," Roosevelt replied. "But it has always been my belief that this country will not be a permanently good place for any of us to live in unless we make it a reasonably good place for all of us to live in. That is the job of a good politician, and I've always tried to apply my life to that principle."

Falcon chuckled. "I'll say this for you, Teddy. If ever I have met anyone who could rightly be called a man of destiny, it is you. I just have a feeling that one of these days I'm going to tell folks that I knew you when."

Roosevelt laughed. "From your lips to God's ear, my friend," he said. "Now, what do you say to a little hunting trip tomorrow?"

"Sounds good to me. What are we going after?"

"Elk," Roosevelt said. "After all, this is Elkhorn Ranch."

* * *

It was raining when they woke up the next morning, but that didn't deter the eager young man from the East.

The cook had prepared a generous breakfast of biscuits, bacon, and eggs, which Falcon and Roosevelt washed down with hot, black coffee. Falcon always did have a good appetite, but it seemed even more stimulated here, in this place.

After they finished the meal, Roosevelt looked through the window and saw that, while the heavy rain had stopped, a light drizzle continued to fall.

"You do have a slicker, don't you?" Roosevelt asked from his position by the window.

"Yes."

"Well, you had better put it on. It doesn't look to me like this is going to end any time soon."

Fifteen minutes later, the two men were more than a mile away from the cabin, riding through the light but steady drizzle. Falcon had gone through blizzards where he'd had to get off and lead his horse, barely managing to survive the storm. A little thing like a light drizzle wasn't going to stop him.

"I think taking an elk is one of the most magnificent things a man can do," Roosevelt said. Those were the first words either of them had spoken in several minutes. "I'm sure you've hunted elk before," he continued.

"Yes, I've hunted elk."

"Of course you have," Roosevelt said. "And even larger and more magnificent game if I don't miss my guess."

Falcon had once killed a bear with a knife. He wouldn't have used Roosevelt's word, "magnificent," to describe that incident, because the bear had attacked him. The encounter left him badly mauled and it was nip and tuck for a while. If it had not been for his wife, Marie Gentle Breeze, and the Indian herbs and cures she applied to kill the infection, he would have died.

They were following along a stream that emptied into the river. The stream itself produced sloughs, and one of them curled back against a beaver dam where the water had pooled and spilled out over the banks to create a small lake.

Falcon saw several birds take flight, and from the agitated way they were flying, he knew they had been frightened by something. He stared into a thicket of aspen trees and saw a movement.

Falcon was about to point it out to Roosevelt when he saw that the young ranch owner had already seen it. The fact that he had seen it as well surprised Falcon, and his respect for this rather fascinating man increased.

Suddenly, the elk broke out of the trees and started across the meadow.

"There he is!" Roosevelt shouted. "You're my guest, he's all yours!"

"No," Falcon said. "He's yours."

By now the elk was three-fourths of the way across the meadow, and Falcon realized that he should have taken the shot when it was offered. He could still bring the animal down, but it might be too late for Roosevelt.

Without a verbal response to Falcon's offer, Roosevelt raised his rifle to his shoulder and aimed.

Falcon wanted to call out to him to shoot now, before it was too late, but he checked the urge. Then he heard the crack of the rifle.

The elk was running in long, ground-eating strides. Falcon saw a little puff of dust fly up from the elk's hide, as well as a tiny spray of blood where the bullet hit. The shot was a perfectly aimed heart-shot. The animal's front knees buckled and he went down headfirst, then tumbled and fell. He tried once to get up again, but he managed only to get the front part of his body up before he fell a second time. This time he was still.

"Good shot, Teddy," Falcon said.

"Thank you," Roosevelt replied, the tone strangely pensive.

Looking toward him, Falcon saw that Roosevelt had lowered his rifle and was just staring at the elk, now still.

"Are you all right?" Falcon asked.

"Yes," Roosevelt replied. He put the rifle back in its saddle sheath, then took off his glasses and began wiping the lenses. He made no effort to approach the elk he had just killed.

"Do you ever . . ." Roosevelt started, but he stopped in mid-question, sighed, then put his glasses back on. "Do you ever have a feeling for the animals you kill?" he asked, completing his thought.

"Yes, I have those feelings all the time," Falcon said. "Even when I need to kill for food, I'm aware of what I'm doing."

"Animals are the innocents of this world," Roosevelt said. "They are God's creatures, just as we are. I don't think we are necessarily superior to them, just different from them. But only man has the intellect to change the environment, and that means we are charged by God to be the stewards of all creation."

"I've never thought of it in just those words," Falcon said. "But now that you put it that way, I reckon I agree with you."

"Yes, well, we are failing in that. I don't know if I will ever be in a position to do anything about it, but if I am, I intend to see that we start living up to our obligation."

Roosevelt took in the great expanse with a sweeping wave of his hand. "What a terrible thing it would be if none of our grandchildren could enjoy this beautiful West because we had failed in our responsibility."

"Somehow, Teddy, I believe you will be able to keep that from happening," Falcon said.

The pensive mood passed and Roosevelt smiled. "Let's go get the elk, shall we? I'll have the cook prepare elk steak for our supper."

It was a week before Childers, Yerby, and Shaw were able to put into operation their plan to kidnap Anna Heckemeyer. They needed to find a time and place where they could take her without being seen, and that opportunity presented itself at about nine o'clock one night.

Never suspecting that she might be in danger, Anna had visited the home of Millie Jackson, a longtime friend. Millie was soon to be married, and after supper Anna stayed for a while, talking with her friend about the upcoming wedding.

It was dark when Anna left Millie's house and started down the street toward her own home. Walking in the dark was not an intimidating experience for her; she had walked all over New York despite the well-known denizens of that city. And yet, as she passed by a large, open lot, she suddenly got a strange feeling of foreboding.

Anna stopped and looked out into the dark shadows of the lot, but saw nothing. She didn't know why she was experiencing this sensation. She knew only that she was, and shivering, she pulled her shawl more tightly around her and quickened her pace.

There was a picket fence at the other end of the open lot, separating it from the adjacent house. Anna hurried toward the fence, thinking it would be the debarkation point for her apprehension. But she was startled when three men suddenly stepped out from behind the fence. Two of them grabbed her, and one put his hand over her mouth to keep her from screaming.

She bit him on the hand.

"Ouch!" the man said. "The bitch bit me!"

"Don't let go of her mouth!" one of the others said. "We can't let her scream."

The third man had a bottle and a cloth, and Anna watched with alarm as he poured liquid from the bottle onto the cloth. That done, he held the cloth up to her nose and mouth.

Anna struggled and tried to twist her head to get away from the cloying smell of the cloth. The man with the cloth clamped it down more tightly over her face, and she felt herself growing dizzy. Her knees weakened, then everything went black.

"What do we do now?" Shaw asked.

"Get her in the buckboard," Aaron said. "We're going to take her out to the shack."

"What if she comes to and starts screaming?"

"We'll put a gag in her mouth."

"Maybe we ought to give her some more chloroform," Dalton suggested.

"No," Aaron said. "Any more might kill her. We need her alive."

Taking her back to the alley, the three men put Anna's limp form into the back of a buckboard. Three minutes later they were out of town. For once, something Aaron planned had gone off without a hitch.

Chapter 20

The first thing Anna noticed when she woke up was that she had a terrible headache. She had never had a headache as bad as this one, and she had no idea what might have caused it.

The next thing she was aware of was the rough texture of the bed. Instead of the smooth satin sheets she was used to in her own bed, this was a very coarse texture, almost like a burlap bag.

And the smells. She was aware of a mélange of fetid, sour odors.

Obviously, this was not her room. But where was she, and how did she get here?

She tried to sit up, then discovered that, wherever she was, she was tied to the bed.

Why was she tied in bed? Why was she here?

On the verge of panic now, Anna looked around to try and determine where she was. But the room, if indeed it was a room, was so dark that she couldn't see anything.

Even the dark was unusual for it was so total, so absent of any ambient light that it was almost overpowering. She had never seen any place as dark as this, and for a moment, she wondered if she was still alive.

"Hello?" she called out. "Hello, is anyone here?"

"I'm here, girl," a man's voice answered from the darkness.

"Who . . . who are you?" Anna asked.

"The name is Percy. Percy Shaw."

Every nerve ending in Anna's body called out for her to scream, but she held the impulse in check, intuitively knowing that panic would only make things worse. She decided to take a conciliatory tone toward her captor, for surely that was what he was. She forced herself to be as congenial as she could.

"I'm pleased to meet you, Percy. My name is Anna."

Percy chuckled, an obscene-sounding laugh that came from somewhere in the darkness.

"I know who you are, girl," he said. "That's how come we snatched you."

"We? You mean there are other people in this room?"

"Not now there ain't," Shaw answered. "Right now there ain't nobody here but me'n you. Aaron and Dalton has gone to take a note to your pa."

"A note? What kind of a note?"

"It's one a-tellin' your pa that iffen he wants you back he's got to come up with some money." Shaw was quiet for a moment. "Oh, yeah, and he's got to let Frank go too."

"Frank? Who is Frank?" Anna asked.

"Frank . . . he's Aaron's brother what's in the territorial prison. Your pa's the one what put him there, so Aaron figured to make your pa tell the folks at the prison to cut him loose."

"Pa won't do that," Anna said. "He won't tell them to let Frank go."

"What do you mean he won't tell them to let Frank go? You ain't tellin' me your pa would just sit back and let you die, are you?"

"I think he will do whatever his conscience tells him

to do," Anna said. "He might give you the money, but I can guarantee you that he will not turn a convicted criminal out of the territorial prison."

"Yeah, well, we'll just see about that," Shaw said.

Anna was quiet for a long moment as she contemplated her situation. She didn't know exactly how her father would react to this, but she was reasonably certain that he would not bargain for her release. He was nothing if not a man of principle. And when it came to being true to his principles, he would do so to the death—or, she realized with a shudder, her death.

"Mr. Shaw?" she called after a few minutes of silence.

"Yeah? What is it?"

"Could you light a lantern, please?"

"Haw!" Shaw replied.

"What is so funny?"

"We ain't got no lanterns," Shaw replied.

"A candle then?"

"Can't do that neither," Shaw said.

"Why not?"

"'Cause I'm lyin' on this here bunk over here and I'm pretty nigh naked. All I got on is my under-drawers."

"I promise I won't peek," Anna said. "I just don't like the dark."

"You ain't got to be scared of the dark with me in here," Shaw said.

"Oh? But aren't you one of the ones who brought me in here? And didn't you just say that if my father doesn't meet your demands you will kill me?"

Shaw chuckled evilly. "Yeah, I guess that's right, ain't it? I mean, I am one of the ones you need to be scared of. But if it'll set your mind to ease, I ain't a-plannin' on doin' nothin' to you now. And I won't do it in the dark."

"Thanks," Anna said.

She was quiet for a few minutes longer. Then she called out to him again.

"Mr. Shaw, I have to go to the privy."

"Just hold it."

"I can't hold it. I had a lot of punch at my friend's house tonight. I have to go."

"Then go."

"I can't. I'm tied to the bed."

"I mean just go right there in bed."

"Please, Mr. Shaw! I can't do that!" Anna said with a shocked voice.

"Then you don't really have to go all that bad, do you?"

"Please. You can go with me and keep an eye on me."

"You mean I can watch you?" Shaw replied, his voice showing a bit of interest.

"I mean you can stay outside the privy and watch to make sure I don't run away."

"Ha!" Shaw said. "There ain't no privy. If you go outside, the onliest thing you can do is just squat down on the ground somewhere."

Anna sighed. "Then you can come with me and watch me squat down somewhere. But please, just let me go."

"All right, but I'm comin' with you," Shaw said with a resigned sigh. "And don't you tell Aaron or Dalton nothing about this."

"I won't, I promise," Anna said.

Anna heard the sound of Shaw getting up from his bunk, then walking over toward her. He ran into something, then let out a yelp of pain.

"Damn, I kicked my toe against the table," he said.

She heard Shaw shuffling things around; then he struck a match. There was a flare as the match caught, then the flare died so that the only light was the single flame of the burning match. The light grew somewhat brighter when Shaw lit a candle. The candle provided a soft, golden bubble of light. It was dim and yellow, but it did serve its purpose.

Shaw walked the rest of the way over to her bed then, and she noticed that he was, as he said, in his underwear. As he leaned over to untie the rope that held her secure, she realized that his almost overpowering body odor was one of the smells she had detected when she first awoke.

Anna sat up on the side of her bed for a moment, rubbing on her wrists and ankles to get the circulation restored.

"Well, you said you had to go, so go," Shaw said. "Don't just sit there."

"Hold on for a moment," Anna said as she continued to rub the rope marks. "It'll take a minute before I can walk. You had those ropes awfully tight."

"Wasn't me that done it," Shaw said. "It was Aaron."

Finally Anna stood up.

"All right," she said. "I'm ready to go now."

"Good."

Suddenly, and without any indication of what she was about to do, Anna sent her foot whistling up toward Shaw's crotch. The point of her shoe caught Shaw in his most tender place and, grabbing his crotch and crying aloud, he doubled over in pain.

Anna saw a nearby chair and she grabbed it, then brought it crashing down over Shaw's head as he was bent over. Shaw went down under the blow.

With a surge of excitement, Anna dashed across the room, jerked open the door, and ran outside. She had no idea where she was or how she would get home, but she didn't care. She was free!

"Here, girl! Where do you think you are going?"

Aaron shouted, grabbing her as, unexpectedly, she ran right into his arms.

Anna had the misfortune of choosing to make her escape at the exact moment Aaron and Dalton were returning from their mission of delivering the ransom note to Anna's father.

"Let me go!" Anna said, struggling with her captor. "Let me go!"

"Well, now, didn't we come along at just the right time?" Aaron asked.

"How did she get away? Where's Shaw?" Dalton asked.

"I hope she killed the son of bitch before she ran out of there," Aaron said.

"You don't mean that, Aaron. He's one of us."

"No, Shaw ain't one of us. Me'n you's blood kin. Only cousins, but that's blood kin. Percy Shaw ain't nothin'."

When Anna did not come down to breakfast the next morning, Judge Heckemeyer wasn't too concerned. He knew that she had visited Millie the night before, and he assumed that she had just stayed over. Anna and Millie had been the best of friends since they were young girls in grade school together, and over the years Millie had spent many nights with Anna, and Anna with Millie.

When they were younger, of course, Judge Heckemeyer always knew where she was because she was careful to ask permission.

Heckemeyer chuckled. Perhaps not asking permission to stay last night was Anna's way of establishing her status as an adult. After all, when she was in New York, she didn't have to ask permission for everything that she did.

Well, of course she didn't have to ask for permission to stay, Heckemeyer thought. But it would have been nice if she had at least shared her plans with him. That way, he wouldn't be worried.

"Judge?"

Looking up from the breakfast table, Judge Heckemeyer saw his housekeeper. There was a strange, pained expression on her face.

"Yes, Sally, what is it?" Heckemeyer asked.

The gray-haired woman who had been his housekeeper since his wife died, many years earlier, held out a piece of paper.

"I found this slid under the door," she said.

"What is it?"

"I think you better read it," Sally said.

Curious, and somewhat concerned by his housekeeper's strange attitude and demeanor, Heckemeyer looked at the note. It was a hand-printed note in large, block letters. The first thing he noticed was that his name was misspelled.

JUDGE HECKMER

WE HAVE TUK YOUR DOTTER. IF YOU WANT HER BAK YOU MUST LET FRANK CHILDERS OUT OF PRISEN AND GIVE US FIVE THOUSEND DOLLARS. IF YOU AGREE TO DO THIS, HANG A RED CLOTH IN YOUR FRONT WINDER. WE WILL CONTAK YOU AGIN WHEN WE HEER THAT FRANK IS LET OUT OF JAIL.

Chapter 21

Judge Heckemeyer sent for Roosevelt as soon as he read the message, and the young rancher was now sitting in the parlor of Heckemeyer's house, drinking coffee and listening to the judge.

"I didn't think anything about it at first," Heckemeyer said. "After all, Anna's a grown woman and Millie has been her friend for many years. I just assumed she stayed over last night. Then this morning I got the ransom note I told you about."

"If you are worried about money, Andrew, I'll gladly pay the five thousand dollars," Roosevelt said.

"No, it's not that," Heckemeyer said with a dismissive wave of his hand. "I'm not worried about the money, I have five thousand dollars. It will break me, but that would be a small price to pay to get my daughter back. It's the other thing I'm worried about."

"The other thing?"

"They are also demanding that I issue orders releasing Frank Childers from prison. I can't do that, Teddy. I won't do that."

"Even if it means Anna's life?" Roosevelt asked.

"Yes, even if it . . . if it endangers Anna." He couldn't bring himself to say "even if it means her life."

"I see," Roosevelt said quietly.

Heckemeyer shook his head. "No, I'm not sure that

you do see," he said. "Teddy, if I issued orders to free Frank Childers, I would be repudiating everything that I have ever stood for. I can't do that."

"So, what do you plan to do?"

Heckemeyer lowered his head and pinched the bridge of his nose. He was silent for a long time before he sighed and lifted his head again. He wasn't weeping, but Roosevelt saw that his eyes were red-rimmed, and filled with the pain of his situation.

"I don't know," Heckemeyer finally said. "Lord help me, I don't know."

"I have an idea," Roosevelt said. "You probably won't like it. In fact, I'm sure you won't like it. But it is a possible answer."

"What is it?" Heckemeyer asked.

"I'm warning you, you won't like it," Roosevelt said again.

"Look, if it will get Anna back safely, I will like it, no matter what it is."

"All right. Send Falcon MacCallister after her."

"What? Are you serious?"

"I told you you wouldn't like it," Roosevelt said.

"Well, you were right. I don't like it. I don't like it at all."

"It's the only way," Roosevelt said.

"What do you mean, it's the only way? There has to be another way."

"I'm sure there is, but nothing comes to my mind right now. What about you? Do you have any ideas?" Roosevelt asked.

"No," Heckemeyer admitted.

For a long moment the two men sipped their coffee, the silence of the room interrupted only by the tick-tock of the old grandfather clock.

"What . . ." Heckemeyer began. He paused for a moment, then continued. "Just what do you think MacCallister would do? For that matter, what could he do?"

"As for what he would do, I believe he would do whatever it takes to get Anna back safely."

"Why would he? I mean, he knows what I think about him."

"Because he is a man of honor," Roosevelt said.

"Ah, yes, I remember you telling me that. Still I can't see him—"

"And he regards you as a man of honor," Roosevelt said, interrupting Heckemeyer.

"How so?"

"Despite how you feel about him, you conducted the trial fairly and honestly. Men of honor see that in each other, Andrew. I believe Falcon MacCallister would go after Anna if you asked him to. And what's more, I believe he would bring her back safely."

"You really think so?"

"I know so," Roosevelt said resolutely.

"All right. I'll ask him. When do you think would be a good time to see him?"

Roosevelt smiled. "How about right now?" he asked.

"Right now? All right, where can I find him?"

"He's waiting on your front porch. Stay right here, I'll bring him in."

Falcon sat on the porch swing while Roosevelt was inside talking to Judge Heckemeyer. Falcon hadn't said anything about it, but he was going to go after the men who kidnapped Anna with or without the judge's blessing.

That was because Falcon knew something that neither the judge, the sheriff, nor anyone else knew. He knew who it was that kidnapped the girl. The note had asked, specifically, for Frank Childers to be released from prison.

Only one person would want Frank Childers released, and that was Aaron Childers. Falcon knew that Aaron Childers was one of the three men he was chasing.

As Falcon sat in the swing, he felt a soft, warm breeze start up, carrying on it the scent of the red roses that grew in such profusion at the end of the porch. A few houses away, he could hear the sound of happy children laughing and playing some game. A little farther down, he heard the ringing of the blacksmith as he pounded on a piece of hot metal, and farther yet, the lyrical whistle of an approaching train.

At moments like these, Falcon envied those men and women who could find satisfaction in living tranquil lives in bucolic settings. A part of him wanted to own a house in a town like this and live quietly.

But even as the thought crossed his mind, he knew that it wasn't what he really wanted, because if he did, he could have it. He certainly had all the money he would need to be able to live such a life. In fact, he had enough money that he could have the biggest and most elaborate home in any place he chose to live in, even a place as large as Denver, or San Francisco.

But he could not do that. He could not settle down. His father once told him that he was born under a wandering star, and when the young Falcon asked him what that meant, his father said, "It means you can never be satisfied by settling down in one place."

"Falcon," Roosevelt said, stepping out onto the porch to interrupt Falcon's reverie. "Could you come inside for a moment?"

Falcon nodded, but said nothing. Getting up from the swing, he followed Roosevelt into the house. The judge lived in one of the nicer houses in Medora. It was a large, two-story, brick house with a wide front porch. Just inside the door was a foyer, with the parlor off one side and the dining room off the other. From here a wide, grand staircase climbed to the second floor. The foyer was open all the way to the ceiling of the second floor, from which hung a long chain, supporting a chandelier filled with dangling crystal prisms that caught the morning sun and projected little splashes of color on the walls.

Judge Heckemeyer was standing just inside the foyer.

"Mr. MacCallister," he said. "Would you come in and visit for a few minutes?"

"All right."

"Coffee?"

"Yes. Black."

The judge nodded at the housekeeper; then Falcon and Roosevelt followed him into the parlor. The judge offered Falcon an overstuffed chair, and as Falcon settled into the dark maroon upholstery, he got the idea that this was normally the judge's chair. The judge had offered it to him, which meant the judge wanted something from him.

Heckemeyer waited until the coffee was brought before he spoke.

"I'm sure you have heard the news about my daughter being kidnapped," Heckemeyer began.

"Yes, I've heard."

"Teddy . . . that is, Mr. Roosevelt, suggested that you might be able to . . . uh . . . get her back."

"I might."

"Then, I'm asking you . . . no, I'm begging you, please do so. I'll pay you any amount of money you want, just . . ."

Falcon held up his hand and shook his head. "I don't want any money," he said.

"All right, I . . . I'm sorry, I didn't mean to demean you by offering money. It's just that . . ."

"You want her back," Falcon finished for him.

"Yes."

"Judge, during the recent trial, you heard Mr. Woodward make reference to the number of men I have killed in self-defense, did you not?"

"Yes, of course I heard it."

"And, if truth be told, you agree with him, don't you? I mean with regard to how many times I find myself in situations where it has been necessary for me to kill."

"I, uh, have some concern about that, yes," Judge Heckemeyer admitted.

"But clearly, if I undertake this mission for you, I may well find myself in this same situation again."

"You mean you might have to kill to save your life?" Heckemeyer said.

"Yes," Falcon said. "Or to save the life of your daughter," he added.

"Then do it," Heckemeyer said. "I know this is unmasking me for the hypocrite I am. Here all this time I have derided you for killing in self-defense, and now I am telling you that I would understand it if you killed the men who took my daughter from me. Understand it? God help me, I would welcome it."

"Do you have the note they left?"

"Yes, it's right here," Heckemeyer said as he handed the note to Falcon. This was the first time Falcon had seen the note, though he already knew what the note said, for the messenger the judge had sent for Roosevelt this morning had told them.

"Have you heard anything else from them?" Falcon asked. "Since this note, I mean."

Heckemeyer shook his head, then pointed at the note. "As you can see there, they say they will get in touch with me again when I have authorized the release of Frank Childers."

Heckemeyer was silent for a moment as Falcon looked at the note.

"I must confess that I am totally at a loss as to what to do now," Heckemeyer said.

"Do you want my opinion?"

"Yes, of course."

"Release Childers," Falcon said.

"What?" Heckemeyer responded in surprise. He shook his head vehemently. "No, I can't do that. I won't do that."

Falcon handed the note back. "Then I'm sorry. If you don't release Frank Childers, there's nothing I can do to help you."

Judge Heckemeyer glared at Falcon. "What on earth are you saying?" He turned to Roosevelt. "Teddy, what is this? You told me he could help me. If the only way to get my daughter back is to release Frank Childers, then I could certainly do that with no help from Mr. Mac-Callister."

"Let me talk to him," Roosevelt said.

"You can talk all you want," Falcon said. "Unless he releases Frank Childers, there is nothing I can do."

"Why must I release Frank Childers?"

"How else are we going to find your daughter?" Falcon asked.

"What do you mean?"

"After Frank Childers is released, he is going to go straight as an arrow to his brother. That's where your daughter is. I'm going to follow him and I'll get Anna back."

"What about Frank Childers?"

"I'll take care of him too," Falcon said.

"What do you mean, take care of him?"

"Do you want your daughter back?"

Judge Heckemeyer nodded.

"Then issue the order releasing Frank Childers," Falcon said again.

Judge Heckemeyer closed his eyes and pinched the bridge of his nose. It did not escape his notice that Falcon had not answered his question as to what he meant by taking care of Frank Childers. The judge held that pose for a long time before he sighed and spoke.

"I don't feel very good about doing this," he said. "But if it is the only way . . ."

"It is the only way," Falcon said.

"Very well. I'll send a telegram ordering his release today."

"No," Falcon said. "Send a letter. That will give me time to get there. I need to be there when they let him out."

"All right."

"Oh, and hang up the red cloth. If Frank's brother doesn't know he's being released, he won't be there to meet him. And if he doesn't meet him, I won't be able to follow them to find out where they are holding Anna."

"All right, Mr. MacCallister. Whatever you say," Heckemeyer agreed.

When Falcon and Roosevelt left the house, they walked down to the Golden Spur. After greeting several of the regulars, they took a table in the back of the room.

"You are convinced that Aaron Childers is the one who kidnapped Anna?"

"He is one of them."

"One of them?"

"There are three."

"My word, I just realized," Roosevelt said. "It's the same three, isn't it?"

"The same three?"

"The three men who attacked me that day. The ones you drove off. They are the ones who have kidnapped Anna."

"I believe that is true."

"It wasn't just a happy circumstance that you came by that day, was it? You were already looking for them, weren't you?"

"Yes, I was."

"Why?"

Falcon told Roosevelt about finding Luke Douglass dying, and his wife, Mary, already dead in a burning house.

"Childers and the other two murdered them," he said. "I made a vow that day to hunt them down and bring them to justice."

"I get the feeling that, regardless of what Judge Heckemeyer might have said today, you were going to go after them."

"I was."

Roosevelt was silent for a moment, then he nodded. "Well, it is indeed a noble cause for someone like you," Roosevelt agreed.

"Someone like me?"

"A roughrider."

Falcon chuckled. "A roughrider? I don't think I've ever heard that term before."

"Of course you haven't. I just coined it."

"What is a roughrider?"

"My definition would be a warrior for justice," Roosevelt replied. "You say that Aaron Childers is one of the bandits. Do you know the names of the other two?"

"Yes," Falcon said. "One of them is Aaron's cousin, Dalton Yerby. The other is Percy Shaw. Shaw is no kin to either of them."

"How is it that you know them?"

"Their names came out in the trial."

"What trial?"

Falcon told how six men had robbed a bank in Belfield.

"I shot two of them," he said. "Ethan Yerby and Corey Childers. Ethan was Dalton Yerby's brother, Corey was Aaron Childers's brother."

"Did you kill them?"

Falcon shook his head. "No, I just wounded them, and not too severely. Frank Childers came back for them and we wound up capturing him and the two wounded men. Aaron, Dalton, and Percy Shaw got away."

"Bully for you," Roosevelt said enthusiastically.

"Yes, well, I was too little, too late. They killed Sheriff Billy Puckett. Puckett was a friend of mine . . . had been a friend of my father's actually. He was a good man who deserved better than to be shot down by the likes of that bunch of thieves and outlaws."

"So now Aaron is trying to get Frank out of prison. What about the other two?"

Falcon told about the jail break on the very day they were to be hanged. He concluded the story by telling that Corey and Ethan had both been killed by Luke Douglass.

"I thought they killed him."

"They killed each other."

"Good for Mr. Douglass. So, what do we do now, and when do we start?"

"We?"

"Yes, of course we. I'm going with you."

Falcon shook his head. "No, you aren't," he said.

"But of course I am," Roosevelt insisted. "In the first place, as I am sure you are aware by now, Anna is of some . . . personal concern to me. And of course, Judge

Heckemeyer is my friend, which means I have every obligation to go. And the fact that these three men once launched a personal attack against me gives me every right to go."

"You aren't going with me," Falcon said again.

"Come on, Falcon, be reasonable. If Frank Childers is released from prison and joins with the other three, that would be four of them. Four against one? Even for you, the odds are quite formidable."

"You aren't going, Teddy, and that's it."

"Would you give me one reason why not?" Roosevelt asked.

"Destiny," Falcon said.

Roosevelt got a strange look on his face. "Destiny? What do you mean by destiny?"

"I told you before, Teddy, you are a man of destiny. Don't ask me how I know it . . . maybe I've been around the Indians so long that I have the medicine. I just know that if something happened to you because of me, I would be cheating not only you, but the world."

Roosevelt laughed nervously. "That's nonsense," he said.

"No, it isn't," Falcon insisted. "And what's more, you know it isn't."

"Even so, that isn't reason enough to keep me from going with you."

"Then how is this for a reason? If you insist on going with me, I'm going to crack you over the head."

"Oh? I believe I've already given you a demonstration of my ability to defend myself," Roosevelt said pointedly.

Falcon laughed. "That you have, Teddy, that you have," he said. "And that's why I know I will be able to keep you from joining me."

"What do you mean?"

"Because I won't fight fair. I'll wait until your back is turned, and I'll club you with my pistol."

Roosevelt rubbed the top of his head; then he laughed, a high-pitched but rich laugh.

"Falcon, my friend," he said. "You make a good argument. All right, I will not try to go with you. At least, not in person. But I will be with you in spirit and prayer."

"That's all I need," Falcon said.

Chapter 22

Aaron Childers was about half-a-mile out of town, but he chose a position that would give him an unrestricted view of the judge's house. Pulling a spyglass from his saddlebag, he climbed up a little hill alongside the trail, lay down on a rock, then looked through the lens.

There it was, in the right front window, a splash of red.

Happily, he climbed back onto the horse and rode quickly back out to the cabin where Dalton and Percy were watching over Anna.

"He's a-goin' to do it!" Aaron shouted as soon as he got back.

"How do you know?" Dalton asked. "Did he give you the money?"

"No, not yet he ain't," Aaron said. "But he's goin' to, 'cause he's got 'im a red cloth hangin' in the front winder just like we told 'im to."

"When do we get the money?" Percy asked.

"Just hold your horses on the money," Aaron said. "We'll get the money after we've got Frank back."

"Seems to me like it ought to be the other way around. We should get the money first, then go get Frank."

"I'm the one making the decision here," Aaron said.

"And as long as I'm making the decisions, we're goin' after Frank first."

"All right," Percy said. "But after we get him, then I think maybe we ought to take us another vote on seein' just who is in charge. 'Cause so far, your bein' in charge ain't worked out all that good."

"All right," Aaron said with a little chuckle. "Soon as we get Frank, we'll take another vote if that's what you want."

"Yeah," Percy said. "That's what I want."

"Percy, you dumb ass," Dalton said. "If we take a vote with his brother here, who do you think is going to win?"

"I . . . I don't know," Percy said. "I guess I just wasn't thinkin' is all."

"That's your problem. You never think. Besides which, he seems to be doin' all right now, don't he? The judge hung up the red cloth, which means he's goin' to do it all. He's goin' to turn Frank a-loose, and give us the money to boot."

"Yeah, but what about them other times when nothin' Aaron did went right?"

"I tell you what, Percy, you don't have to stay around," Aaron said. "Fact is, why don't you just light out now?"

"Before I get my share of the money?" Percy replied. He shook his head. "No, there ain't no way you're a-goin' to get rid of me that easy."

"Then keep your mouth shut and do what I tell you," Aaron said. He looked over toward the bed where Anna sat. "And keep an eye on her, if that's not too big a job for you."

"Listen, she's smarter'n you think. She tricked me," Percy said.

"Hell, Percy, she doesn't have to be very smart to trick you. You're one of the dumbest sons of bitches

I've ever met," Aaron said, and Dalton laughed at the quip.

"You got no call to be a-talkin' to me like that," Percy said.

"I'm goin' to the prison to meet Frank when they let him out," Aaron said. "You two stay here and stay out of trouble."

"We'll be here when you get back, Aaron," Percy said.

"Yeah, I know you will. The question is, will she?" He looked at Anna. "Are you going to give us any trouble?" he asked.

"Oh, don't worry about me," Anna said sarcastically. "I'll have a nice supper cooked for you when you get back."

Aaron laughed. He said to Percy, "I'm takin' your horse."

"What?" Percy said. "What do you mean you're takin' my horse?"

"How else are we goin' to get Frank back here?" Aaron replied. "We sure ain't goin' to ride double."

"But you can't just take my horse."

"Oh, take it easy," Aaron said. "We'll get Frank a horse soon's he gets back."

"I'll go out with you, Aaron," Dalton said. "I 'spect I'd better get on up the hill and keep a lookout for a while. Wouldn't want someone dropping in on us all unexpected."

Both Aaron and Dalton left the cabin, and Percy walked over to the front window to watch them leave. It was a long moment before he spoke.

"I don't care who he is, he don't have no right takin' my horse like he done," Percy said in a voice that was bitter with hatred.

"I can't believe he treats you the way he does," Anna said. "Aren't you all supposed to be partners?"

"Yeah, we are supposed to be partners," Percy said. "But Aaron, somehow he's got the idea that he's the only one that knows anything. And he's always bossing me'n Dalton around."

Anna forced herself to smile. "I admire the way you stand up to him, though. You are much more defiant than Dalton."

"Defiant? What does that mean?"

"It means you are showing him that you are a man, and you can't be treated like a puppy dog."

"Yeah," Percy said. "Yeah, that's the way I feel about it too." He smiled. "You mean you can tell that?"

"Of course I can tell it."

"Ole Aaron, he don't know who he is dealin' with," Percy said. "One of these days I'm going to set him straight."

"I know you will," Anna said.

Percy stared at Anna for a long moment. "What are you doin'?"

"I beg your pardon?"

"You're butterin' me up, ain't you? You're just tryin' to get on my good side so you can trick me again."

"No, I'm not, Percy," Anna said.

"Yes, you are. You done it before."

"I'm sorry about kicking you and trying to escape. I was frightened and I didn't know what was going to happen to me. Now that I know you a little better, I'm not quite as afraid."

"Yeah? Well, you'd better be afraid of me, woman," Percy said forcefully. " 'Cause if you try anything funny again, I'll kill you."

"You don't want to do anything like that, Percy. If you kill me, my father won't pay the money."

"Yeah, well, uh, just don't you try anything else," Percy insisted.

Falcon MacCallister was having lunch when an officer of the prison came into the café and crossed over to his table.

"Mr. MacCallister?"

"Yes," Falcon said.

"I'm told by the warden that you are to be informed as to the exact moment Frank Childers will be released."

"Yes."

The officer shook his head. "I don't know what got into the judge ordering him released. If you ask me, the son of a bitch should've been hung a long time ago."

"When is he scheduled for release?" Falcon asked. He knew that the officer was curious and wanted Falcon to tell him what was going on, but he didn't take the bait.

"At one-thirty this afternoon," the officer said. "Will you be there to meet him?"

"No," Falcon said.

"Then I don't understand. What do you have to do with his release? Does Childers know you are here?"

"No, he does not know and he isn't to be told," Falcon said. "Do you understand me? No one is to be told that I am here."

"All right, if you say so. I'd sure like to know what's going on, though."

Although Falcon wasn't going to say anything at all about why he was there, he decided that he should give the man a little information in order to keep him from asking questions that might get out of hand.

"I'm on a mission for the court," Falcon said. "At this point, that is all I can tell you. I'm sure that, as an officer of the law, you have had to keep secrets before, secrets that, if they got out, could cause someone to lose their life."

"Yes, sure, of course I have," the officer said.

Falcon smiled disarmingly. "Good. The court asked the warden to select a man of honor and trust. I'm glad to see that the warden chose wisely."

"Don't worry," the officer said, an ally now rather than an inquisitor. "Your secret is safe with me."

"Can I buy you a beer?"

"Thank you, no, I have to get back to duty at the prison." The officer started to leave, then he turned back. "Good luck to you."

"Thanks."

Aaron Childers was standing across the street from the prison gate. Leaning against a telegraph pole with his arms folded across his chest, he monitored the comings and goings at the gate.

Most of the arrivals were people who were going about some aspect of business . . . a grocer arrived with a wagon full of groceries for the prison kitchen. A preacher arrived, and a couple of off-duty guards departed.

In every case those arriving or departing had to show identification to the gate guard before they were allowed to pass.

At exactly one-thirty, Aaron saw his brother. Frank walked, unaccompanied, down a long sidewalk that led from the main building to the wall and front gate. Aaron could see him through the gate.

Reaching the front gate, Frank showed the guard a paper. The guard looked at it, nodded, and another guard opened the gate. Frank stepped through it, then stood outside, looking around nervously, as if unsure that it was real, that he was actually free.

"Frank," Aaron called. He didn't leave his position by the telegraph pole.

Hearing his name called, Frank looked across the street and, seeing his brother, smiled and hurried across to him.

"It's good to see you," Aaron said.

"Damn! I knew it had to be you," Frank said.

"What had to be me?"

"I didn't know a thing about this until about fifteen minutes ago," Frank said.

"Fifteen minutes ago?"

"A guard came up to me and told me I was being set free today. At first I didn't believe him. In fact, I'm not sure I believe it now, but here I am."

"What do you say we get out of here?"

"I say let's go," Frank said. He looked back at the prison edifice. "I can't get away from this place fast enough."

"Come on, I've got a couple of horses back at the livery stable. We've got places to go."

"Places to go and a horse to ride. You've no idea how good that sounds. By the way, where's Corey?"

"What do you mean, where's Corey? Don't you know?"

"I heard you broke him and Ethan out of jail," Frank said.

"Yeah, we did. But the two of 'em got theirselves killed."

"Oh," Frank said. "Nobody told me that."

"Come on, we've got a long ride ahead of us."

"Where are we going?"

"We're going to collect five thousand dollars," Aaron said.

* * *

At one-fifteen, Falcon climbed into the hayloft of the livery and looked down the street toward the front of the prison. From here he had an excellent view of everyone who entered or left the prison. And true to the warden's word, Frank Childers exited the gate exactly on time.

Falcon stayed where he was for a few minutes, watching to see if anyone met Frank. At first, he didn't see anyone there, and he worried that perhaps he had made a mistake. Then, across the street, leaning against a telegraph pole, he saw what he had been looking for.

Aaron Childers stepped away from the pole and shook Frank's hand. The two men chatted for a moment, then started up the street toward Falcon, approaching the livery.

Falcon stepped back away from the upstairs loading window to avoid any possibility of being seen from the street. Standing in the shadows, and partially obscured by the stanchion to which the block and tackle for handling the hay was attached, Falcon watched them all the way into the livery barn.

He could hear them talking as they came in.

"So, who's riding with you now?" Frank asked.

"There's only the four of us," Aaron said. "Me'n you, Dalton and Percy."

Frank chuckled. "Percy is still with us?"

"Yes, well, where else would he go? He doesn't have sense enough to get in out of the rain," Aaron said derisively.

"You got that right," Frank answered with a chuckle.

"The horses are back here."

The two brothers continued talking as they walked to the back of the livery. As they moved farther toward the rear of the barn, though, distance rendered their voices first indistinct, and then inaudible.

Falcon stayed in place until the two brothers passed under him a second time, now mounted.

"How far is it?" Frank asked.

"We'll get there tomorrow," Aaron said.

"I don't have any trail gear."

"You can use Percy's," Aaron said. "It's on the saddle."

Falcon watched the two men ride through the shadows, then out into the brightness of day. He waited until he was sure they were well clear before he climbed down to saddle Diabo.

Falcon walked Diablo out of the barn, then bent down to study the hoofprints left by the two horses. One of the animals had a small nick on the U of the shoe of the left rear foot. The other one had a somewhat larger chunk on the left forefoot. Smiling, Falcon stood up, then swung into his saddle. These two couldn't make it any easier to trail them if they were notching trees along the way.

Back at the cabin, Dalton and Percy had switched roles. Percy was now outside, watching the approach to the cabin, while Dalton was inside, keeping an eye on their prisoner.

Anna had managed, by continually working with the ropes, to free her hands. Keeping an eye on Dalton, who was frying bacon, she started working on the ropes that bound her ankles. It was risky because Dalton kept looking back over his shoulder to check on her. Each time he did, Anna would quickly pull her hands back up behind her.

"Don't you be tryin' nothin' now," Dalton warned. "I ain't like Percy. You ain't goin' to get away from me."

"Don't worry, I'm not going anywhere," Anna said. "That bacon smells good."

"Yeah? Well, if there's any left after me'n Percy eat, maybe you can have some."

"Thanks," Anna said.

Dalton turned back to the stove and when he did, Anna reached down to finish untying her ankles. Freeing herself of the last knot, she stood up very quietly and started tiptoeing toward the door.

Just before she reached the door, though, a knife whizzed by and hit the wall in front of her with a solid thumping sound, then vibrated slightly as it stuck there. With a little gasp of alarm she jerked back, then turned toward Dalton.

Dalton was smiling evilly at her.

"I could've just as easy put that knife in your back," he said. He pointed to the bed. "I told you, I ain't Percy. If you try and get away from me again, I'll break one of your legs."

Chapter 23

The night creatures were singing as Falcon made a cold camp that night. A cloud passed over the moon, then moved away, bathing the prairie in silver. Supper was a piece of jerky and a couple of swallows of canteen water. He chewed on a coffee bean as he watched the distant campfire.

Falcon had been able to trail the Childers brothers by following the distinctive shoe tracks left by the horses the two outlaws were riding. Because of that, it had not been necessary for him to ever close to within visual distance.

The campfire ahead of him was theirs, he was certain of that. It was at least a mile away, far enough to enable him to maintain the cloak of secrecy, yet close enough to minimize any possibility of getting him separated from them.

"Why are we leaving a perfectly good campfire?" Frank asked.

"In case MacCallister is following us," Aaron said.

"MacCallister? Wait a minute. That's the son of a bitch that got me, isn't it?" Frank asked. "Why would he be following us now?"

"I don't know why," Aaron answered. "I just know he

has been on our ass from the very beginning. And it wouldn't surprise me none if he wasn't following us right now."

"I noticed that you been lookin' back over your shoulder a lot today," Frank said. "I figured you was just bein' extra careful."

"I was."

"So, did you see him?"

"No."

"So, why are you worried?"

"'Cause he's like a damn Injun. The time to worry is when you don't see him."

Because Anna had managed to get loose twice, Dalton had come up with another way to secure her. He found a small chain and a padlock and he used that to attach her to the bed. In one way, it was more comfortable for her because she wasn't as tightly bound as she had been when tied with ropes. Also, the restraint was only around her left wrist, which gave her a bit more freedom of movement on the bed itself than did the ropes, which had bound both hands and feet.

It was dark outside, and Anna was sitting on the edge of the bed watching Percy Shaw and Dalton Yerby have their supper.

Percy let out a fart.

"You dumb son of a bitch," Dalton said. "Don't you know better'n to fart at the dinner table?"

"I couldn't help it, it just come out," Percy said. He looked over toward the bed. "Sorry 'bout the fart, Miss Heckemeyer," he said.

"What are you apologizin' to her for?" Dalton asked.

"Womenfolk like it when men are polite," Percy said. "Don't you know that?"

"What the hell do I care what womenfolk like? I ain't never had me a woman I didn't pay for, and if I pay for her, then seems to me like it's her job to do what I like. Don't you think that's right, girl?" he said to Anna.

"I really wouldn't know," Anna said.

"In case you high-society-type women don't know nothin' about whores, that's where your menfolk go because you are so cold in bed," Dalton said. He laughed.

"What you tellin' her that for?" Percy said. "She's prob'ly a virgin, she don't know about things like that."

"You a virgin, girl?" Dalton asked. "I hate virgins."

"I'm hungry," Anna said without responding to his taunts. "I haven't had anything to eat all day."

"You want somethin' to eat?" Dalton asked. He reached across the table and picked up Percy's plate, which still had half a piece of bacon and some uneaten beans.

"Hey, wait a minute, I ain't a-finished eatin' yet," Precy complained.

"You're the one wantin' to be nice to her," Dalton said. "Don't seem to me like it'd be too much to ask for you to share your food with her."

Percy stroked his jaw, then looked over at Anna. "All right," he said. "I reckon that'll be all right. But I'll give it to her."

Percy took his plate back from Dalton, then picked up a fork.

"Don't give her no fork," Dalton cautioned.

"Why not? How's she goin' to eat without a fork?" Percy asked.

"She can use her hands," Dalton replied. "You give her a fork and she's liable to use it on you."

"All right, whatever you say," Percy said. He put the fork back down, then took the plate over to Anna and handed it to her.

"Thank you," Anna said. She picked up the bacon and shoved it in her mouth, then did the same thing with a handful of beans.

"Damn, she really was hungry," Percy said.

"It's good for her. Rich bitch like her, she's prob'ly never been hungry in her life," Dalton said.

Percy watched Anna eat for a moment longer; then he started toward the door.

"Where you goin'?" Dalton asked.

"I'm goin' to take a piss."

"Long as you're out there, you might as well take the first watch," Dalton said.

"It ain't my time for watch."

"Take the watch," Dalton said again. "I'll, uh, look out for the girl."

There was something in the tone of Dalton's voice that caught Anna's attention, and she looked up in alarm. Glancing toward him, she saw the look in his eyes.

"All right, but when it comes time to relieve me, you better come out there or I'll come in anyhow," Percy said.

"What do you need to watch for anyway?" Anna asked. "My father has already agreed to all your demands. Nobody is coming after you."

Anna didn't want Percy to leave. She didn't find Percy's company any more desirable than Dalton's, but she had the idea, perhaps unreasonable, that as long as both of them were here, nothing would happen to her.

"She's right," Percy said. "There ain't nobody comin' for us. What do we have to stand watch for?"

"Just get out there and do your time on guard," Dalton ordered. "I'll be out there when it's my time."

Percy paused for a moment, and Anna thought that she saw a glimmer of understanding in him. Maybe if he could see what Dalton had in mind, he would say stay. But her hopes were dashed when he suddenly smiled.

"You goin' to have a little fun with her, ain't you?" he asked.

"What makes you think that?"

"Hell, I can tell it by lookin' in your face. Aaron told us we couldn't do nothin' until after we got the money, remember?"

"Yeah, and he also said he was goin' to be first," Dalton said. "Only he ain't here now."

"Hot damn," Percy said, rubbing his crotch. "Okay, let's do it."

"Get on out there. I'll tell you when it's your turn."

"I want to stay here 'n watch," Percy said.

"You ain't goin' to stay here and watch," Dalton said resolutely. "Get on out there like I said."

"Okay, but don't take too long. Damn if I ain't got me a big hard-on now, just a-thinkin' about it."

Anna watched Percy leave; then she looked back toward Dalton.

Dalton started toward her. His eyes glowed red in the reflection of the candle, and looking into them was like looking through windows into the very fires of hell itself.

"You . . . you don't really want to do this," she said.

"Oh, but I do," Dalton said. "Yes, ma'am, me'n you's goin' to have us some fun."

When Anna saw him coming toward her, her fear became palpable, and she felt bile in her throat. "No," she said in a choked voice. "No, please don't. Your boss said that I wasn't to be harmed."

"My boss?" Dalton chuckled. "Are you talkin' about Aaron?"

"Yes."

"He don't want you killed . . . yet," Dalton said, point-edly accenting the word "yet." "But he was already plannin' on this. Onliest thing is, he wanted to be first."

"No," Anna whimpered. "Please, no."

Anna squeezed her eyes shut, trying, unsuccessfully, to prevent the tears from sliding down her cheeks. Her entreaties fell upon deaf ears, however, for she felt him approaching, then she smelled his foul breath and his body stench as he sat down on the bed beside her.

"Go ahead and cry if you want to, girl," Dalton said, putting his hands on her shoulder and pushing her back. "Fact is, I like it when my women cry."

Anna fell back on the bed.

"No," Anna said. "Please don't do this. My father has acceded to your demands."

"It don't make no difference to me whether your pa come through or not," Dalton said, glaring lustfully down at her. "I been plannin' on havin' me a little of this from the moment we snatched you up. Now the way I look at it, you got yourself two ways of getting' through this. You can either cry and fight me . . . and I got to tell you, honey, I like that. I like that a lot. Or you can do like the whores do, pretendin' that you like it, even though you don't. Either way you do it is up to you."

Anna felt Dalton's calloused hands bunching up her skirt and tugging at her undergarments until she could feel the night air on the most intimate parts of her body. Almost involuntarily, she squeezed her legs together.

Dalton unbuttoned his pants, then put his hands between her thighs. Despite her efforts to resist him, he forced her legs apart.

"There, that's a good girl," Dalton grunted.

Anna felt Dalton's weight press against her bruised and racked body. Then she felt something cold and metallic against her thigh.

It was Dalton's knife! The same knife he had thrown at her earlier. She shifted positions slightly, to allow her to get to the knife.

"There you go, girl," Dalton said. "I knew you would . . . uhn!!"

Anna slipped the knife into Dalton's body. She had presence of mind enough to know to turn the knife sideways to allow it to slide in between his ribs. She pushed it all the way to the hilt.

"What . . . what have you . . ." Dalton asked in a strained voice. He got up, then backed away from her, looking down in shock at his own knife, protruding from his body.

"Why, you bitch! You've stabbed me," he said. He pulled the knife out and when he did, blood squirted from the wound, almost like water from a fountain. He put his left hand over the wound in an effort to staunch the flow of blood, but it spilled through his fingers.

"I'm going to cut your heart out," he said. With the knife in his right hand, he staggered toward her. Before he got to her, though, he fell. He gasped a couple more times before growing silent.

Anna couldn't hear him breathe, and as she looked down at him, she saw that his eyes were open, but already growing opaque.

Anna tried to reach the knife, straining forward with her one free hand. She could brush the tips of her fingers across it, but that was all. She couldn't get hold of it to pull it to her.

She leaned back in frustration, then she saw her undergarments on the bed beside her. Grabbing them she leaned out again, tossed them toward the knife, and pulling on them, managed to drag the knife close enough to reach it.

With the knife in hand, she began picking at the lock

and, after a few attempts, successfully got the lock open. With a little gasp of thankfulness, she started toward the door, then remembered what had happened on her first try to escape. There was only one door in the cabin, but there was a window at the rear.

Moving quickly, Anna went to the back of the cabin. Climbing up on the cabinet, she opened the window, then crawled through. It was a drop of six feet to the ground, but she didn't care.

Getting up from the ground, Anna brushed her hands off, then crept to the edge of the cabin and looked around. She saw Percy sitting up on a rock, looking out toward the approach.

Keeping a wary eye on him, she slipped through the dark to the little lean-to that served as a barn. Because Aaron had taken two horses with him, there was only one horse in the lean-to. If she could get it . . . she could not only use it to get away, she would leave Percy without a horse so he couldn't come after her.

Anna managed to put the bridle on, but when she started to get the saddle, the horse started whickering and moving around.

Looking toward the rock, she saw that the horse had caught Percy's attention. She stepped back into the shadows of the lean-to so he couldn't see her.

Percy stared into the lean-to for a moment, but satisfied that everything was all right, he turned his attention back to the approach. Anna moved back out of the shadows, but she decided it was too risky to saddle the horse.

She wondered if she could ride without a saddle, then decided, why not? She knew that Indians rode without a saddle.

Without a stirrup, she had to climb up on the feeding trough to get mounted. Doing so, she lifted her skirt and straddled the horse. That was when she experienced the somewhat disconcerting sensation of feeling her nakedness against the horse's back. She had not put her undergarments back on.

Too late to worry about that now. Slowly, she guided the horse out of the lean-to. She was several yards away when she heard Percy call out.

"Dalton? Dalton, where are you goin'?"

Anna urged the horse into a gallop, but with no saddle, she was unable to stay on the horse. With the first burst of speed, she was unseated and she fell hard. By the time she got up, Percy was over her with his gun drawn.

"Damn, when you goin' to quit tryin' to escape?" he asked.

When Falcon reached the now-dead campfire the next morning, he realized that his quarry had not camped there last night. The fire had been a ruse to hold him in place.

"Damn," he said, disgusted with himself for letting it happen. He should've come up closer to the fire to see if they had really made camp, but to be honest, he hadn't given Aaron Childers credit for being that smart.

"You got me that time, Mr. Childers," he said under his breath. "But you won't get me again."

Fortunately, their trail was still easy to read, so Falcon began following their tracks, moving more swiftly than he did the day before because there was less chance of overrunning them and giving himself away.

Everything was going well until around noon. At noon a thunderstorm came up and as the rain poured down, it began washing away the tracks right in front of him.

Falcon was about to throw up his hands in disgust

when, about half a mile in front of him, he saw two men leading their horses into the opening of an old, abandoned mine.

"Well, now," Falcon said aloud. "We meet again."

Falcon wasn't quite as lucky in finding shelter as the Childers brothers were. He did find a rock overhang that shielded him from some but not all of the rain. He got Diablo under as much of the shelter as was possible; then he pulled his slicker around him and sat as far back under the rock as he could.

The rain finally eased up around three that afternoon, and Falcon watched as Frank and Aaron Childers reemerged, still leading their horses. After leading them for a few yards, they mounted them, then rode on.

When Falcon reached the mouth of the abandoned mine, he saw that the rain that had washed away the old trail actually made the new trail much easier to follow. That was because there was only one set of tracks now, all previous tracks having been erased.

Chapter 24

"Where's Dalton?" Aaron asked when he and Frank reached the cabin.

"He's lyin' out back," Percy answered easily.

"Lyin' out back? What do you mean he's lyin' out back? Lyin' out back doin' what?"

"Lyin' out back bein' dead," Percy said.

"Dead? You son of a bitch, what did you kill him for?" Aaron asked angrily. "He was my cousin, damn you!" Aaron reached for his gun.

"Hold on there, hold on!" Percy said, sticking his hands out in front of him as if pushing Aaron away. "I didn't kill him."

"Well, if you didn't kill him, who did?"

"She did," Percy said, nodding toward Anna, who, once again, was chained to the bed.

"Wait a minute, don't give me that. Are you tellin' me that little ole slip of a girl killed Dalton?"

"That's what I'm tellin' you," Percy said.

"How could she do that if you got her tied to the bed? What did you idiots do, leave a gun close enough for her to get ahold of it?" Aaron asked.

Percy shook his head. "Wasn't no gun involved."

"Then how did she do it?"

"She stabbed him with his own knife."

Aaron walked over to the bunk and looked down at Anna. "Is he tellin' the truth. Did you kill Dalton?"

When Anna didn't answer him, Aaron slapped her hard. She cried out in pain and, almost instantly, her cheek grew red from the force of the blow.

"This ain't your papa's court, woman," Aaron said. "You ain't got the right to remain silent. Answer me when I talk to you. Did you kill Dalton?"

"Yes. He tried to rape me."

Aaron looked over at Percy. "Is that true?"

"I . . . uh . . . don't know," Percy said. "I was outside. Next thing I knew, I seen her trying to escape. When I brought her back in here, I seen Dalton lyin' on the floor, dead."

"Hey! This shack is on fire!" Frank suddenly shouted, and even as he was giving the warning, the room started filling with smoke.

"What the hell? How did that happen?" Aaron said. "Come on, let's get out of here."

"What about the girl?" Frank asked.

Aaron looked at her restraint. "Where's the key?" he asked.

"The key? I . . . I'm not sure. It may be in Dalton's pocket."

The smoke got worse.

"Well, I ain't goin' out there to look for it," Aaron said. "We've got to get out of here; this smoke will kill us."

"Wait! You can't leave me here!" Anna said, but even before she finished her cry the three men were out the front door.

Anna coughed, then got down on the bed, burying her nose in the blanket in hopes of filtering out some of the smoke. Then she felt someone's hand on her arm and when she looked up, she saw that whoever it was had the key in his hand. He opened the lock.

"They were right, the key was on Dalton. Come on," he said. "We're going through the back window."

It wasn't until then that Anna recognized her rescuer.

"Mr. MacCallister!" she said.

Falcon helped her up and led her to the back of the cabin; then he lifted her up onto the cabinet beneath the already open window.

Falcon shoved her through the window, then climbed through the window behind her. Grabbing her by the hand, he led her away from the burning building, through a thicket of trees, and onto a little dirt road. Here, a single large black horse stood quietly.

"This is Diablo. He'll get you out of here. About two miles down this road, you'll reach the railroad," Falcon said. "Turn left and follow the railroad for about ten miles. That will take you back to Medora."

"Wait a minute. Aren't you coming with me?" Anna asked. "We can ride double."

Falcon shook his head. "I've got some business to take care of first," he said.

"But how are you going to get to town without a horse?"

"I'll borrow one," Falcon said simply.

"Mr. MacCallister, I . . . I can't thank you enough for rescuing me," she said. "You are, truly, a hero."

Falcon didn't answer. Instead, he helped her mount Diablo. Then he snaked his rifle from the saddle sheath and patted Diablo on the rump.

"Take care of her, boy," he said.

Diablo started off at a trot. Then, rifle in hand, Falcon started back through the clump of woods toward the cabin. The cabin was fully engulfed in flames now, throwing out a large radius of heat and sending smoke billowing into the sky.

Falcon saw three men standing near the lean-to. They

had already saddled their horses and were getting ready to ride away. He started toward them.

"It's MacCallister!" Frank said, pointing toward Falcon.

"Shoot 'im! Shoot the bastard!" Aaron said, but even as he was issuing the order, he was mounting his horse. Grabbing the reins of the other two horses, Aaron galloped away.

"Hey!" Percy shouted. "Where at you goin' with them horses?" Percy started running after Aaron. Then Falcon saw a strange thing. Aaron turned and shot Percy.

"Aaron, what are you doing?" Frank called, shocked by what he had just seen. "You're takin' the horses!"

"Sorry, Frank, it's ever' man for himself!" Aaron shouted.

"You son of a bitch!" Frank fired his pistol at his own brother.

"Drop your gun, Frank, and throw up your hands," Falcon shouted.

"The hell I will!" Frank said, aiming his gun at Falcon. "I ain't lettin' you take me back to prison again." He fired, and the bullet actually nicked Falcon's ear. Falcon could feel the sting of it, as well as see a little spray of blood in the periphery of his vision.

"Drop it, Frank, now!" Falcon shouted.

Frank fired a second shot, and though this one didn't nick him, it was close enough for Falcon to feel the concussion of its passing.

Falcon returned fire, shooting once, hitting Frank in the middle of his chest. Frank went down.

By now Aaron had opened up a considerable distance between him and Falcon. Falcon aimed his pistol at him, but realizing that he was out of range, put the pistol back in his holster, then checked on both Frank and Percy. Frank was dead and Percy was dying.

"Why did he do that?" Percy asked in a voice that was wracked with pain. "Why'd he run off on us like that?"

"Because he's a coward, and that's what cowards do," Falcon answered.

"You know what? I hope you get the son of a . . ." That was as far Percy got before he died.

When Aaron reached the top of the ridge, he turned and looked back down toward the burning cabin. He saw both Frank and Percy lying on the ground, and MacCallister standing just over Percy. The cabin was nothing but a burning pile of collapsed timber.

"Sorry 'bout takin' the horses, Frank," he said quietly. "But I figured this way you'n Percy would have to deal with him and that would get me a head start." He turned the other two horses loose, then turned his own horse and galloped away.

After nearly an hour of trailing on foot, Falcon was pleasantly surprised to see a golden palomino standing quietly in a meadow, eating grass. As he came closer, he saw that it was a mare. Was this Douglass's horse?

"Rhoda?" he called.

Upon hearing her name, Rhoda trotted easily over to him.

Falcon began patting the horse on the neck and, looking toward her rump, saw the letter D over an arc. The Rocking D, Douglass's brand.

"It is you, isn't it, Rhoda?"

Rhoda pushed her head against his hand, welcoming the attention.

Falcon pulled the rifle out of the saddle sheath and tossed it aside, replacing it with his own. He mounted the horse.

"Come on, old girl," he said. "Let's go find that evil bastard."

Now that he was mounted, it was much easier to follow Aaron's trail. He hadn't gone too far, though, before he noticed that the horse Aaron was riding had broken stride, badly. Reading the sign told the story. In his desperate attempt to flee, Aaron had ridden his horse into the ground. The hour lead that Aaron had on Falcon meant nothing now.

Falcon found Aaron's horse about half an hour later. The animal was still alive, though only barely. His nostrils were flecked with blood, evidence that Aaron had ridden the horse until its lungs burst.

"I'm sorry, friend," Falcon said to the horse. He patted the animal gently on the neck, and looked into its sorrowful brown eyes. The horse seemed to understand what Falcon was about to do. Falcon put his pistol to the horse's head and pulled the trigger. Mercifully, the horse died instantly.

Falcon poured some water into a hat and held it up for Rhoda, then began walking, following Aaron's trail. The sign continued to tell the story, as clearly as if Falcon were reading it from a book.

Aaron had run as far as he could; then he'd started walking, then he'd started throwing things away. Falcon found the pistol belt, though the holster was empty, which meant Aaron did keep his pistol. Next he found the spurs, then Aaron's shirt, and finally an empty canteen.

Within another mile, Falcon found indications that

Aaron was beginning to have a very difficult time. There were signs that he would fall, crawl a few feet, then get up and lunge ahead a few feet more before falling again.

Falcon heard a train whistle, and realized with a start that he was closer to the railroad than he thought. He knew then where Aaron was going and what his intention was. Aaron planned to hop a freight, and if he did, he would get away.

Falcon remounted and urged Rhoda into a trot. The train whistle sounded much closer now, and Falcon brought Rhoda to a lope. Ahead of him was a long, rather steeply rising slope. The slope was high enough in front of him that it obscured his view of the other side so, though he could hear the train, he still couldn't see it. It also made it more difficult for Rhoda, and the game mare started gasping for breath.

"Don't give up on me now, girl," Falcon said, and amazingly, at his call, Rhoda moved from a lope to a gallop. The train whistled again, this time right in front of him.

Finally, Falcon reached the top of the long slope, and was surprised and disappointed to see that it did not slope down on the other side as he had thought. Instead, it was a steep descent, much too steep to ride down.

Dismounting, Falcon patted Rhoda on the neck. "You've done all I asked of you," he said. "I'll take it from here."

Falcon looked down toward the track. The train he had been hearing was, at that very minute, passing by in front of him. What he saw was a freight train, consisting of an engine and about a dozen boxcars. There was no caboose.

Falcon pulled his rifle out of the sheath and looked back down toward the track.

That was when he saw Aaron, seeing him for the first time since he had last glimpsed him at the cabin. The outlaw, though near collapse, had somehow called upon a hidden reserve of strength. He was running now, and he managed to catch the last car. He hung on the ladder for a moment or two, then climbed to the top.

Falcon sat down on the crest of the hill and, almost leisurely, jacked a round into the chamber of his rifle. He raised the rear sight and slid the gate up to a range marking of five hundred yards. Crossing his legs and resting his left elbow just inside his left knee, he raised the rifle to his shoulder, then sighted down the long, octagonal barrel.

The distance opened to about five hundred yards. He was shooting down, and his target was at an angle and moving at better than twenty miles per hour. It was also a little over a quarter a mile away. To ninety-nine men out of a hundred, it was such an impossible shot that they wouldn't even try.

Falcon took in a deep breath, let half of the air out, then held it. Aaron was standing on top of the retreating boxcar, and he began dancing a taunting little jig. From this distance, Aaron was not much bigger than the front sight itself.

Slowly . . . ever so slowly . . . Falcon began squeezing the trigger.

Aaron had seen Falcon take his rifle from the saddle sheath and sit down on top of the hill. The train was picking up speed now, moving faster than a good horse could gallop. The car was rattling and shaking, and Aaron was having a difficult time standing. He realized that he should get down, not only to help maintain his balance on top of the rapidly moving train, but also to make himself a smaller target. But he felt compelled to make some gesture of defiance, find some way to extract victory from the ordeal MacCallister had put him through. Instead of sitting down, he remained standing and hurled a challenge knowing it wouldn't be heard.

"Look at you now, you son of a bitch!" he shouted. "You killed one of my brothers, and caused the other one to get killed. But now I'm gettin' away and you're left suckin' hind tit! Go ahead and shoot at me if you want to. I'm out of range, you dumb shit!"

Aaron saw a little flash of flame from the end of Falcon's rifle, and he saw the recoil rock Falcon back. He started to laugh at the futile attempt, then, suddenly, and unexpectedly, felt a blow in the center of his chest. He had only a moment to be surprised before he fell from the train, dead, even before his body bounced along the rocky ballast alongside the track.

Falcon MacCallister was not one for parties, and would not have gone to this one if Roosevelt hadn't insisted.

"It would mean a lot to me, Falcon, if you would come," Roosevelt had told him. "It's not only a celebration of the rescue of Anna, it's also sort of an epiphany for me."

"An epiphany?"

"An awakening of sorts, from my long period of grief," Roosevelt said. He took his glasses off and polished them. "There will always be a place in my heart for Alice. But life must go on." Roosevelt smiled. "Of course, I don't have to tell you that, do I? We share that tragedy, you and I."

It was that remark, the "shared tragedy" remark, that convinced Falcon to come to the party. But now, as he dismounted in front of Elkhorn, he began having second thoughts and, had it been anyone else but Roosevelt, he would have remounted and ridden away.

Not one to do things halfway, Roosevelt had hired a band, and the music spilled out onto the lawn where several partygoers were congregating under the trees, or around the gazebo.

One of Roosevelt's hands was cooking half a steer, turning it on a spit over an open fire. Another hand was brushing the glistening steer carcass with a sauce of some sort. Falcon had to admit that the aroma was very enticing.

Roosevelt came outside to welcome Falcon.

"I was beginning to fear that you might not come," he said.

"I confess to having second thoughts about it," Falcon replied. "But a promise is a promise."

"Indeed it is, and that was what allayed my fears," Roosevelt said. "Come, let's go into the house."

As soon as the two men entered the house, the band quit the song it was playing and broke out into a fanfare of sorts. As if by prearranged signal, that brought all the other guests inside the house, where they crowded around in the great room. Then, calling for quiet, Roosevelt introduced Judge Andrew Heckemeyer.

Heckemeyer climbed up on a wooden chair so he would have a commanding enough position to be seen by all in the room. Anna, beaming brightly, was standing beside the chair.

"Ladies and gentlemen," Heckemeyer said. "Those of you who know me might know that it is very difficult for me to ever say I was wrong. In fact, you might even say that I am a little stubborn."

"Stubborn? You, Judge? Surely, sir, you jest," someone said, and the other guests laughed at the sarcasm.

Heckemeyer held out his hands for silence. "All right," he said, "I'm a lot stubborn. Which, I hope, gives more weight to what I am about to say." He looked over at Falcon. "Mr. MacCallister, you, sir, are indeed the stuff of legends, a Western icon, and an American hero. I hereby publicly confess that my former opinion of you was wrong. And I apologize for any negative thing I ever said or thought about you."

"Hear! Hear!" someone shouted, and the others applauded.

"Please," Falcon said, embarrassed by everything. "No apology is needed."

"But you do accept it, I hope?"

Falcon smiled. "I do accept it," he said. When Heckemeyer stepped down from the chair with his hand extended, Falcon accepted it and shook it heartily. That action brought the applause of all present.

"Mr. MacCallister, I hope you know that if there is ever anything I can do for you . . . anything at all, I'll do it," Heckemeyer said quietly.

"Thank you, Judge. I appreciate that," Falcon replied.

Roosevelt climbed up on the chair then, and when he didn't get the immediate attention of all, he put his fingers to his lips and whistled.

The piercing whistle shocked many because it was so loud. Falcon had heard it before, and he just chuckled. The whistle did have the desired effect, though, because everyone grew quiet.

"I also have something to say." He looked at Falcon. "Falcon, I have an appointment for you."

"An appointment?"

"I confess, it is a meaningless appointment unless you would happen to move to the State of New York. But I hope you will accept it with the honor it is intended to convey."

Roosevelt unfurled a scroll, cleared his throat, and began to read.

"In accordance with the authority vested in me as Governor of the State of New York, I, David P. Hill, do hereby appoint Falcon MacCallister to the rank of Colonel of Cavalry in the New York Militia."

Roosevelt lowered the paper and looked at Falcon. "Congratulations, Colonel MacCallister," he said.

"Thanks," Falcon said. "I don't know what to say."

"I knew you wouldn't accept money, so this is all I could think of. I hope you like it."

Falcon smiled broadly. "I do like it," he said. "Colonel MacCallister," he added with a chuckle. "That sounds good. To be honest, I like it more than I probably should."

The others laughed again.

"All right, friends, let the party begin!" Roosevelt said. "We've a lot of work to do tonight. We have half a steer to consume."

With Roosevelt's announcement, many hurried outside to get in line for the barbecue. During the course of the party, so many came by to congratulate Falcon that he finally was forced to slip outside and walk over to the shadows of the far edge of the yard. He was there for but a few minutes when he felt a presence. Turning around, he saw Anna.

"Thank you for Rhoda. She is beautiful," Anna said. "You're sure I can keep her?"

"I'm sure," Falcon said.

Anna was quiet for a long moment before she spoke again, this time in a more plaintive voice.

"I haven't told anyone," she said.

"Told anyone what?"

"That I . . . I killed a man."

"You don't need to tell anyone," Falcon replied.

"I can't get it out of my mind."

"You had no choice."

"That's what I've been telling myself. Still, I'm having a difficult time dealing with it."

"You will have difficulty for a while. But you are a strong woman and you will come to accept that it had to be done."

"How do you deal with such things? I mean, you've killed so many." Anna gasped and put her hand to her lips. "I'm sorry, I didn't mean that the way it sounded."

"That's all right," Falcon said. "It's a good question and, under the circumstances, you have every right to ask."

"All right, I'll ask again. How do you deal with it?"

"When a potato gets rotten, there is nothing left of the original potato. In fact, the rotten so poisons the potato that you have to throw the entire thing away in order to get rid of the rot.

"Men are like that. When their soul becomes infested with evil, there is nothing you can do but get rid of the evil. Just remember, you aren't killing the man, the man has already died. You are only killing the evil."

"Thank you," Anna said, smiling. "Thank you. That will help."

"You're welcome."

"Well, I guess I had better go back to the party now. Are you coming back?"

"In a little while," Falcon said.

After Anna left, Falcon remained outside. A breeze came up, colder than it had been, and he knew that the long, lingering days of a warm fall were about over. It would be winter soon, and snow would close the passes.

He would head south in the morning. He'd never cared much for the cold.

Notes from the Old West

In the small town where I grew up, there were two movie theaters. The Pavilion was one of those old-timey movie show palaces, built in the heyday of Mary Pickford and Charlie Chaplin—the silent era of the 1920s. By the 1950s, when I was a kid, the Pavilion was a little worn around the edges, but it was still the premiere theater in town. They played all those big Technicolor biblical Cecil B. DeMille epics and corny MGM musicals. In Cinemascope.

On the other side of town was the Gem, a somewhat shabby and run-down grind house with sticky floors and torn seats. The Gem booked low-budget "B" pictures (remember the Bowery Boys?), war movies, horror flicks, and Westerns. I liked the Westerns best. I could usually be found every Saturday at the Gem, along with my best friend, Newton Trout, watching Westerns from 10 AM until my mother or father came looking for me around suppertime. (Sometimes Newton's dad was dispatched to come fetch us.) One time, my dad came to get me right in the middle of *Abilene Trail,* which featured the now-forgotten Whip Wilson. My father became so engrossed in the action he sat down and watched the rest of it with us. We didn't get home until after dark, and my mother's meat loaf was a pan of gray ashes by the time we did. Though my father and I were both in the doghouse the next day, this remains one of my fondest childhood memories. There was Wild Bill Elliot, and Gene Autry, and Roy Rogers, and Tim Holt and, a little later, Rod Cameron and Audie Murphy. Of these newcomers, I never missed an Audie Murphy Western, because Audie was sort of an antihero. Sure, he stood for law and order and was an honest man, but sometimes he had to go around the law to uphold it. If he didn't play fair, it was only because he felt hamstrung by the laws of the land. Whatever it took to get the bad guys, Audie did it. There were no finer points of law, no splitting of legal hairs. It was instant justice, devoid of long-winded lawyers, bored or biased jurors, or black-robed, often corrupt judges.

Steal a man's horse and you were the guest of honor at a necktie party.

Molest a good woman and you got a bullet in the heart or a rope around the gullet. Or at the very least, got the crap beat out of you. Rob a bank and face a hail of bullets or the hangman's noose.

Saved a lot of time and money, did frontier justice.

That's all gone now, I'm sad to say. Now you hear, "Oh, but he had a bad childhood" or "His mother didn't give him enough love" or "The homecoming queen wouldn't give him a second look and he has an inferiority complex." Or "cultural rage," as the politically correct bright boys refer to it. How many times have you heard some self-important defense attorney moan, "The poor kids were only venting their hostilities toward an uncaring society"?

Mule fritters, I say. Nowadays, you can't even call a punk a punk anymore. But don't get me started.

It was "howdy, ma'am" time too. The good guys, antihero or not, were always respectful to the ladies. They might shoot a bad guy five seconds after tipping their hat to a woman, but the code of the West demanded you be respectful to a lady.

Lots of things have changed since the heyday of the Wild West, haven't they? Some for the good, some for the bad.

I didn't have any idea at the time that I would someday write about the West. I just knew that I was captivated by the Old West.

When I first got the itch to write, back in the early 1970s, I didn't write Westerns. I started by writing horror and action adventure novels. After more than two dozen novels, I began thinking about developing a Western character. From those initial musings came the novel *The Last Mountain Man: Smoke Jensen.* That was followed by *Preacher: The First Mountain Man.* A few years later, I began developing the Last Gunfighter series. Frank Morgan is a legend in his own time, the fastest gun west of the Mississippi . . . a title and a reputation he never wanted, but can't get rid of.

The Gunfighter series is set in the waning days of the Wild West. Frank Morgan is out of time and place, but still, he is pursued by men who want to earn a reputation as the man who killed the legendary gunfighter. All Frank wants to do is live in peace. But he knows in his heart that dream will always be just that: a dream, fog and smoke and mirrors, something elusive that will never really come to fruition. He will be forced to wander the West, alone, until one day his luck runs out.

For me, and for thousands—probably millions—of other people (although many will never publicly admit it), the old Wild West will always be a magic, mysterious place: a place we love to visit through the pages of books; characters we would like to know . . . from a safe distance; events we would love to take part in, again, from a safe distance. For the old Wild West was not a place for the faint of heart. It was a hard, tough, physically demanding time. There were no police to call if one faced adversity. One faced trouble alone, and handled it alone. It was rugged individualism: something that appeals to many of us.

I am certain that is something that appeals to most readers of Westerns.

I still do on-site research (whenever possible) before starting a Western novel. I have wandered over much of the West, prowling what is left of ghost towns. Stand in the midst of the ruins of these old towns, use a little bit of imagination, and one can conjure up life as it used to be in the Wild West. The rowdy Saturday nights, the tinkling of a piano in a saloon, the laughter of cowboys and miners letting off steam after a week of hard work. Use a little more imagination and one can envision two men standing in the street, facing one another, seconds before the hook and draw of a gunfight. A moment later, one is dead and the other rides away.

The old wild untamed West.

There are still some ghost towns to visit, but they are rapidly vanishing as time and the elements take their toll. If you want to see them, make plans to do so as soon as possible, for in a few years, they will all be gone.

And so will we.

Stand in what is left of the Big Thicket country of east Texas and try to imagine how in the world the pioneers managed to get through that wild tangle. I have wondered that many times and marveled at the courage of the men and women who slowly pushed westward, facing dangers that we can only imagine.

Let me touch briefly on a subject that is very close to me: firearms. There are some so-called historians who are now claiming that firearms played only a very insignificant part in the settlers' lives. They claim that only a few were armed. What utter, stupid nonsense! What do these so-called historians think the pioneers did for food? Do they think the early settlers rode down to the nearest supermarket and bought their meat? Or maybe they think the settlers chased down deer or buffalo on foot and beat the animals to death with a club. I have a news flash for you so-called historians: The settlers used guns to shoot their game. They used guns to defend hearth and home against Indians on the warpath. They used guns to protect themselves from outlaws. Guns are a part of Americana. And always will be.

The mountains of the West and the remains of the ghost towns that dot those areas are some of my favorite subjects to write about. I have done extensive research on the various mountain ranges of the West and go back whenever time permits. I sometimes stand surrounded by the towering mountains and wonder how in the world the pioneers ever made it through. As hard as I try and as often as I try, I simply cannot imagine the hardships those men and women endured over the hard months of their incredible journey. None of us can. It is said that on the Oregon Trail alone, there are at least two bodies in lonely unmarked graves for every mile of that journey. Some students of the West say the number of dead is at least twice that. And nobody knows the exact number of wagons that impatiently started out alone and simply vanished on the way, along with their occupants, never to be seen or heard from again.

Just vanished.

The 150-year-old ruts of the wagon wheels can still be seen in various places along the Oregon Trail. But if you plan to visit those places, do so quickly, for they are slowly disappearing. And when they are gone, they will be lost forever, except in the words of Western writers.

As long as I can peck away at a keyboard and find a company to publish my work, I will not let the Old West die. That I promise you.

As the Drifter in the *Last Gunfighter* series, Frank Morgan has struck a responsive chord among the readers of frontier fiction. Perhaps it's because he is a human man, with all of the human frailties. He is not a superhero. He likes horses and dogs and treats them well. He has feelings and isn't afraid to show them or admit that he has them. He longs for a permanent home, a place to hang his hat and sit on the porch in the late afternoon and watch the day slowly fade into night . . . and a woman to share those simple pleasures with him. But Frank also knows he can never relax his vigil and probably will never have that long-wished-for hearth and home. That is why he is called the Drifter. Frank Morgan knows there are men who will risk their lives to face him in a hook and draw, slap leather, pull that big iron, in the hopes of killing the West's most famous gunfighter, so they can claim the title of the man who killed Frank Morgan, the Drifter. Frank would gladly, willingly, give them that title, but not at the expense of his own life.

So Frank Morgan must constantly drift, staying on the lonely trails, those out-of-the-way paths through the timber, the mountains, the deserts that are sometimes called the hoot-owl trail. His companions are the sighing winds, the howling of wolves, the yapping of coyotes, and a few, very few precious memories. And his six-gun. Always, his six-gun.

Frank is also pursued by something else: progress. The towns are connected by telegraph wires. Frank is recognized wherever he goes and can be tracked by telegraphers. There is no escape for him. Reporters for various newspapers are always on his trail, wanting to interview Frank Morgan, as are authors, wanting to do more books about the legendary gunfighter. Photographers want to take his picture, if possible with the body of a man Frank has just killed. Frank is disgusted by the whole thing and wants no part of it. There is no real rest for the Drifter. Frank travels on, always on the move. He tries to stay off the more heavily traveled roads, sticking to lesser-known trails, sometimes making his own route of travel, across the mountains or deserts.

Someday perhaps Frank will find some peace. Maybe. But if he does, that is many books from now.

The West will live on as long as there are writers willing to write about it, and publishers willing to publish it. Writing about the West is wide open, just like the old Wild West. Characters abound, as plentiful as the wide-open spaces, as colorful as a sunset on the Painted Desert, as restless as the ever-sighing winds. All one has to do is use a bit of imagination. Take a stroll through the cemetery at Tombstone, Arizona; read the inscriptions. Then walk the main street of that once-infamous town around midnight and you might catch a glimpse of the ghosts that still wander the town. They really do. Just ask anyone who lives there. But don't be afraid of the apparitions, they won't hurt you. They're just out for a quiet stroll.

The West lives on. And as long as I am alive, it always will.

<u>BOOK YOUR PLACE ON OUR WEBSITE</u>
AND MAKE THE
<u>READING CONNECTION!</u>

We've created a customized website just for our very special readers, where you can get the inside scoop on everything that's going on with Zebra, Pinnacle and Kensington books.

When you come online, you'll have the exciting opportunity to:

- View covers of upcoming books
- Read sample chapters
- Learn about our future publishing schedule (listed by publication month *and author*)
- Find out when your favorite authors will be visiting a city near you
- Search for and order backlist books from our online catalog
- Check out author bios and background information
- Send e-mail to your favorite authors
- Meet the Kensington staff online
- Join us in weekly chats with authors, readers and other guests
- Get writing guidelines
- AND MUCH MORE!

Visit our website at
http://www.kensingtonbooks.com